D1564893

HANGMAN'S SONG

CHARLES G. WEST

WHEELER PUBLISHING

An imprint of Thomson Gale, a part of The Thomson Corporation

THOMSON

™

GALE

Detroit • New York • San Francisco • New Haven, Conn. • Waterville, Maine • London

LIBRARY OF CONGRESS CATALOGING-IN-PUBLICATION DATA

West, Charles.
   Hangman's song / by Charles G. West.
     p. cm. — (Wheeler Publishing large print western)
     ISBN-13: 978-1-59722-509-0 (lg. print : pbk. : alk. paper)
     ISBN-10: 1-59722-509-6 (lg. print : pbk. : alk. paper)
     1. Large type books. I. Title.
   PS3623.E84H36 2007
   813'.6—dc22   2007002371

Published in 2007 by arrangement with NAL Signet,
a member of Penguin Group (USA) Inc.

Printed in the United States of America on permanent paper
10 9 8 7 6 5 4 3 2 1

For Ronda

CHAPTER 1

She was a frail little woman in appearance, sad of eye with mousy-colored hair streaked with dingy gray. Like so many women who followed their husbands to little homesteads on the prairie, she had aged beyond her years. Hard work and hard weather took a toll on a woman's life. Preacher almost felt justified that his happening upon the tiny homestead was in fact the woman's salvation. After he and his two sons left this place, she would toil no longer. That thought caused him to smile graciously when she offered a dipper of water. "Thank you kindly, ma'am," he said, taking the dipper from her bony hand. "The Lord's blessings upon you," he added.

Mary Weldon stepped back and stood watching the huge man as he turned the dipper up and gulped the water, ignoring the waste that splashed around the sides and soaked his heavy beard. When her husband had called out that someone was coming, she had hurried outside the cabin, hoping that it was Marci and John, her sister and brother-in-law. It was a foolish hope she at once realized. It was far too early in the spring for them to have made the journey. They would most likely arrive toward the middle of the summer. Life would improve a great deal when they got there. The lonely days that stretched end to end were the worst part of Mary's existence. It would be so grand when Marci was there to talk to and help with the work. It would make life a whole lot easier for her husband as well. Franklin and John were close friends and had spent many a night over the past several years planning to start a new life in the west. She and Franklin had decided to go ahead and make the journey. Marci and John had promised they would not be far behind.

She glanced at her husband standing at the edge of the creek, watching the two younger men water their horses. *Strange guests,* she couldn't help thinking. She had no doubt that the savage Indians needed the Word of God, but it seemed a foolish mission for one man and his two sons — especially when the cavalry patrol that passed through the week before had warned her husband that there had been Sioux raiding parties reported since the weather let up. *I reckon they ain't no crazier than we are for trying to make a home here,* she thought. The Indians she had met could certainly use a little religion.

The huge man in the black hat and the heavy bearskin coat handed the dipper back. Guessing her thoughts, he grinned and commented, "Life's kinda hard for a woman out here, ain't it, ma'am?"

"I guess life's hard for most folks," she replied without emotion. "Don't do no good to complain, though."

"No, ma'am, it shore don't, but if you're a Christian woman, your reward will come in Heaven, though you toil here on earth."

"I suppose so," she said with little enthusiasm for the prospects. She hoped the self-proclaimed preacher wasn't about to get wound up for an impromptu sermon. She was thinking about the little pot of stew she had left warming over the fire. It would hardly be enough to feed extra mouths, especially those on the likes of these three. "I guess we're just thankful for the few crops that make it here."

Preacher's grin widened. "Have you accepted Jesus as your savior?" She nodded. "The Lord giveth, and the Lord taketh away. This here's one of them times when the Lord taketh away." With that, he pulled his pistol from the holster on his belt and held it up before her. Puzzled, she stared at it for just a moment before he turned the muzzle toward her and calmly pulled the trigger, sending a bullet through her brain. Mary Weldon's toil on earth had ended.

Down by the creek, Franklin Weldon was startled by the sudden discharge of the pistol. Turning to see his wife crumple to the ground at Preacher's feet, he was paralyzed with shock, unable to even cry out. When he saw the pistol in Preacher's hand, his mind was impacted with the reality of what had taken place. He started to run to his wife, only to be felled by a blow to the back of his skull. Grinning at the fallen man's helpless struggles to get up, Quincy Rix held his pistol to the back of Franklin's head and dispatched him to join his wife.

"Goddamn!" Zeb cried out gleefully, excited by the flow of blood.

"Watch your mouth," Preacher warned. He would not tolerate blasphemous language from his offspring. "Thou shalt not take the Lord's name in vain." He paused then, watching his eldest son's reaction. When Zeb appeared to be properly contrite, Preacher ordered the disposal of the bodies.

"Let's put these poor sinners in the ground, and give 'em a proper service." He cocked an eye in Quincy's direction. "And, Quincy, mind you handle the woman's body respectfully. I don't mind you fondling all over an Injun woman, but these was peaceful white folks."

"We gonna scalp 'em, ain't we, Pa," Quincy asked hopefully, "so's it looks like Injuns done it?" That was the usual routine whenever they struck a miner's camp, a lone trapper, or an isolated homestead like this one.

Preacher Rix cast a patient glance in his son's direction. "Now there ain't hardly no need to scalp 'em if we're fixin' to bury 'em, is there?" Seeing the blank look on Quincy's face, he glanced at Zeb, only to find a similar expression. "If they're underground," he explained, "nobody's gonna know if they was scalped or not." When he saw the light of comprehension finally appear in their faces, he went on. "Now find a shovel and bury these folks, and I'll say a few words over 'em."

While his sons followed his instructions, he turned his attention to the cabin and the possible spoils to be taken. He hadn't expected much in the way of valuables, but he was disappointed to find nothing beyond

11

a few pots and pans, some clothes, and a shotgun. "Dirt poor," he mumbled, angered by their meager existence. Sniffing the air like a coyote, he detected the odor of food. Turning toward the source of the smell, he saw the iron pot hanging over the edge of the coals in the fireplace. He peered into the simmering pot to discover some kind of stew. *Rabbit,* he thought, *or groundhog.* He dipped in his fingers to extract a morsel of meat. *Rabbit,* he decided and looked around for a spoon. After consuming half the contents of the pot, he set it aside for his sons to finish. Looking around him then, he decided to burn the cabin. So he broke a chair in pieces and threw them in the fireplace. When he had kindled a strong blaze, he pulled firewood, furniture, bedclothes, anything that would burn to the fireplace, and stacked the material at the mouth. He stood in the middle of the cabin watching the fire take hold until the blaze began to find the pine sap in the walls. Satisfied that the cabin would go up in flames, he picked up the pot of stew and went outside to join his sons.

Zeb and Quincy made short work of what stew their father had left in the pot. Then they squatted on their haunches to watch the cabin go up. It didn't take long before the pine walls collapsed and the sod of the roof smothered most of the flames. "All right, boys," Preacher said, "finish up that grave, and I'll pray over 'em."

Jordan Gray sat motionless in the saddle, studying the lone plume of smoke snaking up from the distant hills to the south. It was too big to be smoke from a campfire, and too close to the settlements to be an Indian camp. Not being in a particularly curious mood, he was prone to avoid all signs of human contact. He had spent a long, hard winter — mostly in the rugged Big Horns — moving from camp to camp to avoid being discovered by roving Sioux and Cheyenne hunting parties. It had been a difficult winter, with little game to be found in the narrow passes, and a constant search for feed for his two horses. That kind of existence would be hard for most men, but he had adapted to it, moving his camps fast and often. Out of necessity, he had learned to quickly skin and butcher any game he had been fortunate enough to happen upon, packing the meat on his packhorse, and fading immediately into the hills before encountering any curious Indians who might have heard his rifle.

Turning his attention back to the smoke

trailing up into the gray afternoon sky, he considered avoiding it, as had been his custom during the winter months just past. He thought about it for a moment before deciding. As best as he could guess, he could be no more than a long day's ride from Fort Laramie. The smoke he was seeing was most likely from a settler's cabin and might mean someone was in trouble. With that thought in mind, he nudged his horse gently, and the mottled gray mare moved forward again at a slow walk.

His mind alert to the prairie around him, he gave little thought to the reasons for his self-imposed exile to the cold harsh peaks of the mountains. The solitude of the wind-swept towers, where winter temperatures plunged unmercifully, could drive a lone man crazy if it didn't kill him. To Jordan, the time spent alone in the frigid mountains had been a period of healing in his mind. It had been harder on his horses than it had been on him, and much of the time had been spent seeking shelter and food for them. The thought prompted him to reach down and pat Sweet Pea's neck. *Sweet Pea,* he laughed to himself. A more unlikely name for the often belligerent horse, he could not imagine. She had belonged to his old partner and friend, Perley Gates. Perley had named her Sweet Pea in hopes it might help her disposition. It hadn't. But though she might possibly be the rankest-looking horse west of the Missouri, Jordan would wager none could match her for strength and stamina — and she had accepted him. So looks be damned, he wouldn't trade her for any two horses.

Like the heating of iron in the smithy's fire, the winter had served to temper Jordan's soul to a hardness that caused him to give little concern to what might lie ahead. He was even able to at last store the memory of his late wife and son away in a safe place in his mind, to be brought out whenever he chose to remember. It had taken a while for the scar tissue to form over the mental wound left by the violent slaughter of his young family, but in time it had healed. The men responsible for the death of his wife and child were in the ground, slain by his own hand. He no longer questioned the sense of the killings, having come to the conclusion that life itself made no sense. His senses sharpened, his mind attuned to the wilderness in which he rode, he would fight to survive — not for a concern for the future, but merely out of a natural reaction of his own instincts, like that of the wolf or the coyote.

When he reached the gentle line of hills, he discovered that they bordered a wide stream, still swollen with runoff from the melting snow. He paused to survey the column of smoke again. He was close. The fire appeared to be no more than a few hundred yards away, probably beyond the trees that hugged the stream ahead, where it made a sharp bend toward the west. It was then that he saw hoofprints. Coming from the east, they turned to follow the stream toward the foot of the hill, and they left a clear trail through a patch of snow — tracks of three shod horses, not likely belonging to Indians, and something peculiar caught his eye, so he dismounted to take a closer look at the tracks. One of the horses evidently had a slight spur on one shoe, an imperfection that should have been filed off. It was so slight that the owner of the horse probably wasn't even aware of it. Jordan wouldn't have noticed it had it not been for the clear imprint in the snow. In fact, most men would not have noticed even then. But Jordan Gray was not most men. Perley Gates had taught him well when it came to reading sign, and when a man chose to live alone in Sioux country, reading sign often meant the difference between living and dying.

After carefully scanning the way before him, he stepped up in the saddle again and nudged his horse forward, guiding the ungainly mare around the few patches of snow still remaining in the shade of the trees.

As he approached the bend, he heard voices. His immediate reaction was to quickly guide the mare away from the stream and up the slope that separated him from the fire. Pulling his rifle from the saddle sling, he dismounted. Leaving the horses standing in the trees, he made his way to the crest of the small hill.

It had been the cabin of settlers. The logs that had formed the framework for the sod walls and roof had collapsed and were still smoking with small flames burning the remains of a few wooden chairs that had been thrown together in a pile. Jordan cast no more than a glance at the burned-out cabin. His attention was claimed by the three men standing around a shallow grave near a small corral. White men, they appeared to have their heads bowed in prayer. At least, two of them did. The other was the one whose voice Jordan had heard when he approached the bend in the stream. Towering over his two companions, he appeared to be addressing his words toward the heavens. His deep voice boomed out from under the broad rim of a black flat-crowned hat as he delivered his eulogy, his arms outstretched as if besieging the Lord to accept the poor souls lying in the freshly dug grave. All three men wore heavy bearskin coats, so Jordan couldn't help thinking that they presented a picture of a pack of wolves surrounding a kill. He was almost of a mind to withdraw, concluding that there was nothing to be done for whoever occupied the grave, but his suspicious nature dictated a need to know the circumstances of the tragedy.

Moving with the stealth of a man self-trained to survive in a hostile environment, Jordan made his way down the slope, almost to the bottom before the three men knew they had a visitor. Sensing his presence, the tall man jerked his head around to discover the sudden appearance of a stranger who seemed to pop out of thin air. His lead was followed by his two companions. All three stood gaping at the formidable figure dressed in animal skins and carrying a Winchester rifle at the ready. Recovering quickly, the man in the black hat spoke.

"Well, howdy, neighbor. You kinda startled us there. Where'd you come from?" Jordan didn't answer, and the four men stood silently measuring one another for a few moments. Anticipating Jordan's unspoken question, black hat offered an explanation. "Injuns." He gestured with one hand toward the smoldering ruins of the cabin. With the other hand, he motioned for his companions to stay calm. He was smart enough to sense a lethal danger in the wild-looking stranger. "With spring a-comin', the Injuns has been raidin' between here and Fort Laramie." He shook a sympathetic head toward the grave. "I only wish we coulda got here soon enough to help these poor souls. God's will," he added. "It ain't for mortals to question His will. I'm sure these folks has found a better place."

Jordan shifted his gaze quickly around the clearing and back to the three men before him. He had seen the results of an Indian raid before. This didn't have the appearance of one. It was too tidy. However, he had no real reason to disbelieve what he was being told. He fixed his gaze to study the three. The man who had so far been the only one to speak was quite a bit older than his two companions. A full beard, which spread unkempt like a wild bush, was streaked with gray, and it shook with the deep resonance of his voice, like sage in a gentle wind. He was a big man, his massive frame exaggerated by the bulky bearskin coat he wore. Jordan cast a cautious eye at the two younger men. Seemingly vacant of thought, they both gaped stupidly at him, and Jordan wondered if there was half a brain between the two of them. The older man spoke again.

"My name's Nathaniel Rix. Most folks call me Preacher Rix because I've chosen to dedicate my life to bringin' the word of God to the heathens. These here is my boys, Zeb and Quincy." He paused then, as if waiting for his sons to acknowledge their introduction, but they continued to stare at the stranger. "They don't say much," Preacher explained after a moment. Manufacturing a smile, he asked, "Just who might you be, young feller?"

"I might be Jordan Gray," Jordan replied dryly. He was a pretty good judge of men, and he didn't judge this one to be a man you could turn your back on. In fact, he was highly suspicious that the three of them might have had more to do with the funeral just completed than the simple act of burial. "Indians, you say?"

"Yes, sir. Sioux, I suspect, judgin' by the arrow we found in the woman's body." Without taking his eyes off Jordan, he cocked his head to the side. "Show him the arrow, Zeb." Zeb's blank stare turned to a foolish grin, and he moved immediately to obey his father's command. Going over to the corner of the corral where the horses were tied, he pulled an arrow from beneath a strap on the saddlebag. Returning at a trot, he held it out for Preacher to take. Holding it up in evidence, Preacher said, "That's a Sioux arrow for sure."

Jordan couldn't dispute it. He was satisfied that it was a Sioux arrow all right, but what he couldn't say for sure was whether or not they had found it here. There was no trace of fresh blood on it.

"We wiped it clean," Preacher said, anticipating Jordan's thought. Turning to look at the grave, he went on. "Them poor folks never had a chance. I suspect the heathen savages jumped 'em early this mornin'. We come along too late to help 'em, but I'm thankful that the Lord guided me here to say some words of comfort over 'em." He shook his head sadly. "I just wish we coulda got here in time." Then, as if to justify the slaughter, he said, "God's will. The Lord has His plan. It ain't for us to question it. Them souls is better off now than they was tryin' to scratch out a livin' in this wilderness."

Jordan couldn't deny that, but he couldn't rid his mind of the suspicion that Preacher and his sons were responsible for the deaths of whoever was buried in that grave. He had no proof, and there was the remote possibility that everything Preacher had said was the right of it. It left him with a feeling of anger and, at the same time, helplessness. There was nothing he could do for the dead.

Seeking to discourage any thoughts Jordan might have about sharing the plunder, Preacher spoke again. "Dirt poor, they was. They didn't have much, but I reckon what was left is rightfully our'n since we found 'em and buried 'em."

"Yeah, I reckon," Jordan replied sarcastically. "It's kinda unusual the Indians didn't take those horses there. That's what Indians are usually after."

"Yeah, I wondered about that myself," Preacher said, responding to the sarcasm in Jordan's tone. "Could be they was scared off when we rode up."

"Could be," Jordan replied. It was obvious that he would never know what actually happened here. He had nothing to base his suspicions on but his own gut feeling. At any rate, what was done was done, and there was no way he could change it. Maybe the huge man *was* a man of God. It was said the Lord moved in mysterious ways. "I'll be on my way," Jordan announced abruptly.

"Lord be with you," Preacher Rix said as Jordan withdrew from the clearing. "If you're headin' back toward Fort Laramie, you might tell 'em the Injuns massacred these poor folks. I don't know what their names was."

Jordan only nodded in reply, keeping a wary eye on the three until he reached the trees at the base of the hill. Not until he had a few sizable cottonwood trunks between him and the clearing did he turn and quickly make his way back to his horses. Sweet Pea seemed to sense her master's urgency and was off at once as soon as she felt him settle in the saddle. Up over the crest of the low hill and down the opposite slope, leading his packhorse, he guided the mare through a stand of pines, using the base of the hill for cover until he deemed it safe to cut back toward the prairie. He wanted to make sure he was out of reasonable rifle range before exposing his back on the open prairie.

Behind Jordan, Preacher Rix growled, his tone the same as if warning a dog to sit still, "Quincy."

"He's gonna git away, Pa," Quincy complained, his gaze fixed upon the spot where Jordan had disappeared.

"No, he ain't. Just hold your horses. We'll git him." He gave Zeb a warning frown as well. "You boys is too anxious to git your hind ends shot off." Preacher had not missed the steady gaze of the hunter in Jordan's eye and the way the man had carried the rifle in his hands. He would warrant that Jordan had used that rifle before — for more than meat for the table. It was a fine-looking Winchester rifle, and Preacher intended to have it, but he didn't plan to risk getting shot while going about it. "We'll wait here for a spell till it gits closer to dark. He'll be makin' camp pretty soon. That's when we'll git him."

Jordan was not the only soul attracted by the column of smoke in the afternoon sky. Painted Wolf and his companions had also noticed it. Numbering only six, the Lakota hunting party approached the hills cautiously lest they be surprised by a Shoshoni war party or an army patrol. Crossing over to a ridge to the west of the smoke in order to take advantage of the setting sun at their backs, the Lakota hunters dismounted and made their way to the crest on foot.

"White men," Painted Wolf uttered as Red Feather crawled up beside him.

They puzzled over the scene below them:

the charred timbers of the burned-out cabin, the three white men lounging around the ruins. Then Painted Wolf noticed the freshly turned mound of dirt near the corral, and the picture became clear. "They have killed the people who built the house," he said.

"They have fine horses," Red Feather said. Painted Wolf nodded. He had already considered the prospect of taking the three saddled horses and the two in the corral. At the moment, he was calculating the risk involved in doing so. The three men were heavily armed. He and his companions had only two rifles among them, his single-shot Springfield and Red Feather's Henry. Their four companions carried only bows. Red Feather's Henry had a bent magazine, so in effect, it was no more than a single-shot rifle as well. It would be well worth the risk to capture the weapons. It would be a great thing indeed to return to camp with horses and rifles.

"We outnumber them, but we should move farther down the slope to bring our bows in range," Painted Wolf suggested.

Red Feather was not in complete agreement. "I think it would be better if we use our rifles from here. See how the white men lie around. They are easy targets, even at this distance. We could kill two of them before they know we are here." He looked to either side of him to see nods of approval from the others.

"Very well, then," Painted Wolf conceded and slid the bolt back on his Springfield to insert a round in the chamber.

Preacher Rix paused to cock an ear to the wind. Had he heard something on the ridge above the cabin? He wasn't sure. Like a fox, he tested the wind, listening and searching the trees with narrowed eyes. Then he glanced over at his two sons, both sprawled on the ground, Zeb snoring. After a long moment, when he detected no other strange sounds, he decided it was time to leave. "Git up, boys. It's time to ride." He turned to his side, preparing to get to his feet when he felt the wind of the bullet that snapped by his face. Half an instant after, he heard the sharp crack of the rifle, followed almost at once by a second shot and a cry of pain from Quincy.

Quick as a cat, the huge man dived for cover behind the smoking corner post of the cabin. "Zeb! Quincy!" he yelled at his sons. "Take cover!" He turned to see Zeb dragging his brother to safety.

"I'm shot, Pa," Quincy whined.

Preacher, concerned for his youngest, but also busy searching the slope above them, asked, "How bad?"

"Got him in the leg," Zeb answered.

Preacher turned to take a quick look before returning his gaze toward the slope. Quincy was holding the calf of his right leg and rocking back and forth with the pain. The sight served to anger Preacher. With no thought of pity for Quincy's suffering, he was instead filled with indignant rage that Jordan Gray had evidently doubled back to bushwhack them. *Too bad for him he missed,* he thought. *Vengeance is mine, so sayeth the Lord.* It occurred to him then that the shots did not sound like they came from the Winchester Jordan carried. Someone else was taking shots at them. He sharpened his gaze, scanning the hillside for signs of movement. "Keep a sharp eye, boys," he called out. "Quincy, stop that blubberin'. You ain't dyin'."

After a few more moments had passed, two more shots rang out. This time Preacher saw a faint muzzle flash from a pine thicket near the top of the ridge. He immediately drew a bead on the spot and cranked out a blistering barrage with his repeating rifle. Judging by the pause between shots from the hill, he felt pretty sure that there were

27

only two rifles, and they were evidently single-shot weapons. "Zeb," he ordered, "you and Quincy keep pepperin' that thicket near the top. We'll run them bastards outta there."

Up on the ridge, the Lakota hunters suddenly found themselves in an untenable position. Rifle slugs flew around them like angry hornets, clipping branches and smacking pine trunks. All six hugged the ground in an attempt to avoid the stinging assault. It might have been the better plan to work their way in closer to bring their bows in range, but there was no time to debate that at the present. Red Feather's plan might have been successful had it not been for the poor luck to shoot just as their targets decided to move. At any rate, there was no need for discussion as to what action to take at this turn of events. They were drastically outgunned. There was no choice but to withdraw before one or more of the party was killed. Crawling most of the way, they retreated to their ponies and took flight.

"Yonder they go!" Zeb exclaimed excitedly when he caught a glimpse of the Indians near the top of the ridge. He jumped to his feet and emptied his rifle, firing as rapidly as he could.

"After the heathens!" Preacher yelled, and

he and Zeb ran for their horses.

"Pa!" Quincy whined, still sitting beside the smoking cabin and holding his wounded leg.

Preacher gave his younger son no more than a cursory glance. He had blood in his eye, and his only thought at that moment was to kill Indians. "You'll be all right. Stay here and watch them horses. Me and Zeb'll carry out the Lord's vengeance." He wheeled his horse and kicked it hard with his heels, charging up the slope behind the cabin with Zeb close behind.

In his lust for Sioux blood, Preacher forgot about the lone white man on his way to Fort Laramie. He and Zeb galloped across the prairie beyond the line of low hills that shielded Franklin Weldon's cabin. Catching only an occasional glimpse of the fleeing Indians whenever the Lakota hunters topped a rise, he soon realized that his horse was no match for the swift Indian ponies. This only served to frustrate him, and he banged away unmercifully with his heels in an attempt to force more speed out of his rapidly tiring mount. Finally he reined the lathered horse to a stop, searching the land before him. The Indians had disappeared on the seemingly open prairie. He was reluctant to give up the chase, but his anger had at last cooled to the point where he could consider the likely prospect that the Indians might be lying in ambush in one of the many shallow draws ahead. He turned as Zeb pulled up beside him. "They got away. Let's go back and take care of your brother."

He would not realize it until later, but his rabid chase after the Lakota hunters had cost him any opportunity to track Jordan Gray. It had been a costly encounter. A lot of ammunition had been wasted with no meat to show for it. Preacher's concern now was to replace the spent cartridges, and that would mean finding a source better than the settlers he had just buried. Franklin Weldon had been poorly armed.

CHAPTER 2

"Well, look what the cat drug in," Alton Broom exclaimed. "Jordan, how the hell are you?" The affable clerk in the post trader's store came out from behind the counter to shake Jordan's hand.

"Alton," Jordan acknowledged, matching the clerk's grin.

"You look plum wooly," Alton went on. "I swear, I almost didn't recognize you behind all them whiskers and lookin' most like an Injun in them buckskins." He shook his head, amazed by the transformation of the young man he had last seen in early fall the year before. "When you left here, I swear, I didn't think we'd likely see you again. Figured you'd head for Oregon country or Montana, or maybe join the gold rush in the Black Hills."

"Reckon not," was Jordan's simple reply. He was not a talkative man by nature, and the past six months alone in the mountains

31

had reduced his conversation to simple commands to his horses.

Always impatient for news from outside the confines of Fort Laramie, Alton pressed. "Well, where have you been? Sergeant Grant said he had an idea you turned wild, took to livin' like an Injun. From the looks of you, maybe he was right."

Jordan smiled at the mention of the name. Hamilton Grant had befriended him when Jordan had been under suspicion of murdering two people in a bank robbery, even before Jordan was proven innocent of the charge. There were still some at Fort Laramie who were not ready to accept the verdict, not that Jordan gave them much thought. There were others on the post whom Jordan had thought about during the long, hard winter in the mountains: the post surgeon, Captain Stephen Beard, and his daughter, Kathleen. That thought prompted him to unconsciously reach up and stroke his whiskers. He supposed Alton was probably right — he must look pretty much like a grizzly. Then, aware of the pause in Alton's questioning as the clerk waited for an answer, Jordan replied, "The Big Horns, the Yellowstone, the Powder Valley, but mostly the Big Horns."

"Damn," Alton responded. "That's pretty

dangerous country for a white man alone, ain't it?"

"Not if the Sioux and the Cheyenne don't know you're there, I reckon." The image of Kathleen Beard still in his mind, he changed the subject. "I guess I'll go over to the washhouse and clean up a little. That is, if the army don't mind."

Alton shrugged. "I don't think they care if you use it or not. It's too damn cold to take a bath, anyway. You're liable to take a chill and come down with somethin'."

Jordan smiled. "I reckon I'll risk it. I need to see if my razor's rusted up," he joked. "First, though, I need to take care of my horses, see if they'll let me turn 'em in with the cavalry mounts at the stables."

"Maybe. You still ridin' that ornery nag — what's her name?"

"Sweet Pea?"

"Yeah, Sweet Pea. That horse musta took a nip outta every horse in the corral when you had her in there before."

Jordan couldn't help but grin when he pictured the belligerent mare in his mind. "Sweet Pea ain't real sociable — that's a fact."

"See much Injun sign on your way in from the Big Horns?" The question came from a corner of the dimly lit room, surprising

Jordan. He had not even glanced that way when Alton had claimed his attention. Turning now to see who had asked the question, he was almost startled when he saw the man seated at the corner table, quietly working on a bottle of whiskey. At first Jordan thought he was seeing a ghost, for the man bore a striking resemblance to Perley Gates, the old man who had schooled Jordan in the art of staying alive in the wilderness.

"Some," Jordan answered, "mostly small huntin' parties, but I came across one burned-out cabin with two folks dead." He paused a moment before adding, "I ain't sure it was Injuns that done it. There were three white men there when I got there. They claimed it was the work of Sioux warriors. Fellow claimed he was a preacher. He was praying over their grave when I showed up."

"That feller was in here last week," Alton said, "him and his two sons. Quotin' a lot of stuff from the Bible. I reckon it was from the Bible, though I ain't one to know. They were drinkin' hard liquor with the rest of the sinners." Remembering his manners then, Alton laughed and said, "Speakin' of sinners, this here's Ned Booth." He turned toward the man seated at the table. "Ned's plannin' on headin' out pretty much the same way you just come from."

Ned Booth got up to extend his hand to Jordan. "Well, nearbout the same country," he said. "I'm headin' out to the Black Hills in a day or two, soon as I catch up on my drinkin'."

"Jordan Gray," Jordan said, taking the hand extended. It was easy to see how he had first thought he was looking at Perley Gates. The man could have been Perley's brother, or maybe his son, for as he stepped into the light of the doorway, Jordan could see that he was a good bit younger than Perley had been. He even wore the same type of floppy hat with a flat crown, like Perley's, and buckskin shirt and pants. But the unruly hair sticking out from under the hat was more brown than gray. "You might run into a little snow yet," Jordan offered.

"I expect I might," Booth allowed. "Buy you a drink?"

"Thanks just the same," Jordan replied, "but I think I'll go on over and get cleaned up." He nodded to Alton and turned to leave. "Maybe I'll take you up on it if I see you later on."

"I ain't ever seen him around here before," Booth commented as he and Alton stood watching Jordan head across the parade ground.

"He's a good man," Alton said. "Been through some hard times for a man that young. I expect he'd be a good man to have at your back if you was in trouble."

Leaving the wash house, Jordan met a young private hurrying across the parade ground to find him.

"Are you Jordan Gray?" the private asked.

"I am," Jordan replied, somewhat surprised, since he had been on the post no more than a couple of hours.

"Captain McGarity sent me to find you. He said if you wouldn't mind, he'd like to talk to you."

"Is that a fact?" Jordan responded, wondering why the post adjutant wanted to see him. He knew Paul McGarity. He seemed to be a fair man, even considering the fact that it was McGarity who had ordered Jordan's arrest for the bank incident at Fort Smith. The captain had been truly apologetic when it was proven that Jordan had had nothing to do with the robbery or the murder of the two bank employees. He was simply doing his duty, and Jordan understood that.

"Yes, sir," the private replied. "He's at the adjutant's office. I can show you the way."

"I know where it is. Tell your captain I'll

be along directly."

The young soldier hesitated. He had expected immediate reaction to the captain's request, which to him was a direct order. Reading the confusion in the private's face, Jordan smiled. "Tell McGarity I'll be there in a few minutes. I don't wanna come with soap and a razor in my hands."

"Yes, sir," the private said, relieved when he realized that Jordan was not refusing to accompany him. "I'll tell him you're on your way."

"Come in, Gray." Paul McGarity got up from his chair to greet Jordan. "Thanks for coming by." He offered Jordan a chair across from his desk. "Looks like you've taken to the wilds since I last saw you," he commented, looking Jordan over. "Alton Broom said you were on the post."

"Yep, I rode in this mornin'," Jordan replied, then went on to report the massacre he had stumbled upon on his way to Laramie and the three white men who were already at the scene. "The old man called himself Preacher Rix. He claimed it was Sioux that done it — hard to say."

McGarity shook his head sadly. "Weldon," he uttered softly. "From where you say the cabin was, that would be the Weldons' place." He thought for a moment before continuing. "That fellow Rix passed through here a couple of weeks ago. I didn't talk to him, but I saw him and his sons at the post trader's. If I recollect, I believe Alton Broom said the man was a missionary or something. Sorry to hear about the Weldons. We'll need to send out a patrol to check it out."

Jordan didn't respond, but he wondered what good it would do to send out a patrol. It was too late to help the poor folks lying in the grave near the smoking ruins of their cabin. He also wondered why McGarity had wanted to talk to him. He and the captain were hardly close friends.

"I understand from Alton that you've spent the winter in the Powder River and Big Horn country." Jordan nodded, but made no comment. McGarity went on. "Some of our scouts have seen some signs of hostile activity heating up now that the winter is starting to let up, and now there's this incident you just told me about. But we don't know where the main concentration of hostiles is. Since you've spent the winter in that country, maybe you could give us an idea as to what's going on." He paused to study Jordan's face, wondering if the soft-spoken young man held any grudges for his part in Jordan's mistaken arrest. "Colonel

Bradley would be most appreciative of your help," he added, referring to the post commander.

As for Jordan's disposition, he had no time for grudges. He had never personally met the post commander, Lieutenant Colonel Luther Prentice Bradley, and he would be very surprised if the colonel really knew him.

"We could put you on the payroll as a scout," McGarity added when Jordan failed to answer right away. "We'd provide food for you and forage for your horses. Whaddaya say, Gray? A man like you, what else are you gonna do?"

A man like me. The comment caused Jordan to wonder what the captain meant by that. He had never given thought to the issue. He supposed that someone like McGarity could easily lump him in with the trappers and scouts who wandered aimlessly over the mountains and prairie, with no thought beyond next week. What was he going to do with the rest of his life? In truth, he had avoided thinking about it. One thing he was certain about, however — he was damn sure not going to try farming again. He had hired out to work on a farm when he was a boy because there had been nothing else to do. He had tried to farm his own land after he had married because it was the only way to provide for his wife and young son. Now, with his wife and son in the grave, victims of lawless raiders, he loathed the thought of settling down in one spot to scratch out an existence raising corn and beans — which prompted another question he was at a loss to answer. Why had he returned to Fort Laramie? Was it because Kathleen Beard was here? He immediately dismissed the thought from his mind.

"All right," he abruptly replied. "I reckon you're right. I don't have anything else to do. Might as well give it a try."

"Splendid!" McGarity replied. "Colonel Bradley will be grateful. I'll walk you over to meet Lieutenant Wallace. You'll be working for him."

Lieutenant Thomas Jefferson Wallace turned when he heard Jordan and Captain McGarity approaching. Seeing that it was the captain, he immediately stiffened to attention. Wallace was West Point, and perhaps the only officer on the post who revered military discipline fervently. He was a handsome man, as tall as Jordan, with wavy blond hair. He was so perfectly cast in his uniform that Jordan could not imagine him wearing casual attire. Wallace was the executive officer of M Company, Second Cavalry. He had already established himself as a confident young officer, eager for combat with the hostiles. "Morning, sir," he greeted McGarity smartly and snapped a stiff salute, while eyeing the man in buckskins warily.

"Good morning, Thomas," McGarity returned with a salute somewhat more casual. "I've got a new scout that'll be working with you. Lieutenant Thomas Wallace, Jordan Gray. Jordan here knows the Big Horn and Powder River country pretty well."

"Jordan," Wallace acknowledged. "Glad to have you aboard. We can always use a man familiar with that area." He extended his hand. The lieutenant's greeting was delivered in a polite but stiff manner. He, like almost everyone else on the post, was familiar with the name Jordan Gray, and he was somewhat surprised to hear Jordan was assigned to him as a scout.

Jordan shook his hand and replied, "Tom."

"Thomas," Wallace at once corrected. "We may as well start off on the right foot. I prefer my scouts address me as Lieutenant Wallace. It's important to keep proper discipline, especially in combat."

Jordan took a moment to consider the

young officer before replying. "Right, Lieutenant," he finally replied, "and you can call me Mr. Gray." He briefly considered suggesting that the lieutenant could kiss the part of his anatomy that contacted his saddle. But when he caught a sideways glance from McGarity, he decided the brash young officer's remark was more amusing than provoking.

Taken aback by Jordan's obvious exception to his remark, Wallace said, "Right. Well, *Mr.* Gray, let's hope you know the country as well as you claim."

There was a definite spark of conflict between the two young men, hardly a good beginning, and McGarity wondered if he had made a mistake in assigning Jordan to M Company. *Oh, well,* he decided, *they'll either work it out between them, or I'll transfer Gray to another company.* He knew Wallace would be leading a patrol out to investigate the Weldon murders, probably the next day. Maybe they would end up shooting each other. Truth be known, McGarity didn't care much for Wallace either. It might be a good thing for the brash young officer to work with a scout like Jordan Gray. McGarity had an idea that Jordan wouldn't hesitate to tell Wallace to go to hell if he took a notion to.

"Very well, then, Gray," the lieutenant said, after McGarity informed him that he would be taking a patrol out to the Weldon place. "We'll ride out day after tomorrow. That'll give you time to get yourself settled. You can report to Sergeant Grant at the cavalry barracks when you're ready. Do you know where the barracks are?"

Jordan nodded, pleased to hear that he would be working with Hamilton Grant. "The long building I passed on the way in, next to the stables." Wallace nodded. Jordan then turned to McGarity. "Anything else you need from me, Captain?"

"That's all, Jordan. I'll fill Lieutenant Wallace in on the raid on Weldon's place. I expect that will be your first job as a scout, to lead his patrol back there."

"I heard you were back," a grinning Hamilton Grant said as he turned to see Jordan approaching the stables. "I was just lookin' at that ragged piece of gristle you call a horse, and I told Macy here there wasn't but one man in the whole territory that would ride a horse like that." He stepped forward to meet Jordan, his hand extended. "You're sure a sight for sore eyes, Jordan. How are you?"

"Sergeant Grant," Jordan responded

warmly and shook the burly sergeant's hand. "I reckon I've been better, but I just found out I'll be workin' with you," he joked, "so things might get worse."

Grant laughed. "Yeah, the lieutenant told me you were gonna be assigned to our company as a scout. Say hello to Macy here. Macy and I served together under Stonewall Jackson in that little disagreement between the North and the South." Macy stepped forward and shook Jordan's hand.

Jordan had learned something about Hamilton Grant's background when he had been incarcerated in the Fort Laramie guardhouse, awaiting trial. He had developed a genuine friendship with the gregarious sergeant, sparked probably by the fact that Grant believed him when he proclaimed his innocence. He learned that Hamilton had held the rank of captain in the Confederate Army and, like many others, decided to serve in the Union Army at a reduced rank after the surrender. Jordan had found it rather ironic that Hamilton's last name was Grant, not a popular name in the Rebel Army. Ten years had passed since Lee's surrender at Appomattox, years that saw Grant move up in rank to that of First Sergeant of Company M. In private, Macy still addressed him as Captain, although

Grant never encouraged him to do so. Less concerned with military ranking, Jordan simply judged the husky sergeant to be a good man, and he had been on the verge of reconsidering the offer to sign on as a scout until he learned he would be working with him.

Part of the afternoon was spent with Hamilton Grant, during which Jordan was filled in on the normal routine of the civilian scouts. At the present time, he learned, he was the only white scout attached to M Company, the other six being Crow Indians. Afterward, when Grant had other duties to attend to, Jordan moved his gear into a small storeroom behind the stables. This eight-by-twelve room would serve as his quarters on the post. Grant had arranged it for him. It suited Jordan just fine. If he had been given the choice, he would have probably moved his horses and his gear some distance downriver to set up camp. But Grant pointed out the fact that he needed to be close in case he was needed in a hurry.

At Hamilton's invitation, Jordan joined the first sergeant for supper, where he met several other members of M Company. They offered polite greetings of welcome, but Jordan guessed by the open stares of curiosity that his reputation had preceded him. The fact that he had at one time been a guest in the guardhouse awaiting trial for murder was not exactly a secret either. Fort Laramie, like all army posts, kept very few secrets. So it was well known among the military population that the new scout was the same man who had brutally slain a man less than a year before. The troopers who had witnessed the scene had talked about the grisly execution. So Jordan was not surprised that there would be a tendency on the part of the soldiers to keep a respectful distance from him. In fact, Grant and Macy were the only troopers who felt comfortable around him.

Supper finished, Grant walked with Jordan back to the stables. Crossing the parade ground, they approached the bachelor officers' quarters, affectionately known among the officers as Old Bedlam. The clear sounds of a string quartet could be heard emanating from the room at the rear of the building. Hamilton explained that the building was the social hub of the post, where the officers held parties and dances. He said he had heard that some of the young officers were hosting a spring social that evening.

As they neared the building, they came up behind a couple walking toward the front steps. In the fading half-light of evening, the couple was unaware of Jordan and Hamilton until Hamilton spoke. "Good evening, ma'am . . . sir." He saluted when the couple turned to acknowledge the greeting.

Jordan was stunned when the young lady turned to face them. "Kathleen," he blurted.

Kathleen Beard seemed equally startled for a moment before recognizing the broad-shouldered figure in buckskins. "Jordan?" She then gasped, hardly believing her eyes. Recovering quickly from the surprise, she said, "My goodness, I wasn't sure that was you. You look like an Indian in this light," she teased.

Not sure how to reply, Jordan simply shrugged and said, "I reckon."

"You know each other?" This question came from Kathleen's escort, whom Jordan had scarcely noticed, his gaze having been captured by the image of the woman who had filled his thoughts on many a cold winter night. Jordan glanced at the young man. *Wallace. Kathleen's escort is Lieutenant Wallace.* Now Jordan had another reason to dislike the arrogant young officer, this one stronger than the others. From the look on the lieutenant's face, it was obvious that Wallace was not pleased to learn that Kathleen knew his newest scout.

"Are you on your way to the party?" she

asked, knowing full well that he wasn't, but unable to resist the opportunity to tease him.

"I hardly think so," Thomas Jefferson Wallace answered for him. "The bachelor officers' quarters are off-limits to enlisted men and scouts" — he paused for emphasis — "Indian or white."

Jordan ignored the rude remark, his gaze captured by the warm smile on Kathleen's face. "Sergeant Grant is giving me a hand gettin' settled," he said. Then shifting his gaze momentarily to the impatient officer, he added, "After I get my gear settled, I might come back to see if they need any servants for your party."

Kathleen laughed, but finding no humor in Jordan's joke, Wallace scowled and insisted, "Come, Kathleen, we're missing the dancing." He then directed an order in Grant's direction. "Carry on, sergeant."

"Yes, sir," Grant replied, making no attempt to hide the grin on his face. But Jordan remained motionless, his eyes locked on Kathleen's.

"Come to see me tomorrow," she said, placing her hand on Jordan's forearm. "I'm anxious to hear how you've been."

"We'll be leaving in the morning on patrol," Wallace immediately inserted, obviously irritated by the lady's hand on Jordan's arm. "I don't think *Mr.* Jordan will have time for visiting."

"That's a fact," Jordan said, his eyes still captive of her gaze, "but I'd be pleased to visit when we get back."

"That's a promise," Kathleen replied, her smile lighting the gloom of evening. "It's nice to see you again," she called over her shoulder as Lieutenant Wallace took her arm and led her toward the steps.

Jordan stood transfixed until he felt a tug on his arm. "Looks like you and the lieutenant have somethin' in common after all," Hamilton Grant remarked, thoroughly amused by anything that served to get Wallace's goat. "Give you somethin' to talk about on patrol."

Jordan turned his gaze away from the steps. "We're just friends. She nursed me back to health after I took a couple of bullets in the shoulder." He didn't care to comment further, especially to express his disappointment to see that she was keeping company with a man as arrogant as Wallace. In spite of reminding himself that he had no stake in Kathleen Beard's life, it still angered him that she was being escorted by the lieutenant.

CHAPTER 3

Sergeant Grant had advised Jordan that the patrol would not start out until after mess call, but Jordan was awake before sunup. He heard the bugler blow reveille. Then, in about thirty minutes, there was another bugle, which he would later learn was stable and watering call. With Sweet Pea saddled and ready, he was waiting at the mess tent when Hamilton Grant arrived at seven o'clock, just as the bugle sounded mess call.

"You said the patrol was leaving first thing this morning," Jordan said when Grant walked up to join him. "With all the bugles blowin' and everybody runnin' around, I thought for a little bit that the patrol had left without me."

Grant laughed and replied, "You're new to army routine. Everything has to be done on schedule. Lieutenant Wallace likes to start out with a good breakfast under his belt, so he'll be ready to go after the troops are fed."

"Seems like an awful lot of fuss to me," Jordan said, a smile on his face.

"It's the army way," Grant returned.

"You don't look like you're ready to ride," Jordan observed.

"Hell, I'm not going anywhere," Grant replied. Jordan had assumed that his friend would ride with the patrol, but as first sergeant, Grant would remain to carry out administrative duties in the company orderly room. Reading the surprise and disappointment in Jordan's eyes, the sergeant reassured him, "Macy will be riding with you. He's a good man. You can count on him in a fight." He paused then, wondering if he should say more. "You should get along with Wallace. I warn you, though. He thinks he can wipe out the whole Sioux nation with one company of men."

From his brief exposure to the lieutenant, Jordan wasn't surprised at all, and he again had second thoughts about signing on as a scout. *What the hell?* he decided. *I'll go on this patrol and then decide if I'm gonna be a scout or not.*

After breakfast, the patrol formed on the parade ground. Four mounted Crow scouts sat watching the soldiers as the troopers milled around with no apparent show of urgency. With a quick tip of his finger to his hat, he bade Hamilton Grant farewell and wheeled Sweet Pea around to join the detachment. Pulling up before the four Crow scouts, he reined up a safe distance away lest Sweet Pea take a nip out of one of the ponies' flanks. The Indians eyed the scruffy-looking horse in open curiosity. In a few minutes, Lieutenant Wallace appeared, riding an immaculately groomed blue roan. The troopers responded to his presence, forming up in formation. Wallace hardly glanced in Jordan's direction as he waited for Macy to report the patrol ready to ride. When all was in order to the lieutenant's satisfaction, he led the detail out in a column of twos. The Crow scouts followed the column, and Jordan brought up the rear. With no instructions from the lieutenant, he was not sure where his position should be. After leaving the post behind, Wallace ordered the Crow scouts out on the flanks. With still no specific instructions as to what was expected of him, Jordan rode up to the head of the column.

"Do you want me to lead you to that homesteaders' cabin?" Jordan asked the lieutenant. It was his impression that it was the sole reason for his being on the patrol.

Wallace cast a condescending glance in

Jordan's direction. "It won't be necessary, Mr. Gray. I know full well where the Weldon place is."

"Then what the hell am I doin' here?" Jordan responded, unable to hide his irritation.

The two young men glared at each other for a long moment before Wallace replied, "You're here to learn. I'm told that you supposedly know the Big Horn country. Maybe you'll be useful when we send patrols out in that area. As far as the present operation, you'd do well to watch the Crow scouts." That said, he turned his eyes to the front, dismissing his new civilian scout.

Before this is over, you and I are going to have a little tussle. The thought must have been apparent on Jordan's face because Macy pulled up alongside him. "You ain't the first one that wanted to kick his arrogant ass," he whispered low. Macy's remark served to cool Jordan's anger a bit, and he gave the corporal a slight smile and a nod of his head. *Maybe so, but I might be the first one that gets the job done,* he thought.

The patrol — fifteen enlisted men, one officer, four Crow scouts, and one white scout — arrived at the Weldon place about midmorning the second day out. Jordan would have thought the distance could have been covered in one full day's march, but he was learning firsthand that the military moved in a grinding sequence of orders and procedures. When the charred ruins of the cabin were in sight, he nudged Sweet Pea out ahead of the patrol. Three days before, when he had encountered the three white men, there had been no opportunity to scout the area without risking his neck. Now he wanted to examine the tracks around the cabin before the soldiers added their own.

There was an abundance of prints around the small clearing, some old, some fairly new. Most were from shod horses, but there were a few from unshod horses, which made Jordan wonder if his hunch about Preacher and his sons might be a little suspect. Still, it was a strong gut feeling he had experienced when he had faced the three white men, so it was hard to concede to Preacher's version of the tragedy. He stood up to meet the patrol as they rode into the clearing.

"Sioux," one of the troopers called out after retrieving an arrow from a corner post of the cabin. It had been so obviously planted that Jordan had not even noticed it when he rode in ahead of the soldiers. He took a good look at it as it was being handed to Wallace, and he was willing to bet that it was the same arrow Preacher's son had fetched from his saddle strap.

Wallace turned the arrow over and over, examining it closely. "It's Sioux all right." He glanced over at Jordan. "You agree, Gray?" It was obvious from his tone that he was baiting his new scout.

"I agree that what you've got in your hand is a Sioux arrow, but I ain't sure this was the work of a Sioux war party."

The lieutenant formed a slow smile as he gazed at Jordan. "Still think this was done by white men, right?"

"Looks that way to me," Jordan replied.

Wallace dismounted then, and pointed to the tracks that Jordan had been examining when the patrol rode up. "Unshod," he said. "Indian ponies."

"Maybe so," Jordan had to admit.

"Sioux war party," Wallace pronounced confidently, and handed the arrow to Jordan. He then took a cursory look around the tiny homestead before ordering the Crow scouts out to look around the surrounding hills. "See if you can find which way they left here," he told Iron Pony, the only one of the Crows who spoke English. With a dismissingly smug glance aimed at Jordan, the lieutenant walked over for a closer look at the ruined cabin.

"Sir," Corporal Macy asked, "can the men boil some water for coffee and take a little break while the scouts are out?"

Wallace paused to consider. "Granted, Corporal. A little coffee wouldn't hurt."

Jordan walked over to the trooper who had found the arrow and asked to see exactly where he had picked it up. The soldier pointed to the corner post, about halfway up on the charred timber. "About here?" Jordan asked, pointing to the area indicated. The trooper nodded. Jordan looked closely at the burned post, searching for the exact spot where the arrow had been implanted. All he could find was a small indention, nothing like the scar an arrow shot from a bow would make. With his hand, he sank the arrow into the wood, and backed away, leaving the arrow stuck in the post. "About like this?" he asked the soldier again.

"Yes, sir, I reckon," the trooper replied, failing to see the relevance of Jordan's questions.

Jordan nodded thoughtfully, convinced that it was more than likely the same way the arrow had been planted before. He still had no explanation for the unshod tracks around the clearing, however, and that troubled him. While the men took advantage of the break, he walked over to the corral.

He had barely stepped into the churned-up mud of the small enclosure when he discovered that most of the tracks he saw were from an unshod horse. He was certain then that the tracks found around the cabin were not from Indian ponies. Franklin Weldon's horse was unshod, not that unusual for a white man living so far from a blacksmith.

Feeling it his duty as a scout, he informed the lieutenant of his findings. Clearly skeptical, Wallace listened patiently before voicing his doubts. As he was about to convey them, Iron Pony rode up. "We found 'em," he announced proudly. "Up on the ridge, tracks of five, maybe six ponies."

"Shod?" Wallace shot back.

Iron Pony shook his head. "Not shod — Indian ponies."

With a smug smile, formed for Jordan's benefit, Wallace turned to Macy. "We'll give the men fifteen minutes more and then mount 'em up. Then we'll follow the hostiles' trail. We might even get lucky and run them to ground."

While the soldiers drank their coffee, Jordan climbed the hill to take a look at the tracks Iron Pony had found. "Left ponies here," the Crow scout said as Jordan approached a stand of pines near the top of the slope. "Went on foot here," Iron Pony

57

continued, leading Jordan a dozen or more yards away to a thicket of young pines. Then the somber Crow scout stepped back, offering nothing more.

"Damn!" Jordan softly exclaimed, looking around him in the thicket. It looked like a war had been waged there. Fresh tree limbs lay about on the ground, trunks on many of the young trees showed chips and scars, still new. Dropping to his knee, he looked closely at the pine straw. It told him that someone had lain close to the ground there, no doubt because someone else had been shooting up the thicket. *Maybe Preacher Rix and his two half-wit sons,* he thought. Getting to his feet, Jordan followed the signs back to where the horses had been tied. Then he walked a few yards down the opposite side of the ridge and stood looking out over the prairie in the direction the Indians had obviously fled.

When he turned around, it was to find Iron Pony staring intensely at him. When their eyes met, the Crow warrior nodded his head as if to confirm what Jordan had deduced. Jordan was aware then that the other three scouts were watching him with the same interest shown by Iron Pony, and he realized that they had apparently been evaluating his ability to read sign. Evidently they approved, for all three solemnly nodded their heads. Jordan turned back to Iron Pony. "There was a hot fight here," he said. "I'm thinkin' maybe a Sioux huntin' party came up on the three white men I met here before."

"Maybe so," Iron Pony agreed. Gesturing toward the scarred trees around them, he added, "Too many bullets for one man."

Jordan climbed in the saddle and rode down the slope. The Crows followed on their ponies. About halfway down the hill, they reached the point where other tracks from shod horses mingled with those of the fleeing Indians'. So Jordan had a pretty clear picture of what had taken place. "I expect we'd best go back and tell the lieutenant what we've found," he said. Iron Pony nodded.

"You're still trying to tell me there's a preacher going around murdering home-steaders?" Wallace asked impatiently after hearing Jordan's report. "And now he's fighting Indians as well?"

"All I'm tryin' to tell you is what probably happened here," Jordan replied without emotion. "The Crow scouts agree."

Clearly irritated, Wallace glanced at Iron Pony, then back at Jordan. "The Crows will agree to anything you want them to. They'd say it was preachers, Mormons, or Commanche if they thought that's what you wanted." The lieutenant was certain that the Weldons had been massacred by Sioux raiders, just as other small ranches and homesteads had been hit in the area. He had no time for half-baked theories from the likes of Jordan Gray. Turning to Macy, he ordered him to get the men mounted. "We'll go after these murdering savages," he said as he strode over to his horse. "I don't think we'll find any gun-toting missionaries, though." The shod tracks that joined those left by the Indian ponies simply told him that the Sioux had stolen horses from Weldon.

"Waste of time," Jordan couldn't help commenting. "Those tracks are at least two days old."

Just about to step up in the stirrup, Wallace paused and turned to face Jordan, clearly angry. "Dammit, man, I'll decide what's a waste of time and what isn't. The mission of this patrol is to investigate this Indian attack, and that's what we're going to do. We've all been properly entertained by your wild imagination, but I suggest you take a position at the rear of the column, and maybe you'll learn something."

Jordan stood motionless for a few moments, surprised by the arrogant young officer's scathing verbal attack. It was clearly out of proportion to the facts that Jordan had pointed out. He glanced at Iron Pony, but the Crow scout averted his gaze to the ground, unwilling to support Jordan's position. Jordan didn't blame him. The Crows did not want to risk losing their jobs. Jordan harbored no such fear. The small taste he had of working for the army was already bitter on his tongue. After a long moment of silence, during which the lieutenant stood glaring at him, Jordan finally responded, "Lieutenant, when's the last time somebody told you to kiss their ass?"

"What . . . ? Why, you impudent . . ." Wallace sputtered, mortified to be talked to with such disrespect for his rank. Those troopers closest to him were now frozen dead still, watching the confrontation with some amusement while inching closer so as not to miss anything. This served to fan the flames of Wallace's anger even higher. In a fit of infuriation, he grabbed his riding crop from his saddle strap and took a step toward Jordan.

"If you're plannin' to use that crop on me, you'd best think on the idea some more," Jordan advised, his voice calm, his words even and unhurried.

Though soft and without apparent anger,

the buckskin-clad scout's tone had a lethal quality that caused Wallace to freeze in his tracks. He looked around him, dismayed to realize that none of his command appeared ready to defend him, content instead to be spectators to the confrontation. Burning with indignation and frustration, he nevertheless retained the good judgment to avoid engaging Jordan in a fistfight. "You're fired!" he finally blurted. "You no longer are employed as a scout for this patrol."

"Suit yourself." Jordan shrugged, having already decided that being an army scout was not necessarily in his future plans.

Seeking to quickly end the mortifying confrontation and regain his air of authority, Wallace stepped up in the saddle. "Let's move 'em out, Corporal Macy."

"Yes, Sir!" Macy replied smartly and wheeled his horse to carry out the lieutenant's command. As he turned, he winked at Jordan and nodded his approval.

Jordan acknowledged the nod and backed Sweet Pea away to give the corporal room. Within a matter of minutes, Macy had the patrol ready to ride. A casual spectator now, Jordan sat his horse and watched the column file past him and proceed down the slope. *Following a trail that's at least two days old, maybe three,* he thought. It was a waste of time. The half dozen Sioux who had left those tracks were probably back on the reservation by this time. Jordan was convinced that they had nothing to do with the bodies occupying the grave below him in the clearing, anyway. *Well,* he thought, *I didn't have much of a career as an army scout.* He shrugged and decided it was best to find out right away that he wasn't suited to the vocation. Had it not been for the fact that his packhorse and most of his possessions were back at Fort Laramie, he would have turned Sweet Pea's head toward the northwest to the Big Horns. Even as he thought it, a vision of Kathleen Beard invaded his mind. Unwilling to admit to a strong interest there, he told himself that he would return to Fort Laramie only long enough to collect his horse and possibles.

CHAPTER 4

"I thought you was on patrol with Lieutenant Wallace," Alton Broom called out when Jordan passed the post trader's store. Standing on the step outside the store, he bent down to shake the ashes from his pipe, tapping it against the wall, then stood up again, awaiting Jordan's reply.

"I was," Jordan returned.

"Well, what in the world are you doin' back here?" Alton asked impatiently. He peered around Jordan to see if the patrol might be following behind. "Grant said you was to be gone for five days."

"I was fired," Jordan answered, offering nothing more in the way of embellishment. "I came back to get my things."

"Well, I'll be go to hell," Alton uttered, finding it hard to believe. He agreed with Sergeant Grant's impression that Wallace couldn't get a better scout. "It ain't none of my business, but how'd you ever get crossways with Wallace?"

"It ain't hard to do," Jordan replied, but declined to go into detail about his altercation with the pompous young officer. Alton was still curious, but didn't push it when it was obvious that Jordan was not going to discuss it. "Which is the doctor's house?" Jordan asked, changing the subject abruptly.

"Captain Beard?" Alton responded. "The post surgeon's house is the first one just past the bachelors' quarters. Are you ailin'?" he asked, thinking that might have something to do with Jordan's early return to Laramie.

"No, I'm all right. He patched me up once for a gunshot wound in Fort Gibson. I just thought I might wanna let him take a look." It was a lie. His wounds had healed long ago, even though he still carried a slug deep in the muscles of his shoulder. It wasn't the doctor that he wanted to see.

"I expect you'll most likely find him at the hospital this time of day," Alton said.

"Much obliged," Jordan said, nudging Sweet Pea with his heels, ending the discussion, and leaving Alton to scratch his head, his curiosity frustrated. Jordan hadn't really wanted to see Captain Beard at all. In fact he hoped he wouldn't be home.

He slow-walked Sweet Pea past the bachelor officers' quarters, still making up his mind whether or not to present himself to the captain's daughter. She had specifically asked him to call on her when he returned from the patrol, but now he was wondering if she had really meant it. *Why in hell would she want to see me?* Maybe she was just being polite to a former patient. *Why in hell would I want to see her?* He had to stop and think about that. He was in no position to call on a young lady.

He suddenly found himself in front of the doctor's house. He pulled Sweet Pea to a stop before the porch and sat there trying to decide to dismount or wheel about and head for the stables. *Don't be a damn fool,* he told himself and turned away. He was about to give Sweet Pea a hard heel when he heard her voice behind him.

"Jordan?" Kathleen called from the doorway. Startled, Jordan pulled back on the reins. "Were you coming to see me?" She walked out on the porch. "You looked like you were about to ride off. I declare, it seems every time I see you, you're running off somewhere."

"No . . . I mean, yes, I thought I might stop by to see you," he stammered, feeling a warm glow creeping up the back of his neck.

"Then why were you going to ride away?"

When it was obvious that the young man was too flustered to answer, she asked, "Is the patrol back? Thomas said he would be out for five days."

"I expect they'll be a couple of days longer." That did not answer her question, and he could see that she was waiting for a full explanation. "I just came back alone."

"I don't understand," she said, a puzzled look upon her face. "Are you all right?" He assured her that he was. "Come on inside," she directed. "It's too chilly to talk out here."

He tied Sweet Pea's reins to the corner porch post and followed her inside. As soon as he crossed the threshold, he felt out of place. Kathleen had done an elegant job of making a comfortable home for her father and herself. The living room was furnished with delicate pieces, no doubt shipped from New Orleans or St. Louis, with braided carpets on the polished wood floor. Jordan cast a nervous eye about him at the dainty crocheted doilies gracing the chair backs and the sofa. He had not seen such elegance since he was a young hired hand on his father-in-law's farm. And, just as he had felt he did not belong then, such was his feeling on this day, when memories of his late wife came back to him. He suddenly found himself fighting panic. Sensing it, Kathleen suggested they go to the kitchen and sit at the table.

"I was just thinking about making a cup of tea," she said, her smile radiating warmth that served to dispel his discomfort. "Would you like a cup?"

"Why, I reckon," he stuttered. He would have preferred a cup of coffee. He could not recall if he had ever had a cup of tea. In his present state of nervousness, he would have gratefully accepted anything she offered.

He sat at the table, watching her every move as she placed a kettle of water on the stove to boil. Reaching into a cupboard, she took a china teapot down from the shelf and placed it upon the table along with two cups and saucers. Jordan's feeling of panic began anew as she reached for a tin of ground tea. He was suddenly aware of his rough buckskin shirt and trousers, and he fixed his gaze upon the delicate china cup before him. What if he was clumsy and broke it? Sensing his insecurity, she sat down opposite him while waiting for the water to boil.

"Now tell me about your disagreement with Thomas," she said, still smiling. He had not suggested that there had been one, but she could easily guess that there had.

She knew that the lieutenant could be hard to get along with for a wild spirit like Jordan Gray. And their meeting the other night had left little doubt that the two young men had developed an immediate dislike for each other. She was also fairly confident that she could be the main reason for their conflict. It did not give her any satisfaction, for she truly held each in high regard. In fact, she had spent a great deal of time with Lieutenant Thomas Jefferson Wallace lately, and she was certain that a proposal of marriage would soon be forthcoming. It was a matter that she had given considerable thought of late. She was not getting any younger, and Thomas seemed destined for success in the military. She had spent her life in military garrisons as the daughter of the post surgeon, so it was a lifestyle she was comfortable with.

Gazing at Jordan now, as his eyes nervously scanned his surroundings, she could not help but be reminded of a hawk trapped in a cage. There was something about this wild hawk that touched a special place deep in her heart, a fascination that drew her to him. She wished it were not so. It would make things a great deal simpler for her, for she feared she was going to be called upon to choose. And, really, there was but one sensible choice for a girl in her situation. She knew what life as Thomas Wallace's wife would be like. Who could say what life with Jordan Gray would be like? She wondered if he ever even thought about the future. Her thoughts were interrupted by the sudden whistling of the kettle.

She got up from the table and poured the boiling water into the teapot. "We'll let it steep for a bit," she said cheerfully. "Now you were going to tell me what happened between you and Thomas that sent you back here early."

Reluctantly, he related the disagreement between himself and the lieutenant with no embellishment of the details. "We just don't see eye to eye on a lot of things, I guess," he summed it up. "They didn't really need me as a scout, anyway."

"Thomas can be difficult to understand at times," she conceded, "but he's really a good and kind man at heart." She found it important to defend the lieutenant, although Jordan's facial expression indicated that he was not convinced. She studied the somber young man seated at her table, looking so desperately out of place, and she again felt a sense of awe and the fascination of being close to an untamed creature. He did not possess the finely chiseled features of her handsome lieutenant, yet there was admittedly a rugged beauty in the tawny-haired, broad-shouldered young scout reminiscent of the lethal beauty of a mountain lion. Fearful, lest her thoughts lead her in a foolish direction, she abruptly got up to pour the tea.

There was a protracted period of silence while the two young people sipped the hot liquid. Jordan, still afraid he might drop the delicate cup, squeezed the fragile handle between thumb and forefinger. The handle was not large enough to loop his finger through. In his mind, he pictured the prim and proper Lieutenant Wallace in his place. He was sure the lieutenant was probably right at home sipping tea from delicate china. The picture served to irritate him, and he decided he might as well find out how things stood between Kathleen and Wallace. Never having been accused of being subtle, he blurted out, "Are you and the lieutenant seein' each other serious-like?"

Damn you, she thought, for she had hoped to avoid the subject. She would have preferred not to admit her relationship with Thomas. She held no desire to deceive Jordan. It was just that she had been telling herself that she had not made that decision when, in fact, she actually had. Now, after his blunt question, she was forced to tell him the truth, even though reluctant to. "I guess you might say that," she admitted. "Thomas has been calling on me since we came here."

His expression did not change, but the disappointment was apparent in his eyes as he absorbed her answer. *Only a fool would have thought otherwise,* he thought. Fashioning a faint smile for her, he said, "Well, I reckon you could do a lot worse for yourself."

Damn you, Jordan Gray. Why don't you do something about it if you want me? She immediately scolded herself for thinking such thoughts, for she knew that if he had suddenly taken her in his arms, she would not have resisted. And she would have never forgiven herself for allowing it. She had to listen to her practical sense. There was a future with Thomas. What could she expect with Jordan? A cave in the mountains? At best, a tent on an army post while he was employed as a scout? She could not commit to a life like that. "Father says that Thomas has a great future with the army," she commented lamely. "West Point graduates have the best opportunity for advancement."

He nodded solemnly, as if deeply considering her remark. "Well, you know I wish you the very best," he finally said. He placed the china cup carefully on the saucer. "I expect I'd better go. I've got to get ready to travel." With that, he stood up and placed his chair back under the table.

Feeling his disappointment, as well as a stabbing hollow feeling in her own heart, she rose to accompany him to the door. Wanting to tell him something to ease his hurt, she placed a hand on his arm and said, "You know, you'll always have a special place in my heart." As soon as the words came out, she knew she should not have said them, for the hurt deepened in his eyes. He paused at the door to look directly into her eyes, and for a moment, she was sure he was going to speak, but he didn't, leaving his thoughts unsaid. "Where will you go?" Kathleen couldn't help but ask.

"I don't know — the Black Hills maybe." He flashed her a smile then. "Maybe I'll find some of that gold everybody's talkin' about." He had really given no thought as to what he was going to do. The Black Hills just happened to pop into his mind at that moment. Now, when he thought about it, he decided, *Why not? But right now, I think I could use a drink.*

There were two horses tied to the rail in

front of the post trader's store when Jordan walked up, leading Sweet Pea. One was saddled, the other loaded with packs. Out of consideration for their welfare, Jordan tied Sweet Pea to the porch corner post, well away from the other two. Inside, he encountered the man he had met several days before talking to Alton Broom. Both men turned to greet him.

"Come to get that drink I owe you?" Ned Booth asked with a welcoming grin.

Jordan, his mind heavy with self-disgust for having had thoughts of approaching Kathleen Beard, tried to grin in return. "I could use a drink, even that poison Alton sells." He paused, then said, "Matter of fact, I'd prefer that poison."

With a wink for Booth, Alton went to the bar to fetch a bottle and glass. "What's the occasion, Jordan? I don't recollect you ever buyin' a drink of liquor. Are you celebratin' somethin'?"

Jordan couldn't help but respond with a bitter laugh. *Yeah,* he thought, *I'm celebrating being a damn fool.* "I'm celebratin' leavin' this place, I reckon."

"Hell, you just got here," Alton remarked. "You leavin' already? Where you headed this time?"

Jordan shook his head thoughtfully. "I

don't know. I'm just goin'." He tossed the drink down, grimacing from the fiery trail it left in his throat. "Damn, that stuff's awful. Gimme another." He turned to Ned Booth. "Now I'll buy you one."

"Thanks just the same," Booth replied, "but I'm all caught up on my drinkin'."

Jordan tossed the second drink down, squinting his eyes almost closed until the fire subsided. "I reckon I've caught up with mine, too," he announced when Alton held the bottle poised over the empty shot glass. "I don't guess I need a snootful of that stuff."

Booth, who had been studying the young man closely, spoke up then. "Why don't you come with me? I'm headin' out for the Black Hills. I could use a partner. It ain't all that healthy, a man alone in that country. We might even strike it rich, and if we don't, why, hell, what have we lost?"

Jordan had to consider the prospect for no more than a moment. "I've never been to the Black Hills, but I've heard plenty about the place, some good, some bad. I reckon it's time I see for myself."

Booth's face lit up with a wide smile. "Well, I can show you around 'cause I've spent a fair amount of time in that country. 'Course, I ain't been back since the hills got overrun with prospectors, so I reckon we'll both have somethin' to see." He extended his hand. "So it's a deal then?"

"I reckon," Jordan replied and shook his new partner's hand.

"Then let's get the hell outta here!" Booth exclaimed with a grin. "We're burnin' daylight standin' here jawin' with the likes of Alton Broom."

In less than an hour's time, Jordan cut his packhorse out of the cavalry corral, packed his belongings, and was ready to ride. Ned Booth watched his new partner's movements as Jordan readied himself for the trail. He decided right away that he approved of Jordan's cross-strapping of his packhorse's load, balancing the packs to make it easier on the animal. He settled his concentration upon Jordan's saddle horse then. He could not recall having seen a more homely beast. Curious as to why a man chose to ride a horse that looked more like a shaggy mule, he studied Sweet Pea closely, taking note of the animal's broad chest and full body, and the constant flickering of the ears, first this way, then another, indicating the horse was alert to everything around it. "That's a pretty stout horse you're ridin'," he decided.

Jordan was surprised by the comment. Sweet Pea was never paid a complimentary remark by someone just introduced to her. He decided that Ned had a pretty good eye for horses. "Yep, she'll usually get the job done, but her disposition needs some work. Take care not to let your horses stand too close to her, especially her left side. She'll take a nip outta anything that crowds her."

With Jordan's possessions packed on his horses, the two new partners set out for Ned's camp by the river. After some discussion, they decided to wait until morning to start. "Startin' out on a new adventure is always best first thing of a mornin'," Ned opined. "Besides, that'll put us at the Niobrara River about dark, and that's a good spot to make camp."

Alton Broom stood on the step of the post trader's store, watching until they were out of sight. "I swear, if I didn't have a wife and young'uns to worry about, I'd go with 'em," he muttered to himself.

CHAPTER 5

"I'm much obliged to you fellers for sharin' your grub with me and my boys. It's especially gratifyin' to me to find Christian men in this land of the heathen, what with my youngest needing to rest his leg." Preacher Rix sucked the last particles of meat from the prairie hen's leg and tossed the cleaned bone into the fire. He had volunteered no explanation for the bullet wound in Quincy's leg, leaving one to speculate on the circumstances that resulted in his son being shot. Leaning back against a rock, he wiped the grease from his hands on his bearskin coat and relaxed while he sucked the remnants of his repast from his teeth. With a broad smile of satisfaction, he studied the two miners who had generously shared their supper with him as well as providing a fairly clean cloth for Quincy's leg. Glancing at his sons, who were oblivious to anything but the few remaining beans they were scraping from the iron pot, his grin became even wider.

"Been a spell since you folks et?" It seemed a logical question to ask, judging by the ravenous appetites exhibited by his surprise guests. The miner, a tall, lean man with a snow-white beard, exchanged a quick glance with his partner, who was equally astonished by the three strangers.

Ignoring the question, Preacher asked one of his own. "You boys strike it lucky?"

"Not a thing," the white-bearded miner answered, shooting a warning glance at his partner, a younger man who, in turn, echoed the older man's answer.

Preacher studied their faces for a few moments, doubting the honesty of their answers. "Then it don't make a lot of sense to stay here in this hollow, does it? I mean, if you ain't findin' no gold."

The miner was about to reply when they were distracted by the empty iron pot rolling on the ground, where it had been carelessly tossed aside after Zeb and Quincy had scraped the last bean from it. Like two hungry bears, Preacher's sons sniffed around the campfire as if looking for anything else edible. Their actions brought a grin of amusement to their father's face. The two miners looked at each other in disbelief. Looking back at Preacher again, White Beard answered his question. "We was about to pack up and leave this creek when you fellers rode in."

"That a fact?" Rix replied. "Where you headed?"

White Beard looked at his partner, not sure he wanted to say. "Word is, a feller named Pearson struck color north of here in a place they call Deadwood Gulch. We thought maybe we might try our luck there."

"We're on our way there, ourselves. Ain't we, boys?" Preacher shot a glance at his sons with a slight nod of his head. They understood and took a few casual steps to position themselves behind the two miners.

Fearing the three might be thinking about traveling with him and his partner, White Beard quickly responded, "We ain't hardly packed up yet, since we ain't in no particular hurry."

His smile still firmly in place, Preacher said, "There ain't no need to pack up your earthly possessions. The Lord has other use for them. You're as ready as you're gonna get for your journey."

Confused by what seemed to be a nonsensical remark, White Beard turned to look over his shoulder at Zeb, who had moved directly behind him now. The dull-witted son returned the look with a foolish grin. White Beard turned back to face Preacher, looking for an explanation.

"The Lord giveth, and the Lord taketh away," Preacher offered the doomed man. "You're about to be took away."

White Beard opened his mouth to speak, but his words were choked off by a sharp gasp as he recoiled from Zeb's knife thrust deep into his side. Stunned by the sudden attack, he rolled over, almost landing in the fire while trying to reach his shotgun propped against a nearby rock. "Jim!" he cried out to warn his partner. "Look out!" His warning was followed almost instantly by the sound of a pistol as Quincy put a bullet in the back of Jim's head.

Preacher casually kicked the shotgun out of White Beard's reach and stood watching while the wounded man flailed about on the ground, trying to grasp the knife handle protruding from his side. The blade, while not deep enough to cause a mortal wound due to the thickness of the coat White Beard wore, was lodged in the muscle of the man's side. "Finish him, son," Preacher calmly instructed. "You shoulda used your gun like your brother did."

"I wanted to do it with my knife," Zeb complained.

"Well, you shoulda cut his throat then," Preacher said.

Still intent upon killing the man with a knife, Zeb called out to his brother, "Quincy, throw me your knife." While he waited for Quincy to draw his knife from his belt and toss it on the ground before him, his victim started crawling toward the horses.

With no concern for the man's attempt to escape, Preacher called after him, "This would be a good time to ask the Lord for forgiveness of your sins."

"Damn you, you've kilt me," White Beard sobbed as he continued to crawl, the pain in his side searing him like fire.

"Ask for forgiveness," Preacher said. "Don't go to meet your Maker with blasphemy on your sinful lips."

"Damn you," White Beard repeated.

With Quincy's knife in hand now, Zeb let out a triumphant yell and jumped astraddle White Beard's back. Attacking again and again, he slashed the man's throat repeatedly until White Beard collapsed to the ground dead.

"It coulda been a whole lot quicker," Preacher remarked critically. "Let's see what the Lord has provided," he said, already rummaging through the miners' packs.

"Can we scalp 'em, Pa?"

"Yeah, go ahead. Make it look like the heathen Injuns done 'em in." He finished ransacking the miners' belongings while his two sons gleefully went about their grisly business. Finding nothing of real value in the packs, he began a search of the rocks and dead logs around the camp, looking for evidence of a rock out of place or a patch of disturbed soil. Frustrated when the search yielded no evidence of a secret hiding place, he paused and lifted his deep voice toward the heavens. "Guide my hand, Lord. Show me where these two miserable sinners hid their gold." He felt certain that there had to be some of the precious dust hidden thereabouts. The camp was apparently two or three weeks old, and he figured the two miners would not have remained there for that length of time had there been no show of color. "Throw them scalps in the fire, and help me find the treasure," he ordered.

Zeb and Quincy watched for a few moments, fascinated by the sizzle of the two scalps as they curled up in the flames. Preacher had to scold them both for dawdling when he had given them a command. Preacher was patient with his boys, even considering the tardiness with which they seemed to approach maturity. Zeb, the eldest of the two, would soon be thirty-five, as near as Preacher could remember, and he still had to be told what to do. Quincy, a year younger than his brother, was not as smart as Zeb. An impartial bystander would have no doubt expressed it another way: Quincy was even dumber than his brother. It was too bad Quincy's brain had not grown as rapidly as his hulking body. Preacher shook his head sadly when he thought about it. It wasn't the boy's fault. If he hadn't lost his mother at such an early age, he might have turned out differently. It wasn't the boy's sin, but that of his mother. Zeb was the spitting image of his father, but Quincy favored his mother's cousin more than Preacher, a disturbing fact that bothered Preacher from the day the child was born. Then, one night, he had received a vision of his wife's cousin having carnal knowledge of the boy's mother. Preacher awoke from the sinful dream, knowing the Lord had seen fit to enlighten him. It was soon after that night that the Lord had provided the occasion for Preacher to slay both sinners. It was then that he felt the hand of the Lord upon him, as well as the satisfaction he derived upon the taking of life. With his two young sons he left Missouri behind, seeking out sinners on the new frontier.

"Pa, there ain't no gold here," Zeb complained. "We done looked under ever' rock and stick. There ain't no gold."

"It's here. I can smell it." Preacher was not ready to give up the search. He was convinced that the two miners would have broken camp long before this if they had not been successful. He looked around the campsite, his eyes darting from one corner of the clearing to the opposite. "Quincy!" he suddenly blurted. "Grab that shovel and drag that fire over." The only place they had not looked was under the coals of the fire.

Preacher watched anxiously as Quincy scattered the coals and charred pieces of wood from the bed of ashes. "Brush them ashes outta the way and dig that dirt up under 'em," Preacher ordered. Quincy dug a hole about a foot deep, extending the sides wider and wider until it became evident that there was nothing buried under the fire. "Dad blame it!" Preacher complained. "I woulda bet my soul them boys had struck it, but I reckon I was wrong." He threw up his hands in surrender. "Let's get on our way. There's still plenty of daylight left. Take whatever you need, and remember the Lord has provided."

"I want me them boots," Zeb stated, gazing at the younger miner's corpse. "They look about my size."

Preacher glanced again at the boots. Almost knee-high, they were of a type common to miners of that day, with low heels and laces to the top. He had fancied them himself, but had quickly determined that they were too small for his feet. "Well, take 'em then, and let's be on our way."

Zeb wasted no time in unlacing the boots, and with a foot planted on the dead man's crotch for leverage, he pulled the boots off. In his haste to liberate the boots, he failed to notice the two small pouches of gold dust that dropped out of the pants legs to rest on the ground.

"What about them mules?" Quincy asked.

Preacher paused to consider, then ordered, "Put a rope on one of 'em and bring him along. I don't want to bother with no ornery mules. If we don't see nothin' better before dark, we'll butcher him for supper." Quincy did as he was told, and soon the three were on their way, their horses loping along the narrow valley floor. The encounter had not been bountiful, but they had something to show for their trouble: some extra utensils, a fine pair of boots for one of his boys, and something for supper. Preacher judged it to be worthwhile.

■ ■ ■ ■

Jordan and Ned Booth started out from Fort Laramie on a frosty April morning, with the last clear notes of the bugler sounding stable and watering call hanging on the crisp cold air. For the first hour, they accompanied a muleskinner, an acquaintance of Ned's, who was driving a two-wagon load of supplies to Fort Fetterman. Jordan was beginning to wonder if Ned knew every soul west of the Missouri. They bid the teamster farewell at Goose Creek when he followed the trail to the northwest, and Jordan and Ned struck out to the north. Increasing the pace after leaving the slow moving mules, Ned planned to make the Niobrara River before dark. With no trail to follow, and none needed, the two partners held their horses on a true north course, making their way through scattered patches of sagebrush and prickly pear cactus. A chilling north breeze blew fresh on their faces, giving notice that Old Man Winter was reluctant to concede the stage to spring. Though riding easily in the saddle, both men were alert to the prairie around them, constantly scanning the endless expanse of rolling plain for any sign of Sioux hunting parties.

It was almost dark when they reached the banks of the Niobrara and their first night's camp. The river ran clear and not deep enough to make the crossing difficult, so they made their camp on the other side. "One of the prettiest rivers you'll ever see," Ned declared. "She's got some sassy spots downstream a-ways, but she's pretty much a lady. I've been down her almost to the Missouri."

Jordan nodded in reply, making no comment, but he wondered if there was anyplace west of the Missouri that Ned had not visited.

In three days' time, they reached the Cheyenne River and the feet of the dark peaks that had loomed upon the horizon for many miles before. Even at this point, it was easy to see why Indians of various tribes had regarded the Black Hills as sacred land. For generations now, it had been Sioux territory, they and the Cheyenne having banished other tribes, and they regarded it as their spiritual home. The quiet mystique of the towering mountains, which looked so out of place in the heart of an endless prairie, seemed to silently warn a stranger that this was a special place. Jordan could not help but feel that he and Ned, and all white men, were trespassers.

They followed the river in a generally eastern direction for a short distance. Leaving the river then, Ned led them northward again into a valley that took them into the heart of the mountains. Steep slopes, covered with dark pines and rocky ledges rose up from the valley floor on each side of the riders as the mountains closed in to form a narrow passage that eventually led to another valley, this one with a busy stream that bisected it. They had progressed more than halfway up the valley when Jordan spotted a hoofprint near the edge of the stream.

"Damned if it ain't," Ned declared. "Shod, and it ain't that old." He unconsciously took a quick look around him. "Looks like somebody else is tryin' their luck in this valley."

They continued on along the streambank for about one hundred yards before Ned pulled up again and pointed toward the peak above them. High above the cliffs, a circle of buzzards formed their macabre wheel. " 'Pears like the boys has found somethin' for dinner," Ned commented dryly. "Hard to say whether it's on this side of the mountain or t'other."

They continued following the stream as it wound around the foot of the mountain until the narrow passage broadened to form a grassy clearing. Near the head of the clearing, a solitary mule stood watching them approach. Both men pulled up to take a closer look before proceeding. After a brief moment, Ned pointed to a cluster of rocks beyond the stream. "Yonder" was all he said. Jordan nodded, having seen the bodies at almost the same time.

After making sure the mule was the only living thing in the camp, Ned and Jordan rode in and dismounted. The bodies of the two white prospectors lay in grotesque poses in evidence of their violent deaths. Both had been scalped, one shot in the back of the head; the other appeared to have been hacked to death with a knife. While at first it appeared to be the work of Indians, there were some things that didn't quite add up. Obviously, both men had been killed by someone who must have taken them by surprise. Otherwise they would not have been killed at such close range. The scattered remains of a campfire, and the freshly dug hole where the fire had been, didn't look like something a party of Lakota Sioux would have done.

Ned knelt down among the charred limbs and ashes. After a few seconds, he asked, "How many Injuns you ever seen take a scalp and throw it in the fire?" He held up a scrap of singed hair, still attached to a charred piece of skin, for Jordan to see. "These boys was done in by white men, maybe their own partners, but I don't think it was Injuns that done it."

Something curious caught Jordan's eye near the corpse of one of the miners. The man's boots had been removed, and lying on the ground, partially hidden by the victim's pants leg, was a small pouch. Jordan knelt down to examine it. "How many white men would kill somebody and leave their gold dust behind?" The word *gold* immediately got Ned's attention, and he came to see what Jordan had found.

"Well, I'll be . . ." Ned uttered, as he peered into the small pouch. "It's gold dust all right." Then he pointed to the corpse's other leg. "And there's another'n."

What was puzzling at first, but became crystal clear to Jordan after a moment, was the scene that had taken place here. Looking around him at the camp, he saw that everything was turned upside down. Obviously, the killers had torn the place apart looking for the little pouches that were lying right under their eyes. "Pull the boots off of the other one, and I wouldn't be surprised if you find a couple more of these," he said.

Ned felt around the boot tops of the other

body. Jordan was right, for he felt two pouches resting in the trousers where they were tucked into the boots. He removed the boots and examined the small hide sacks. "Looks like they trusted each other," Ned commented. "They hid their gold in the same place." The four pouches looked to be evenly split. He tossed two of them to Jordan. "Well, it didn't take us long to strike it rich, did it? I didn't figure on doin' it this way, though — them poor devils."

"I guess we can put 'em in the ground," Jordan said. "That's the least we can do for 'em."

"Hell, that's what them boys is for," Ned replied, nodding his head toward the ring of buzzards circling overhead. "Buzzards gotta eat, too."

"I reckon," Jordan said, "but I feel like we oughta do somethin' for these poor fellows, considerin' they gave us the gold they worked for." He picked up the shovel lying near the hole that had once been a campfire. "I'll do the diggin'. The grave's already half dug, anyway."

"I'll take a turn," Ned relented with some reluctance. If he had any religion, part of it was a strong disdain for any form of manual labor. "I ain't took on a preacher for a partner, have I?" he chided.

The word *preacher* struck a strong chord in Jordan's mind, for at that moment he happened to be looking at a hoofprint left in the soft dirt that had been shoveled aside. He had seen a similar print before at the burned-out cabin where he had happened upon the self-proclaimed preacher and his two sons. The spur was not as evident as before, bearing testimony that it was gradually wearing down. But it was still distinguishable to Jordan's eye. "I've got a fair idea who did this piece of work," he finally commented, and then he went on to explain as he took up the shovel and began to dig.

"A preacher, huh?" Ned grunted. "Don't surprise me none."

By the time Jordan finished the grave, it was getting along late in the afternoon. The sun would soon be blocked out by the steep peaks that formed the tiny valley, so they decided to camp there for the night. Ned was curious to see if he could strike any color in the rocky stream since the two prospectors had evidently taken some dust there. While Jordan made camp, Ned took a pan and tried his luck. When darkness finally settled in the valley, he gave up. "They musta cleaned this stream out," he declared. "I didn't aim to stop here anyway. The real strikes have been up north of here."

The next morning, they continued on their way, leaving the little valley behind. For the next two days, they made their way from one narrow valley to the next. Tall, rugged mountains stood silent, seemingly watching the two white men, as they pushed farther and farther into the sacred territory of the Sioux. Both men seemed to feel the spiritual presence that dwelled in the cliffs and rocks above them. Even the hawks that occasionally circled to watch their progress refrained from calling out. Winter had not left the mountains, even though it was well into April now. So it was with great relief that the two travelers finally came into a much gentler country of grassy meadows and dark ponderosa slopes. There was sign everywhere of pronghorn antelope and deer, even some elk sign. The two new partners decided it was too much to pass up, so they made camp by a stream that curved around the foot of a high hill and took some time to hunt for fresh meat.

"How much farther is this gulch we're lookin' for?" Jordan asked as he and Ned relaxed before the campfire after filling their bellies with fresh venison.

"Near as I recollect, about another day and a half or two days," Ned answered. "I only been there myself once before." He watched his young friend for a few moments as Jordan looked around him, seeming to absorb the spirit of the place. "It's easy to see why the Injuns think this country is special, ain't it?"

Jordan nodded. He was thinking he could easily spend a long time in this gentle land, where there was plenty of game to hunt and lush grass for his horses. Gold had never been a lure for him. In all likelihood, it was doubtful he would have teamed up with Ned if he had not simply been searching for any distraction to take his mind off Kathleen Beard. He turned and looked toward the north. The next day would find them entering more rugged country again. He was reluctant to leave this oasis among the mountains, but Ned was anxious to see if there was as much gold as the rumors had promised. So at morning light, he saddled Sweet Pea again, and they rode north.

Deadwood Gulch was not hard to find. Miles before reaching the narrow canyon, named for the multitude of dead trees on the slopes, Ned and Jordan struck trails from every direction, all converging on Deadwood. Late arrivals, as they were, found a town of tents and shanties already crowding together on both sides of a stream with larger, more permanent structures

95

already in the early building stages. All were prospecting for gold, although all were not actively digging it out of the ground. For there were already saloons set up in large tents, gambling houses, even prostitution establishments. As Ned put it, "Some dig it outta the ground. Some dig it out of the prospectors." Jordan readily agreed. There were some so anxious to get their share of the prospectors' earnings they were operating their businesses from the backs of wagons, too eager to wait for a structure to be erected. It was a lawless community, and Jordan could easily understand why Ned had been happy to find a partner to watch his back. Every man carried a gun, either wearing a pistol or cradling a rifle or shotgun. The town reminded Jordan of a great carnival, something to marvel over for a short time, but no place for a man who craved the solitude of the high mountains.

Jordan and Ned guided their horses to a half-finished building near the middle of the muddy thoroughfare and dismounted. "Ain't this somethin'?" Ned blurted, the first comment either of the partners had offered since riding into the bustling town. "I don't know 'bout you, but I could use somethin' to eat. I'm gittin' a little tired of deer meat."

"You can get some good home cookin'" down the street at the Trough." The voice came from behind them, and they turned to see a man coming from behind the building. He had obviously overheard Ned's remarks. "My name's Sweeney," he said. "This here's my place. It's gonna be the best saloon in Deadwood, and I hope you boys will come have a drink when I get her built."

"Why, shore," Ned replied. "I expect we might. Where'd you say we could get a home-cooked meal?"

"The Trough," Sweeney replied. "Two women run the place. It's next to the blacksmith." He pointed toward the end of the muddy street. "I ain't seen you fellers around. You just get here?"

"Rode in this minute," Ned answered. "Figured we'd see what all the fuss was about." He nodded toward Jordan. "This here's my partner, Jordan Gray. My name's Ned Booth."

Sweeney shook hands with both men. "I reckon you boys will be lookin' to stake a claim. There ain't nothin' left around the spot where John Pearson first struck color, but most of the newcomers have been workin' the streams farther up the gulch. You might try your luck there."

"Much obliged," Ned replied. Turning to

97

Jordan, he said, "Come on, partner, let's go git us some of that home cookin'."

Sweeney stood watching while the two men climbed into their saddles and, leading their packhorses, started down the street. His gaze settled upon the broad shoulders of the younger man. Jordan Gray — he'd remember the name. Gray had not spoken a word, content to let his older partner do the talking, but Sweeney had detected the keen look of awareness in the young man's eyes. A random thought struck Sweeney then: Jordan Gray rode the ugliest horse he'd ever seen.

Hattie Moon stepped outside the small shack that served as a kitchen for the Trough, a cup of coffee in her hand. Wearing nothing more than a cotton petticoat under her apron, her underarms were wet with perspiration, a result of working over a hot stove for most of the afternoon. Faint wisps of steam wafted up from her bare arms when she emerged into the chill spring air that lay heavy in the narrow canyon. Her pudgy cheeks glowing scarlet from exposure to the heat from the stove, she took a few deep breaths, filling her lungs with the cold air.

The iron stove was Hattie's living. She and

her late husband, Horace, had hauled the stove all the way from Omaha in a four-by-eight covered wagon. With no money to pay for their fare, much less freight on a two-hundred-pound iron stove plus their other household possessions, they could not afford the luxury of train travel. She thought about that now as she sipped the bitter black coffee.

Poor Horace, she thought. *He just didn't have the backbone to make it in this new land.* It was now two years since Horace had died. Consumption, the doctor had said. But Horace had never really been right ever since being kicked in the head by a mule. It had been rumored around Deadwood that Hattie had done Horace in herself. Hattie had never made any attempt to set the record straight, her reasoning being that a little reputation couldn't hurt in a wild place like Deadwood Gulch. It might possibly give someone pause to think before trying to take advantage of a woman.

She glanced up when her partner, Maggie Hogg, came out of the huge tent that filled the role of dining room for their eating establishment. As skinny as her partner was round, she walked with the swagger of an army sergeant. "I could use a cup of that, myself," Maggie said, eyeing Hattie's coffee.

There was still over a quarter of an hour before she would flip the sign over on the front of the tent from NOPE to YEP.

"It's gettin' a little rank," Hattie replied. "I haven't started a fresh pot yet. I'm fixin' to put it on in a minute, soon as I get my breath."

"Hell, the ranker, the better," Maggie said. "I've been kinda draggin' my feet all day for some reason."

Like Hattie, Maggie was widowed after she and her late husband had homesteaded a few acres close by Horace and Hattie's farm. Her husband was shot to death in an argument over a card game. Maggie grieved for a day or two until she really thought about it. Then she decided it was not such a great loss after all. About all he had been good for was drinking and gambling. She and Hattie, finding themselves in like situations, decided they were better off without their husbands and determined to team up and make the best of it. They packed everything they could in their wagons and headed for the gold fields. Together they had proven to be a tough team. They had found that a business that served good cooking was well received in a town made up predominantly of men. The cooking was no-frills, straight-up meat and potatoes, such vegetables as were attainable, depending upon the season, and lots of cornbread and coffee. It was served by Maggie Hogg, wearing men's pants tucked into a pair of miner's boots amid a noisy chorus of good-natured ribbing and flirting from the customers. Most of the clientele were regulars, paying in gold dust by the week, the payments weighed on Maggie's balance scale. There was some general speculation that the scale was weighted a shade heavier in Maggie's favor, but the men didn't begrudge a touch of larceny by the two widows.

"Well, I expect we'd better feed 'em before they tear the tent down," Hattie finally uttered. She dumped the last bit of coffee from her cup and went back into the kitchen to start a fresh pot.

As usual, there was a line waiting outside the tent. Near the front were two newcomers Maggie could not remember having seen before. "Evening, boys," she greeted her customers. To the two strangers, she directed her next remark. "You can park them guns on the table inside the tent flap. I don't feed nobody wearin' guns at my table."

"Fair enough," Ned replied with a wide smile for the lady and immediately unbuckled his gun belt. "I hope the grub ain't so bad that you have to use that to make sure the customers eat it," he teased, nodding toward the forty-four she wore on her hip.

"You just make sure you behave yourself, old man, so's I don't have to use it on you," Maggie replied, matching Ned's grin with one of her own.

"She wears that to make sure nobody skips out without paying up," a man behind Jordan said and laughed at his own joke.

"You're the only one I need it for, Homer," she returned with a laugh.

Jordan dutifully propped his Winchester next to the other weapons and seated himself at the table. Ned paused before sitting down beside him, changed his mind, and moved to the stool at the head of the table, a better position to keep his eye on his and Jordan's guns. The man Maggie had called Homer leaned toward Ned and said, "That there is where Bull Brady always sets."

Ned raised his eyebrows. "Is that so?" He glanced around him and, seeing no one who appeared to be claiming the chair, asked, "Is he here?"

"Don't see him," Homer replied. "I was just givin' you a little advice. Bull's kinda set in his ways."

Ned glanced at Maggie, who had paused to hear the exchange. When her eyes met Ned's, she shrugged and said, "You pays your money, you sit wherever you can find a seat. All seats are the same. The food ain't no different." She turned and left the tent to help Hattie bring the food in.

"I reckon Mr. Brady ain't here to claim his favorite place," Ned remarked and seated himself at the head of the table. He winked at Jordan and grinned.

Jordan was far more interested in enjoying a good supper cooked by a woman to care who sat where. He raked his memory, but could not remember when he had last sat down at a table to eat food prepared by someone other than himself. He turned his plate right side up, pausing a moment to study the knife and fork beside it before sitting back to await the banquet. He didn't have to wait long. A few moments later, Maggie entered the tent again, carrying a pot in one hand and a platter in the other. She was followed by Hattie, who began filling coffee cups from a large pot. At almost the same time, the front tent flap parted, and a huge man with oxlike shoulders thrust his massive body into the dining room. It wasn't necessary to inform strangers that this was Bull Brady. Jordan wasn't particularly interested in the late arrival, his attention was captured by the large pot of stew in Maggie's hand.

There were a few nods of fearful acknowledgment from some at the table, which Bull ignored as he swept the room with what could only be described as a defiant grin. Then his gaze lit upon Ned Booth and settled there. His eyes narrowed, forming a dark frown, and he stomped purposely to the head of the table. "Git up. You're settin' in my place."

Ned Booth was not a big man. In fact, Bull made about two men Ned's size. But Ned was not one to suffer bullies in any form. He looked up at Bull and grinned. "I reckon you have to get here early if you want a special seat, friend. Yonder's an empty place." He pointed toward the other end of the table. "Now, if you don't mind, you're standin' in the lady's way."

Maggie wisely stepped back out of the way as Bull's face clouded up like an approaching thunderstorm. "I ain't your friend, old man," Bull blurted. "Git your scrawny ass outta my place before I break your back."

"No call for that, boys," Maggie said. "If you're gonna act like dogs, take it outside."

All eyes were upon Ned as he casually reached over and took a biscuit from the tray Maggie was still holding, his gaze never leaving that of the huge man hovering over him. Jordan watched, curious to see how far

Ned was going to take it.

After a long moment, Ned spoke. "Why don't you be a good boy, sonny, and set down over there so we can all enjoy our supper?" Without pausing, he directed his next remark at Maggie. "That stew looks plum edible, ma'am. What kinda critter did you cook up in that pot?" Maggie didn't get a chance to respond.

"Damn you, you old fool, I gave you fair warnin'," Bull roared and reached for a handful of Ned's buckskin shirt. Ned's reaction was to douse the big man's face with the steaming hot coffee just poured by Hattie.

Shocked by the burning liquid, Bull jerked back, almost releasing Ned's shirt. Recovering immediately, he was now enraged. Roaring like a wounded grizzly, he clamped down on the shirt again and dragged Ned off the stool, knocking it over in the process. The men on either side of Ned scrambled off the bench to avoid being swept up in the huge bully's rage. With no intent of giving in, Ned took a couple of swings at his adversary, the blows landing harmlessly on Bull's massive shoulders. In the general confusion that followed, amid the shuffling of benches, stools, and chairs, and the fruitless haranguing by both women to take it outside, Jordan sat unmoved for a long moment, calmly studying his partner's predicament.

"Now, you old fart," Bull threatened, "let's see how sassy you'll be with your head caved in." He drew back a massive fist, but he never threw the punch, for his wrist was caught and held motionless in the air. Stunned by the sudden vise that had captured his wrist, Bull jerked his head around to confront the person who had dared to interfere.

With a little half smile on his face, Jordan spoke in low, even tones. "The man wants to sit in that place. It's best to just leave him be and go sit somewhere else."

Bull couldn't believe what he was hearing. He tried to pull his wrist free, but Jordan's grip was unyielding. "Who the hell are you?" he demanded.

His words still without emotion, Jordan answered, "I'm the man whose tryin' to keep you from makin' a big mistake. Now leave him alone, and sit down and eat your supper."

Bull's face flushed with rage that was now building to a fast boil. Releasing Ned's shirt, he spun around to confront Jordan, at the same time taking a wild swing with his free hand. It was intended for Jordan's nose, but

Jordan anticipated it and easily ducked under. Before Bull could recover from his wide miss, Jordan hammered away at the bigger man's gut with a series of lefts and rights, doubling him over in an effort to protect his midsection. Striking with the speed of a rattlesnake, Jordan delivered to Bull's face a half dozen telling blows, which flattened his nose and left him staggering blindly backward, swinging his fists awkwardly, but finding nothing but air.

His rage tempered only slightly by the utter feeling of frustration, Bull hesitated for a moment, his eyes glazed in disbelief as he peered out from under bloody brows. The eyes that returned his gaze were steady and cold, evaluating the damage done, waiting for the stricken animal's next charge. Those who witnessed the fight would later tell of being reminded of a wolf taking down a wounded buffalo. There was not a sound in the huge tent except the heavy breathing of the massive bully, as the regulars at the Trough were held in stunned silence, in awe of a spectacle they never thought they would see.

Aware then of the eyes watching his humiliation at the hands of the somber stranger, Bull determined to mount another charge into this buzz saw of flailing fists.

Though his mind was reeling, he knew if he could lock Jordan inside his massive arms, it would be a different story. He would break his back. Jordan knew the same thing. Consequently, when Bull launched his unsteady charge, Jordan stepped aside and, with one foot extended, tripped the desperate man. Bull crashed to the plank floor of the tent, causing those spectators on that side of the long table to scramble out of harm's way.

"All right," Maggie Hogg pleaded loudly in an attempt to assert her authority, "that's enough!" She reached for her forty-four only to discover an empty holster. In the confusion of the fight, Ned had deftly slipped the weapon from her belt. He now stood just behind the fallen bully, watching as Bull struggled to get to his hands and knees. The big man's motions were slowed considerably by the many blows he had taken to the head, but he was still determined to fight. He remained in that position for a few long moments while the customers stood back watching, mesmerized by the sight of the belligerent bully on his knees.

Gradually, Bull's spinning brain began to settle, and he pushed himself up on his feet again to face Jordan. Like a wounded grizzly, he uttered a low warning growl and braced to mount another charge, but was halted abruptly by the sudden explosion of the forty-four right behind his head. He jerked his head around to see Ned Booth holding Maggie's pistol in the air.

"That's enough, like the lady said," Ned commanded, bringing the pistol down to aim directly at Bull's face. "Now, if you think this little tussle is worth gittin' your head blowed off, you just go right ahead and make another move, 'cause shore as I'm standin' here, I'll send you straight to Hell. I ain't et a honest-to-God home-cooked meal in I don't know how long, and because of your little fit, my supper's gettin' stone cold."

Bull stood motionless, held by the cold lifeless muzzle of the pistol staring him straight in the eye. In truth, he had had enough of his tangle with the broad-shouldered young stranger, but his shame at having been beaten caused him to consider risking an attempt to charge the old man.

"Go ahead, try it," Ned said, reading Bull's thoughts.

The old man's tone was enough to make Bull reconsider. After all, he reasoned, it wasn't worth the chance of getting shot.

And, he promised himself, there would be another time. "You won this round," he finally conceded, "but we ain't dealt the next hand yet." Then he looked at Jordan, standing calm and poised. "You were lucky this time, but we'll run into each other again."

"Always a pleasure," Jordan replied.

Hattie, having positioned herself by the firearms table, stood waiting to hand Bull his gun belt as he walked out. Wiping his bloody nose with the sleeve of his shirt, he paused to accept the weapon, a moment's indecision flashing through his brain. Anticipating such a moment, Hattie opened her hand to reveal five cartridges she had removed from the weapon. She held her hand out to him, and he merely grunted an angry response as he accepted his bullets.

Jordan and Ned walked to the entrance and stood watching until Bull got on his horse and rode away. "I reckon we taught him a lesson," Ned commented. "I was fixin' to give him a good ass kickin' when you jumped in."

"I could see that," Jordan replied.

The threat over for the time being, they returned to the table, where they were confronted by Maggie Hogg. Hands on hips, she awaited them. "I'll take my pistol now," she said to Ned. After he dutifully turned it over, she continued. "Now I reckon you'll wanna finish your supper before you mend the hole you put in my tent."

Ned shot a quick glance up toward the top of the tent. His grizzled face took on a sheepish grin as he spotted the small black hole in the canvas. "It's just a little bitty hole," he said in defense of his actions.

"It weren't there before," Maggie insisted.

"I can mend it for you, ma'am," Jordan interjected. "Let's eat now before that stew gets any colder."

Order restored, the customers who had been on that side of the table when the fight started picked up the bench that had been overturned, and pulled up to the table again. Those on the other side, having never vacated their seats, were well ahead in the consumption of the victuals.

True to his promise, when supper was finished, Jordan stayed to repair the damage done by Ned's warning shot. "How the hell are you plannin' to fix it?" Ned asked.

"I ain't sure," Jordan replied as he studied the little bullet hole near the ridge pole, some fifteen feet high at the peak. "It woulda been a helluva lot easier if you'd shot a hole in the side of the tent."

"Well, I didn't wanna hit somebody," Ned said in defense of his actions.

"You didn't have no business grabbin' my pistol in the first place." They turned to discover Maggie Hogg standing behind them. "Here's a piece of canvas to patch it with." She stood with them, staring up at the hole while Jordan contemplated the best way to fix it. After a few moments, she said, "Hell, you're too big to go crawlin' around on top of my tent. You're liable to make a bigger hole than the one we've already got." With an air of one accustomed to running things, she turned to Hattie Moon. "Hattie, what's Lem Edwards' youngest boy's name?"

"Jimmy?" Hattie replied.

"Yeah, Jimmy. He ain't no bigger'n a possum, but he's a smart little fellow. He'll scramble up on that tent and fix it. We'll send somebody to fetch him."

While young Jimmy Edwards scampered up on the tent with a large needle and twine from his daddy's saddle shop, Ned took the opportunity to become better acquainted with Maggie and Hattie. He apologized for putting the hole in their tent, but the women conceded it was worth it to see somebody take Bull Brady down a couple of notches. Jordan, mainly a silent spectator, couldn't help but be amused by Ned's obvious attempt to charm the ladies. Although Hattie was more generously endowed with feminine padding, it was the bony Maggie who had evidently stirred a romantic interest in the old mountain man.

Ned, aside from finding someone to practice his charm upon, had witnessed confirmation of a feeling he had felt upon first enlisting Jordan as a partner. He remembered Alton Broom's remark that Jordan would be a good man to have at your back. The young man was not only one a partner could count on — he was a force to be reckoned with when called to action. Ned shook his head in awe as he reflected upon the cool, workmanlike manner in which Jordan had handled Bull. *Yes, sir,* he thought, *I got me a real mountain cat for a partner.*

CHAPTER 6

At Hattie's suggestion, Ned and Jordan rode toward the upper end of the valley, and followed a busy stream called Hard Luck up into the hills, almost to the point where the water was first flushed out of the rocky hillside. "That's where I'd set up camp if it was me," she had advised. "A couple of fellers set up there last fall, but the Injuns run 'em off. Ain't nobody tried their luck there since." She had cast a warning eye in Ned's direction. " 'Course, it's a little bit risky being that far from everybody else. The same thing might happen that run them first two fellers off."

The thought of being away from the already thriving town of Deadwood appealed to Jordan. He'd take his chances with the Indians. Having spent the winter just past in the midst of Lakota territory, he was accustomed to living on the edge of danger. He deemed it far more satisfactory than living in a noisy mining camp. Following the meandering course of Hard Luck Creek, they had passed a dozen or more claims with owners busily working the stream. The voices of the prospectors carried up and down the stream as they shouted out instructions to each other or laughed at some comment from a partner. Accompanying this was the ringing of picks and shovels in the gravel and the hammering of sluice boxes being built or repaired, even this late into the evening. It was a din that soon offended Jordan's ears. It was the sound of greed with no respect for the sanctity of the land. *No wonder the Sioux are so upset,* he thought, and he admitted to himself that he had no real desire to search for the gold that was supposed to be abundant here. The reason he had agreed to accompany Ned was really because he had not seen the Black Hills — that and the desire to rid his mind of Kathleen Beard. That last thought caused him to reconsider. Maybe a noisy mining town was what he needed to drown out thoughts of Kathleen with that arrogant lieutenant. Rather than follow his impulses to ride as fast as Sweet Pea could carry him to the solitude of the mountains, he determined to stick it out for a while, at least until he had helped set Ned up.

Once their camp was established, and the horses taken care of, Jordan set out on foot for a look around. It didn't take long to see how easily a Sioux war party had slipped in and caught the previous occupants of the site by surprise. The hillside was covered with heavy stands of ponderosa pine that cloaked the numerous outcropping of rock formations. "We'd better sleep with one eye open," he murmured to himself. When he returned to the camp, Ned was already sifting through the fine gravel in a small pool formed by the water as it emerged from the rocks.

"Are we rich yet?" Jordan asked.

"Not so's you'd notice," Ned replied, never taking his eyes off the pan.

During the next few days, the results were much the same, with no real show of color. But Ned stayed at it, working the little stream from dawn to dusk, an occasional hint of gold incentive enough to hold his interest. On an average of every other night, he would ride into Deadwood to keep company with the two ladies running the Trough. After the first two nights, Jordan stayed in camp, preferring the solitude of the mountain. In a matter of days, however, Jordan grew restless. Mining was not in his blood. Ned, understanding the young man's inability to ignore the irresistible call of the mountains, suggested that Jordan should take it upon himself to provide food for the camp. It was Jordan's salvation. For at least half a day, every day, Jordan would saddle Sweet Pea and head up into the mountains to hunt. The camp soon became overstocked with venison, to the point where Jordan would occasionally ride downstream to share the meat with other claim holders. The bounty was graciously accepted, for like Ned, these men begrudged time away from their search for wealth.

Ned had the fever, and when he finally sifted out a few sizable grains of pure gold, he was helplessly snared, even though the yield was insignificant. The only calling that was strong enough to overpower his lust for the elusive dust was the urge to visit Maggie Hogg. Jordan couldn't help but notice the way Ned's eyes seemed to sparkle whenever Maggie came over to the table to make conversation. Judging by Maggie's coquettish smile for Ned, Jordan was convinced that there was a definite spark between the two that might lead to something. An occasional amused side glance from Hattie told Jordan that she detected a little something developing between their two partners as well.

Bull Brady was never there on the few occasions the two partners showed up together at the Trough, which was just as well as far as Hattie and Maggie were concerned. They had no wish to chance a reoccurrence of the clash between Jordan and Bull. According to Maggie, the belligerent bully had been back only a few times, seating himself at the head of the table, speaking to no one, silently brooding as he ate his supper. It was her guess that he was still feeling the shame of his defeat. No one of the other customers dared to glance his way, and the conversation at the table was reduced to a few whispered requests to pass the salt. Bull had been a disturbing force before his encounter with Jordan Gray. Now, with his nose still crooked, and scars over his eyes not yet healed, he was more threatening than before, keeping the ladies' customers cowed and uneasy. Maggie was afraid he was going to scare away most of her regulars. The satisfaction she and Hattie had enjoyed over seeing the bully properly put in his place was rapidly being replaced by a feeling of regret that the incident had occurred. Still, it was hard to fault Jordan for what had happened. "You'd better watch your back," she advised Ned one evening at supper. "That man ain't likely to forget the whuppin' your friend gave him."

"I reckon I can handle anything that jasper starts," Ned replied with an obvious show of bravado.

"You ain't as young as you used to be," Maggie reminded him. "You'd just better watch your back."

Ned reared back as if insulted, then favored Maggie with an impudent grin. "I might not be as old as you think," he said, "for fightin' and most other things, if you know what I mean."

"Your mouth's about to get you in trouble," Maggie replied with a girlish giggle.

"I don't brag about nothin' I can't back up," Ned stated with a definite air of confidence. "I just might be carryin' your ticket to paradise between my legs."

"Is that so?" Maggie replied. "You better watch out, old man. I might call your bluff."

It was destined to happen. Maggie and Ned had been sniffing around each other for some time now, and one evening when Ned and Jordan came in town for supper, the opportunity presented itself. As had become her custom, Maggie sat down on the bench across from Ned and Jordan to indulge in idle conversation. On this night, she mentioned the scarcity of vegetables, and the problem it caused in preparing meals. "There ain't much homecooked about the grub if it ain't much more'n meat and beans," she complained.

"I know where there's some wild turnips," Ned volunteered. "I seen 'em on the other side of Hard Luck."

His comment surprised Jordan. As far as he remembered, Ned had never been on the far side of the creek for any purpose beyond emptying his bowels. He wondered if Ned would even know a wild turnip if he saw one. Maggie, on the other hand, found the comment interesting.

"Is that a fact?" she said. "I reckon I could take the wagon up there in the mornin' and dig up some, if you could tell me how to find 'em."

"Why, I reckon I could do better'n that," Ned replied. "I'd be glad to show you where they are." Then, for fear she might decline the offer, he added, "It'd be a little too hard to try to tell you where they are."

Playing the game out, Maggie smiled graciously, and said, "That's mighty nice of you, Ned, but I wouldn't wanna put you to no bother."

"No bother at all," Ned was quick to respond. "We'll go after them turnips tomorrow."

"Well," Maggie said, pretending to appear undecided, "I guess we do need some kind of vegetable." She looked at Hattie, who had paused to listen in. "I could hitch up the wagon after breakfast — wouldn't hurt to try to spice up the meals a bit."

Hattie said, "I guess it couldn't." Well aware of what was actually going on, she rolled her eyes and, shaking her head, returned to the kitchen. Jordan turned away from the romantic sparring of the couple, well advanced into their middle years. He was unable to hide the grin plastered on his face. Neither he nor Hattie had been inconsiderate enough to point out that it was hardly the time of year to dig wild turnips. But then again, he was sure Ned and Maggie were aware of that.

So it was that, on the following morning, Ned Booth sat on his horse, patiently waiting by the fork where Hard Luck Creek joined the stream that ran the length of Deadwood Gulch. At a little past ten o'clock, Maggie appeared, driving a team of mules. Ned didn't own a pocket watch, so he didn't know what time it was, just that it seemed a whole lot later in the morning. He beamed a wide grin of relief when he saw her.

"I ain't sure you can get a wagon very far up this creek," he said. "The trail ain't that wide once you get about half way up the mountain. We might have to leave it partway, and go the rest of the way on horseback."

As Ned had predicted, the trail became extremely narrow, and very steep in many places. There was no question Maggie's wagon could not make it. Ned suggested that they could leave the mules and ride double on his horse, but Maggie voiced concern about leaving her team and wagon for somebody to steal. "I know a good place to leave it," Ned volunteered. They turned back then, and Maggie followed Ned down the trail again for a few hundred yards to a grassy clearing by a little spring. "You can leave it here," Ned said. "They oughta be all right."

"The hell they will," Maggie retorted. "I'm tired of playin' games. You been sniffin' around me ever since you set foot in Deadwood." She had grown tired of bouncing over the rough trail, pretending she was looking for turnips. There weren't any turnips up on that mountain. She knew it. He knew it. And the more she thought about what they had really wanted total privacy for, the more she felt they were acting like schoolchildren. She climbed down from the seat and wrapped the reins around a tree. Looking up at Ned, who wasn't sure what was about to happen, she reached over behind the seat, pulled a large buffalo robe from under it, and spread it in the back of the wagon. Giving Ned a wink, she said, "Soft as a featherbed — I'm too damn old to bump my bottom against the bare boards of a wagon bed." Ned remained in the saddle, stunned by her blatant remarks. "Well," she scolded, "are you gonna get down from there or not?" When he still did not respond, she asked, "This *is* what you come up here for, ain't it?"

At last able to respond, sure now that they were both thinking the same thoughts, Ned was quick to reply, "It sure is, but I reckon I figured I was gonna have to work a little to get at it."

With impatience registered on her face, she spoke matter-of-factly. "Ned, I've got to get back and help Hattie in the kitchen. We both know what we want, and it's been a long time for me — since my husband died, in fact. So let's get on with it."

"It has for me, too," he admitted. Then he threw a leg over and stepped down from the saddle, grinning from ear to ear. He looped the reins through the wagon wheel, then reached over and patted the buffalo robe. "Yessum," he chortled, "soft as a feath-erbed."

"Shuck them clothes, and let's see if there's anything in there worth all this trouble," Maggie said. "But first, I'd advise you to tie them reins to the tailgate. If my mules was to happen to bolt of a sudden, they might break that horse's neck."

Still grinning, Ned did as she advised, although he saw little risk in the mules bolting. They were both grazing contently upon the grass. After he retied the reins, he started undressing, while keeping a fixed eye upon the lady, who was doing the same. After the outer clothes were shed, it appeared to be pretty much a draw as far as sexual appeal was concerned. Both paused a moment at that point to appraise the other. They were both wearing long underwear, Maggie's new and freshly washed, obviously a pair she saved for special occasions. Ned's, on the other hand, were faded and gray, drooping at the knees and elbows. There was a button missing on one corner of the back flap, so they sagged to one side.

There was a moment of hesitation on Maggie's part at the sight of her eager swain. "You ever think about washin' them long johns?"

"Shore," he replied while working at the

buttons, failing to see the relevance of her question. "When they start to itch, I think about it." He didn't bother to mention that thinking about washing them was as far as he usually got.

She considered that for no more than half a second before attacking her buttons, overpowered by her own internal itch. *Beggars can't be choosers,* she thought. In a matter of seconds, they were standing before each other, naked and shivering in the chill spring air, each appraising the other. Eager to get to the serious business, Ned lunged for her, his hands groping her bony ribs and hips. In his uncontrolled ardor, he caused her to bump her bottom against the edge of the wagon bed. "Wait a minute, dammit!" she complained. "Help me up on the wagon. I'm freezin'. Let's get under the robe."

Distracted by the sight of Maggie in her middle-aged glory, Ned had been oblivious to the cold. He noticed then the chill bumps standing all over the lady's pale skin. At that moment, in that degree of animal heat, however, she could have been Cleopatra in his eyes. Nothing short of an earthquake or an Indian attack was going to stop the wheels of passion already in motion. As gently as he could manage under the circumstances, he helped her up on the robe. He climbed up beside her and doubled the robe over them. Skeptical that her lover's equipment was functional, Maggie was relieved to see signs of life in Ned's lower regions. Ned seemed to be relieved as well.

With neither party willing to waste time on tender passion, the job was done in a businesslike manner, swift and noisy, with an abundance of grunting and heavy breathing. The buffalo robe was flung aside as both parties were soon bathed in sweat. Long absent from the mating ritual, Ned emptied his chamber early. But in his desire to please, and in an effort to maintain his pride, he stayed in the saddle, riding as hard as he could manage, until the lady's prayers were answered. When she finally arrived, she uttered a primal scream that caused the mules to bolt, pulling the wagon several yards before being stopped by the securely tied reins.

Spent, and feeling as if near death, Ned rolled over on his back to catch his breath. *I'm too old to do this,* he thought, but he had to smile, thinking of his conquest. There was no time for more than that one thought, however, before he was rolled off the wagon when Maggie jerked the robe out from under him. "Get up," she said. "I've got to get back to the kitchen. Hattie'll be pulling her hair out."

It had ended as abruptly as it had started. Maggie hustled back into her clothes and was driving her team of mules back down the trail while Ned was still fumbling around trying to button his underwear. Pleased that he had been able to satisfy the lady, even at the near cost of his life, he grinned widely, just for himself. He took his time climbing back into his shirt and pants, and pulling on his boots, his mind tracing back over the entire encounter. Walking up to his horse, he said, "Good thing Maggie stopped me from tying you up to that wagon wheel." Then he stopped to think, *Wonder how she knew them mules would jump like that?* It occurred to him then that he might not be the first old man with whom she went hunting for turnips.

Jordan Gray looked up from the meat he was tending over the fire when he heard Ned's horse splash through the stream. He didn't say anything until Ned had dismounted, walked over to the fire, and sat down wearily. With the hint of a smile on his face, Jordan spoke. "I swear, Ned, you look plumb tuckered out. Diggin' for turnips must be hard work."

"The older you get, the harder it gets,"

Ned replied with a heavy sigh.

For several days after the hunt for turnips, Ned seemed content to stay in camp and work the claim. Jordan suspected that his partner's itch had been sufficiently scratched to last him a while. It was probably just as well that they stayed away from the Trough for a time. Jordan was aware of the possible danger from Bull, which Hattie and Maggie had warned him about, but he was not one to worry over it. He took the normal precautions whenever he camped in dangerous country, whether threats might come from Bull Brady or a Sioux war party. His honest feeling was that Bull was not inherently an evil man — just a bully — and the odds of getting bushwhacked by him were slim. Ned was not so sure. He tended to agree with Maggie that they should both watch their backs.

The object of Hattie and Maggie's concern was consoling himself by working feverishly at his claim. The unexpected beating at the hands of Jordan Gray had produced a shocking effect upon the huge man, to the point where he had suffered a considerable loss of his once invincible confidence. No man had ever bested him in a fight of any kind, and Jordan had done it with such ease

128

that Bull wondered if he had somehow been tricked. The more he thought about it, the more he began to be convinced that Jordan had simply taken him by surprise. Surely in a rematch, the results would be far different. With that settled in his mind, he turned his thoughts to another problem, this one of financial concern. "There ain't no gold here," he blurted, suddenly fed up with the constant digging and sifting with no measurable result.

Bull had not been lucky in his choices of sites. This was the third claim he had worked with no more than four or five ounces of gold from the lot. How could it be, he wondered, that farther down the same creek there had been several strikes, and yet he struck nothing but sand and gravel? Angry, he threw his shovel down and turned his face toward the heavens. "Why?" he roared, his deep voice filling the narrow gulch with echoes that bounced from rock to rock, seeming to mock his cries of anguish. "Damn you," he roared again, cursing the canyon and the stream. "I work as hard as anybody. Why can't I strike it?"

"Maybe you need to put your trust in the Lord," a voice fully as deep as his own came back.

Startled, Bull turned toward the sound,

instinctively snatching up his rifle in the process. Searching quickly from right to left, he saw no one at first. Then the voice spoke once more. "You got no call to take up your rifle." Then he saw three mounted riders wearing heavy bearskin coats. Leaving the cover of the pines, they walked their horses slowly out into the open.

Cautious, Bull cocked his rifle and held it ready. No one who knew of his reputation as a belligerent ever approached his claim. "Who the hell are you?" Bull demanded.

The rider in the middle responded. He was larger than the other two, fully as big as Bull, and obviously the eldest. "I'm a man of God," he proclaimed. "Folks call me Preacher Rix. These here are my sons, Zeb and Quincy." He fashioned a crooked smile for Bull's benefit. "Sounds like you ain't havin' much luck with your prospectin'."

"I reckon I ain't," Bull replied. He was prone to add, *If it's any of your damn business,* but he restrained his tongue since the man was a preacher. There were few things that Bull held in respect. Preachers fell among that group, a fact more of superstition than genuine respect.

Since it was apparent that an invitation was not likely forthcoming, Preacher asked, "Mind if we step down?" His original plan, while watching the camp from the trees before, was to simply shoot the man from a distance. But first he had chosen to wait in hopes he might see where Bull hid his treasure. After having heard Bull's desperate lament, however, Preacher had decided it a waste of time. There was no sense in alerting any other prospectors who might be in hearing distance of a shot if there was no prospect of a payday for him and his boys. Maybe they could at least get something to eat. They had eaten nothing but wild game for the past several days.

"Reckon not," Bull answered, keeping a wary eye on the threesome. Anybody could claim to be a preacher. He kept his rifle handy just in case. Preacher Rix had a fearsome look about him. Bull decided that if he was a preacher, he could give the devil quite a tussle. He wasn't sure about the man's sons. The one Preacher had called Zeb had what Bull would describe as weasel eyes, flitting all around constantly as if searching for something. The other son, Quincy, was possessed of a vacant look and a half grin that would indicate intelligent thought had never taken root behind the bushy eyebrows. He limped on one bandaged leg. Hoping to discourage a visit and the prospect of a sermon, Bull said, "I ain't got no grub. I et my dinner about an hour ago."

Preacher answered with a wide smile. "Well, that's all right, friend. We've got a little meat left. Since you already got a fire goin' there, we could cook up some of it — even share it with you if you're still hungry. Pronghorn — Zeb shot it this mornin'. It was a right good shot, too. Right behind the critter's head — musta been seventy-five or a hundred yards off, weren't it, Zeb?"

Zeb's gaze settled on Bull for a long moment, and he nodded in answer to his father's question. A faint smile creased his jaw, but he said nothing. Bull began to wonder if it might have been a mistake to let them step down. As a precaution, he kept his rifle in one hand while Preacher and his sons cut some strips of antelope to roast over the fire.

"Looks like you run into a little hard luck," Preacher offered in way of conversation. Bull's hand automatically went up to gingerly touch his broken nose, but he declined to explain the appearance of his face. Preacher paused for Bull's reply. When there was none, he went on. "Hope it ain't because of strong drink and sinnin'. I'm here to preach on the sins of drinkin' and fightin', tryin' to save the souls of the heathen, Injuns and whites alike."

"Is that so?" Bull responded, making little effort to disguise the sarcasm in his tone. "Well, mister, you got your work cut out for you."

"How about you, friend?" Preacher asked, his fierce dark eyes locked on Bull's in an accusing stare. "Have you accepted Jesus as your savior?"

Bull grunted impatiently before answering. "I've accepted this here rifle as my savior, and I expect you'll find most of the men in Deadwood with the same religion."

A thin smile slowly formed on Preacher's face. "Is that a fact? Well, looks like I've come to the right place." He pulled a strip of meat from the flames. "Eat up, boys. We'd best get about our business, and let this man get back to his."

Bull was anxious to see the three uninvited guests depart, but he was cautious not to turn his back to them. He stood aside, rifle still in hand while Preacher and his sons ate the roasted meat. When they had finished, Preacher wiped his hands on his heavy coat and summoned his two offspring to mount up. "Let's get on our way, boys." He stepped up into the saddle before a final word for Bull. "Lord's blessings upon you, friend."

Bull merely grunted in reply, happy to be

done with them. He turned to go back to his sluice box. It was a fatal mistake. Zeb's bullet caught him right between the shoulder blades, and he crumpled heavily to the ground, mortally wounded.

"Woo-hah!" Quincy sang out excitedly.

His father, who had been surprised by the shot, pulled up on the reins and turned toward his eldest. "I swear, Zeb, you do beat all. Did I tell you to shoot him?"

"No, sir," Zeb replied sheepishly, his eyes still on the fallen man, "but he was a heathen, same as the others."

"That don't make no difference. I oughta whip you for pullin' that pistol. Anybody in earshot'll come runnin' when they hear that shot." He looked down to make sure Bull wasn't moving. "It was a clean shot, though. Fetch that rifle. Quincy, take a quick look in that there tent. See if there's anythin' worth takin'. Be quick, boys. We need to leave this place before some of his neighbors show up."

"Pa, he's still breathin'," Zeb called out as he pulled the rifle from Bull's hand.

"Well, finish him off. We don't want him doin' no talkin'."

Quincy, on his way to Bull's tent, stopped to complain. "Let me do it, Pa. Zeb's already shot him once."

Zeb, grinning at his brother, immediately pointed Bull's rifle at the back of the wounded man's head and pulled the trigger. The harsh bark of the Henry rifle prompted Preacher to urge his sons to hurry. "Git mounted. We ain't got time to hang around here now. If he's got friends, they'll be comin' to see what the shootin's about."

Bull didn't have any friends, but the shots were heard by a solitary hunter searching for signs of elk in the next canyon. Jordan paused to listen when he heard a pistol shot. He didn't think much of it until a few minutes later he heard the report of a rifle. This gave him pause to consider the possibility that someone might be in trouble. He decided to take a look.

Leading Sweet Pea, he crossed over the ridge and made his way down through the pines to a point where he could get a view of the canyon beyond. At first glance, the narrow gulch appeared to be empty, but as he scanned the length of it, he spotted a thin wisp of smoke lazily drifting up from behind a screen of low brush. Leaving Sweet Pea in the trees, he continued to descend the slope until he reached the bottom. It was a camp all right. As he had figured, the smoke he had seen was from a campfire. Beyond it, he spied a tent, half hidden by the thick brush beside a narrow stream. But there was no sign of anyone around. Deciding it safest to announce his presence, he called out, "Hello the camp! Anybody home?" There was no answer, the breeze rustling the leaves of the willows beside the stream the only sound to be heard. He scanned the canyon floor from left to right again. Whoever had been there was now gone. After a few minutes more to make certain, he left the cover of the trees and approached the campsite.

Before he reached the fire, he discovered the body. It had been rolled over the low lip of the stream and was lying half in the cold mountain water. He at once dropped to one knee and brought his rifle up ready to fire while he quickly looked around him again. The silence of the canyon remained unbroken. Satisfied that he was not in danger of being the next victim, he returned his attention to the dead man. Although the corpse was lying facedown, the bulk of the body told him who it was. To be certain, he reached down and pulled the shoulder over to get a look at the face. It was the man they called Bull all right. A strained look of agony frozen upon his face was evidence of his last desperate moments while he awaited the final shot that sent him from this world. It wasn't hard to figure out: shot in the back, then executed while he lay wounded. It was a tough way to go. Jordan couldn't help but pity the poor man who still wore the marks of the beating he had suffered at Jordan's hand.

Jordan was not the only person who had heard the shots. He had started looking around the camp for sign when he heard the horses approaching from downstream. In a few moments, two riders came into view, miners from the look of them. Jordan stood up and waited for them to approach. He recognized one of them as a stout, gray-haired man who had been at the Trough the day he had fought with Bull. Upon seeing Jordan standing beside the tent, the man spoke.

"Heard the shootin' down at our claim," he said. Jordan gestured toward the body with a nod of his head. "Damn," the man uttered. "Bull?" Jordan nodded again.

"Damn," the man's partner echoed.

"Looks like he got it in the back," Jordan offered and turned to lead them to the body. As soon as his back was turned, he heard the unmistakable sound of a rifle being cocked. He whirled back around to discover the barrel looking directly at him.

"Shore looks that way," the gray-haired man said, his voice emotionless. "I reckon you settled your score with Bull. Ain't none of us sorry to see ol' Bull with his toes turned up, but we don't hold with no back-shootin' sons of bitches here."

"You've got it all wrong, mister," Jordan said, his tone equally emotionless. "I just got here a couple of minutes before you did. I heard the shots same as you."

"Is that a fact?" The gray-haired man shot a quick glance at his partner. "He just got here a couple of minutes ago. Whaddaya think about that, Harvey?"

Harvey, his pistol drawn and leveled at Jordan, stroked his chin in an exaggerated gesture. " 'Pears to me he got here a tad sooner than that — soon enough to settle ol' Bull's hash."

"You're dead wrong," Jordan insisted. "I've got no reason to kill a man. If I'd killed him, I wouldn't have stood here and let you ride up."

"I expect you didn't have time to run by the time you saw us," Gray Hair replied. "Now suppose you lay that rifle down real gentle. Make any funny moves and I'll shoot you where you stand. Shoot you now, or hang you later — makes no difference to me, but we've about had our fill of murderin' claim jumpers around here."

Realizing they were not prone to hear his side of it, Jordan considered the chances of getting the jump on the two of them. His rifle wasn't cocked. He might be fast enough to cock it and get one of them, but the other one would certainly put a bullet in him. "You're makin' a mistake," he repeated and laid the Winchester on the ground. "Suppose we let the law settle this."

"The law?" Harvey blurted with a laugh. "We're the law, me and Sam, judge and jury. Miner's law is the only law in Deadwood, and you was caught red-handed. Whaddaya say, Sam?"

"Guilty," Sam replied without hesitation. "I say hang him so other outlaws will see what kind of welcome they git in Deadwood." He grinned at Jordan. "There you go, Mr. Backshooter. There's your fair trial. Keep that gun on him, Harvey, while I git down."

Jordan had little choice but to stand there helpless while Sam prepared to dismount. They had the drop on him, and at this point, he wasn't sure what his next move should be. But he was certain of one thing, he had no intention of being led meekly to the slaughter. "Back away from that rifle,"

Sam ordered as soon as his feet were on the ground. Jordan complied without protest, taking a couple of steps back. His eyes constantly shifting back and forth between the two miners, he waited for his chance. The only option he could see was to overpower the one called Sam. But could he do it before Sam's partner shot him? *I guess I'm about to find out,* he thought. "Watch him, Harvey," Sam cautioned as he bent over to pick up Jordan's rifle.

"I got him," Harvey replied confidently.

Jordan waited until Sam picked up his Winchester and had a rifle in each hand. Then, with the swiftness of a mountain lion, he launched his body. The sudden attack caught Sam by surprise just as he was about to straighten up again. The force of the impact drove both men flailing against Sam's horse, causing the startled animal to rear in fright. Harvey tried to react quickly enough, but had his hands full trying to control his equally startled horse. By the time he reined the horse around again, Jordan and Sam were in a desperate struggle to gain control of Sam's rifle, Jordan's Winchester having been dropped on the ground once more. Harvey tried to wheel his horse in position to get a clear shot at Jordan, but the two men were rolling under

Sam's horse, and the confused animal lurched against Harvey's horse in an effort to avoid them. Desperate at that point, Harvey took the shot anyway, but his horse reared when Sam's horse slammed against it, causing him to miss wildly, the bullet finding purchase in the animal's left hind quarter. The horse screamed and reared again, this time its front hooves landing on the other horse's rump. In the confusion, Jordan managed to overpower Sam, taking him from behind and clamping an arm under his chin. Sam had to release the rifle and grab Jordan's arm with both hands in a frantic effort to keep his windpipe from being crushed.

With the rifle now in his possession, Jordan continued to clamp down on Sam's neck, holding the desperate man in front of him as a shield against Harvey's pistol. As for Harvey, he had his hands full trying to keep from being thrown from his horse. When he finally regained control of the startled animal, it was to confront the business end of Sam's rifle leveled at him. He hesitated, not sure what to do.

"Drop your pistol if you want to live," Jordan advised. Uncertain still, Harvey didn't move. "If you shoot, you're gonna hit your partner, and I'll cut you down with this rifle. Make up your mind before I choke his wind off for good." Harvey seemed paralyzed with indecision. Finally, Sam managed to screech a desperate plea that moved Harvey to drop his weapon. "Now get off the horse and back away from the pistol," Jordan commanded. As soon as Harvey dismounted, Jordan shoved Sam, gagging and stumbling, into his partner. "Now start walkin'," he ordered, gesturing toward the north end of the canyon. "If I see you lookin' back, I'm gonna put a bullet in your butt."

The two miners did as they were told, walking as fast as they could manage toward the head of the gulch. Jordan watched for a few moments before discarding Sam's rifle and picking up his own. Both men jerked their heads around when they heard him cock the Winchester. He immediately dusted their heels with a shot in the dirt behind them, causing them to look straight ahead again. They picked up the pace without having to be told.

"Whaddaya think he's gonna do?" Harvey whispered as he and Sam walked nervously toward the far end of the canyon.

"Whatever the hell he wants," Sam replied, his irritation amplified by the hoarseness in his aching throat. Unlike his partner, he no longer feared for his life, reasoning that Jordan would have shot them already if that was his intention.

"You think he's stealin' the horses?" Harvey whined.

"I expect so, at least the sound one." Forgetting Jordan's instructions not to turn around, he stopped, faced Harvey, and demanded, "What the hell did you shoot my horse for?"

"Well, dammit, I didn't go to do it. My horse bucked."

Sam was about to reply, but at that moment, both men realized that they had stopped walking, and no shots had been fired. They turned around and looked back toward the camp. He was gone. Both horses were standing waiting, Sam's wounded horse off to one side of the stream. "Well, he might be a murderer, but looks like he ain't a horse thief," Sam commented dryly. "Come on, we'd better spread the word that we got another outlaw on our hands. He may have just been after Bull, but Bull ain't the only one that's been dry-gulched lately. There was them two fellers south of Deadwood last week. Don't it seem peculiar to you that this same feller we caught standin' over Bull's body is the same one that told everybody about findin' the other two? We'd

143

best tell Ben Thompson to call a meetin' of the vigilance committee."

Ned Booth paused as he bent over his pan filled with the fine gravel from the narrow stream. Not sure if he had heard something or not, he listened for a moment before deciding it was nothing. Just as he was about to turn his attention back to the gravel in his pan, he caught a movement out of the corner of his eye. Startled, he spun around, his hand automatically going to the handle of his pistol. "Dammit, Jordan," he cursed, angry for a split second. "One of these days I'm liable to shoot you — sneakin' up on a man like that."

"I'm sorry," Jordan replied. "I wasn't tryin' to sneak up on you. I guess you were just too busy to notice."

"Hell, I knowed it was you," Ned lied. Truthfully, he knew Jordan just naturally moved as silently as a Blackfoot warrior. Ned hated to admit, even to himself, that his ear wasn't sharp enough to detect his partner's presence until Jordan was practically stepping on his heels. Even the mangy horse Jordan rode seemed to tiptoe through the trees. Ned looked over Jordan's shoulder toward Sweet Pea. "I don't see no meat across the saddle. No luck today?"

"I had luck, I reckon — all of it bad."
Then he proceeded to relate the series of
ill-timed incidents that had resulted in his
confrontation with the two miners.

Ned listened, deep concern showing in his
face. He set his pan on top of a low table
rock that had been split down the middle
by some ancient storm. "I swear, Jordan,
trouble seems to think it's your next of kin."

There were immediate decisions to be
made. Jordan was inclined to ride into
Deadwood to set the record straight, but
Ned convinced him that would be tanta-
mount to suicide. "There ain't no law in
Deadwood. More'n likely they've got a
vigilance committee, and they'd string you
up for your trouble." He thought for a moment. "I'd best go into town and find out
who's the man that runs things. You better
lay low for a spell till I can talk to 'im. The
quicker we get this straightened out, the
better. I've seen these things get outta hand
if these boys get to drinkin'. One time in
Montana I seen 'em hang a stranger just
rode into town and stopped at a feller's
camp to water his horse. Nobody saw the
feller for two days, so they figured the
stranger had kilt him. They strung him up,
right in the middle of town. The next day
the feller he was supposed to have kilt

showed up. He'd been up in the mountains hunting for elk."

"I didn't kill anybody," Jordan protested. "If I run, it'll look like I did."

Ned persisted. "Jordan, if you don't, they'll send a lynching party up here lookin' for you, and when they're liquored up real good, they ain't gonna take time to find out if you're guilty or not." Ned sounded pretty confident that he knew what he was talking about, so Jordan finally gave in. "The best thing, boy," Ned assured him. "You pack up some possibles and head back up in the mountains. I'll get right on into town and try to talk some sense into whoever's the big dog. I'll meet you tomorrow about mid-day and let you know how things are." He paused to think for a moment. "You know that little waterfall where you surprised them two pronghorns? I'll meet you there."

Jordan was reluctant to leave Ned behind. "What if they think you were in on it?"

"Hell, I ain't worried about that. Them two fellers who saw you at Bull's claim know I weren't there. I'll be all right. Now get goin' before some crazy vigilantes come ridin' in here."

"All right then," Jordan said. "I'll leave my packhorse here." He gathered up a few things and packed them in his saddle bags.

146

"You be careful, old man," he cautioned as he stepped up in the saddle. Turning Sweet Pea's head toward the towering mountain behind him, he touched a finger to his hat-brim in a farewell gesture and gave the mare his heels.

CHAPTER 7

Hattie Moon turned to see who had just come into her tent. "Well, where have you been for the last couple days?" she asked. "You're a little too late for supper. We was just clearin' the dishes away. I can fix you up a little somethin' if you're hungry, though."

Ned favored her with a grateful smile. "I wasn't plannin' to make it to supper tonight, but I could eat, long as I'm here."

"Where's that young partner of yours?" she asked, already aware that Jordan was in trouble, but waiting to see what Ned had to say about it.

"That's what I come into town about," Ned replied. "I'm afraid some fellers think he bushwhacked that Bull feller, and I need to set 'em straight. I told him to head for the hills till I can find out what's goin' on."

"Well, you were right to tell him that. Harvey Perkins and Sam Morris came in here to get Ben Thompson. They said they rode up on your partner standing over Bull's body. They said they tried to take him, but he got the jump on 'em."

"Who's Ben Thompson?"

"He's the head of the vigilance committee. He didn't even finish eatin'. They went right out to round up the rest of the committee and call for a meetin'."

"Where would that be?"

"Over at Sweeney's saloon."

"They don't do nuthin' without they get liquored up good first." This came from Maggie who had overheard the conversation from the kitchen. She entered the tent, and plopped her bony backside down on the corner of the table, one leg propped on a chair. "Did Jordan do for ol' Bull?"

"Hell, no, he didn't," Ned at once replied. "He come up on Bull's camp no more'n a few minutes ahead of them other two fellers."

"That ain't the way it looked to Sam and Harvey," Maggie said. "They said they tussled with him till Harvey shot Sam's horse, and Jordan got the jump on 'em." She couldn't suppress the hint of a smile when she said it, visualizing the scene and the two fumbling miners.

"Ha!" Hattie blurted. "It's a wonder they

149

didn't shoot each other, them two."

"I better git on up to Sweeney's before they go off half-cocked," Ned decided.

"You want me to fix you a plate?" Hattie asked.

"I reckon not. I'd best git on over there." He paused. "Maybe a piece of that corn-bread, or a cold biscuit I could take with me." Hattie reached for the platter and broke off half of the remaining cake of corn-bread. "Much obliged," he said, stuffing a generous mouthful in without pause.

Maggie placed a hand on Ned's arm. "You'd better watch yourself, Ned. They might figure you were part of it." She released him then. "I ain't heard no pistols shootin' in the air, so I know the meetin' ain't over yet."

Although the meeting was not yet con-cluded, it had reached a high pitch. The late Bull Brady had suddenly been elevated to a status approaching beloved by his fellow miners. And as the level in the whiskey bottles receded, the degree of righteous demand for vengeance went up. Ben Thompson took his position seriously and was generally determined to make sure the committee had the right of it. Since there was no formal law in Deadwood, it had become necessary to form a vigilante organization to protect the prospectors from the type of crime that had victimized Bull Brady. Murderers had to know they would not be tolerated in Deadwood. Perkins and Morris were adamant in their testimony that Jordan Gray was caught red-handed. But Ben knew that the two partners were not above embellishing a story to make it more acceptable. Ben wouldn't be sure until another witness stepped forward.

Unnoticed by the noisy gathering, a giant of a man stepped quietly into the back of the crowded saloon. Pulling back a chair from the rearmost table, he settled his imposing bulk and motioned for his two companions to take seats on either side of him. Content to watch the progress of the hastily called committee, he listened with interest to each man who spoke. It appeared that the consensus of opinion was that young Jordan Gray was the guilty man — that is, until one Ned Booth burst into the meeting.

"Hold on, here!" Ned shouted out over the din of voices, and everyone turned to see. "You boys are about to git all lathered up over somethin' that didn't happen the way these two fellers said."

"Hell, you're his partner," someone in the

middle of the room shouted, his comment echoed by several other voices.

Ben Thompson held up his hand. "Let's hear what he has to say."

"Those of you who've met Jordan Gray know he ain't the kind to bushwhack a man. He was huntin' elk when he found Bull murdered." Ned went on to tell the story just as Jordan had told him. The longer Ned talked, the more inclined Ben was to believe him. He had met Jordan the week before, and Jordan didn't strike him as the kind to commit such a dastardly crime. Sensing their appointed leader was wavering, the gathered men began to grumble among themselves, most of them already strung tight enough to ride after Jordan that very night.

"He done it, all right," a deep unfamiliar voice rose above the din. All eyes turned toward the rear of the room to discover a large mountain of a man in a heavy bearskin coat making his way forward. His imposing appearance brought an immediate silence to the crowded saloon and the mob parted to provide a passage for him. "I seen him when he killed that man, and this feller was with him." He nodded toward Ned. His statement caused an angry eruption of voices.

Ned couldn't believe what he was hearing. "Why, that's a damn lie," he blurted.

"Hold on!" Ben Thompson shouted trying to restore order. It took a few minutes before the mob settled down again. When there was quiet once more, Ben turned to the dark stranger. "Just who might you be, mister?"

"Rix is my name," Preacher replied, his voice rumbling like thunder. "Reverend Nathaniel Rix. Me and my boys was on the far side of the ridge when we heard a gunshot. We rode up to the top to take a look and seen him shoot that poor feller in the head after he was already laying on the ground wounded."

"You're a preacher?" Ben asked, not sure he had heard correctly.

"I am, sir. Me and my sons have been travelin' the territory, bringin' salvation to the heathens."

Ben thought that over for a brief second. It was a rare thing, indeed, to find a preacher in Deadwood. Then he thought about the statement the preacher had just made. "You say Ned, here, was with Jordan Gray when he shot Bull." Preacher nodded. "Sam and Harvey say Gray was alone," Ben said.

Preacher paused no more than a second before answering. "This feller," he said, indicating Ned, "was holdin' the horses back in the trees. They wouldn't have hardly seen him, but we could see him plain as day. I just wish we could have got down that mountain soon enough to help out, but there weren't no quick way down from where we sat." His comment stirred some of the mob to call for Ned's capture right then.

"It'd take a preacher to make up a lie that big," Ned said, angry as well as baffled as to why the man would concoct such a tale. Then it occurred to him that Jordan had told of finding a mysterious preacher and his sons burying a man and woman at a burned out cabin near Fort Laramie. That was pushing coincidence a bit far. He turned to face his accuser. "You lying son of a bitch, you and your two boys killed Bull, didn't you?"

The atmosphere in the crowded saloon became intense once again as the vigilantes began to work up to a fever pitch. The mob looked to the stranger for his answer to Ned's accusation.

Preacher smiled calmly and replied softly, "I reckon if me and the boys done it, we'd be long gone from here by now, instead of coming here to see that justice was done. Besides, I ain't the one caught standin' over the dead body."

Doing his best to maintain control of the meeting, Ben called again for quiet. Then he asked Ned, "Where is Jordan Gray?"

"I couldn't rightly say," Ned replied. "He ain't at the claim, is all I can tell you."

"Took off, has he?" Preacher gave voice to the thought that was rapidly taking form in everyone's mind.

"He didn't have much choice," Ned protested. "Them two lame brains was ready to hang him on the spot. He was gonna come in here to set you straight, but I told him to lay low for a spell till I could talk some sense into you folks."

"Figurin' that nobody saw you hidin' back in the trees," Preacher added, fanning the flames of suspicion he had ignited.

"Why, you lying son of a bitch . . ." Ned blurted and lunged for Preacher. He was immediately set upon by several of the men gathered close around him and taken bodily to the floor. He proved to be a handful, however, as he fought those who held him and almost succeeded in freeing himself before Barney Lipscomb grabbed his coattail and pulled him back. The coat was ripped in the process, tearing an inside pocket and dropping a leather pouch on the floor. Ben Thompson immediately reached down to retrieve it.

"Well, lookee there," Sam Morris clucked. "How much is in there, Ben?"

"I don't know," Ben replied when he was sure the boys had the old man under control. "Maybe ten or twelve ounces."

This caused rampant speculation among the gathering. They all knew that it was highly unlikely that Ned could have panned that much dust in the short time since he and Jordan had arrived on the scene. Harvey Perkins was the first to speak. "Looks like ol' Bull was pullin' more dust outta that creek than he let on." He thought about it a second, then added, "And I expect that's just this here feller's half of the split."

"I come by that dust honestly," Ned protested to Ben. "I took it off a couple of dead miners me and Jordan come up on back down the valley a ways."

"I expect you probably did," Ben replied.

"You got it all wrong," Ned exclaimed in frustration. "They was already dead when we found 'em."

"Looks pretty plain to me," Preacher commented. "Ain't much doubt who killed your friend." He raised his eyes to the ceiling of the saloon and proclaimed, "Vengeance is mine, sayeth the Lord. Thou shalt not kill."

"Amen, Reverend," Sam Morris said. "I

got a rope on my saddle. We can string this murderer up right now." Most of the gathering shouted their endorsement of his suggestion. The righteous men of Deadwood were set on a hanging. Ben Thompson was the only one who voiced a cautionary thought.

"According to Sam and Harvey, this old man wasn't the one that did the actual shooting."

Sam, already impatient to see Ned swing, proclaimed, "He was part of it, just as much as if he pulled the trigger. Besides, Jordan Gray's done lit out. He mighta got away, but by God, we got his partner."

There was no need to take a vote. By this time, almost every man there was anxious to see a hanging. They crowded in around Ned, many hands grasping his arms and legs, and carried him outside. No amount of pleading from the old man could dissuade the mob from their intent to demonstrate to all would-be murderers the folly of preying upon Deadwood miners. His pleas for reason ignored, he tried his best to resist, struggling against his captors and cursing the lot of them with every breath. All of his efforts were to no avail. His hands tied behind his back, he was hoisted up on his horse and led to a solitary cottonwood in the center of the gulch. When it was apparent that he was helpless to prevent his execution, he finally calmed down and sat waiting to meet his fate.

"It might go easier on you in the next world if you was to tell us where Jordan Gray is," Ben Thompson suggested.

With the calm demeanor of a man resigned to face his Maker, Ned looked down at Ben. "You can kiss my ass." Then he took a look around at the faces staring up at him. "I'll see every man here in Hell — a curse on the lot of you for hanging an innocent man." He had no sooner gotten the words out when the horse bolted, leaving Ned swinging back and forth from the cottonwood limb, his feet kicking frantically.

The sudden start of the horse caught everyone by surprise, and Ben looked back to see Preacher Rix standing with a quirt in his hand. When Ben's eye caught his, Preacher smiled and said, "You men have done the right thing. We can't let outlaws get away with murderin' innocent folks."

A late arrival to the lynching, Hattie Moon was stopped dead in her tracks when she saw Ned's horse charge out of the mob. "What have you damn fools done?" she demanded. Sam Morris, a foolish grin plastered across his dingy face, informed her of what had taken place. "That ol' man ain't murdered nobody," she protested. "You damn fools are the only ones murderin' anybody."

"You don't know what you're talkin' about, Hattie," Ben Thompson implored. "You weren't here to hear all the evidence."

"That old man didn't have it in him to murder anybody. Cut him down, Ben."

"We'd best not, Hattie. Looks like he's still breathin'. Besides, we want him to hang there for a while so everybody can see what happens to outlaws in Deadwood."

"Damn maniacs," she uttered, knowing there was little to do for Ned now. As she watched, his limbs finally stopped trembling, and he was still.

"He put a curse on all of us just before he swung," Harvey Perkins whispered softly in her ear.

She turned to look at him. Knowing how superstitious Harvey was, she couldn't resist saying, "I expect the curse will get all of you then. A dead man's curse is hard to shake." The look in Harvey's eyes told her that her comment had the effect she intended. She hoped he would worry himself to death over it. Hattie had not known Ned Booth long, but she was certain that he and

Jordan had nothing to do with Bull Brady's death.

Soon the spectacle of a hanging lost its entertainment value, and the mob thinned out, most of the people heading back to Sweeney's saloon to congratulate themselves on their action. One of the men got a board from behind the saloon and hung it around Ned's neck with the inscription THE PRICE FOR MURDER IN DEADWOOD. Later that evening, when things had quieted down, Hattie Moon and Maggie Hogg drove a wagon to the tree and cut poor Ned down. The two of them managed to load his body onto the wagon and take it back to the Trough, where it lay until Manual, their hired hand, took it up the valley to bury it. A dark figure, standing in the shadows at the back of the saloon, watched the efforts of the two women to salvage some degree of dignity for the late Ned Booth. Unseen in the darkness of the shadows, a wide smile creased his heavy beard. The whole episode had gone quite well from Preacher's point of view. It had succeeded in taking any suspicion from him and his sons. He was especially pleased with his influence upon the will of the lynch mob. *The Lord helps them what helps themselves,* he thought to himself and turned to fetch his sons.

■ ■ ■ ■

Jordan peered up at the sun. It looked to be considerably past midday. Maybe he and Ned got their signals crossed, but he was certain that Ned had said to meet him by the waterfall. There shouldn't have been any confusion about it. Where he now sat was almost the same spot where two pronghorn deer were grazing when he jumped them one afternoon. They were so surprised that he had easily shot one of them and could have gotten the other one if Ned and he had needed the meat. No, this was the right place. Maybe Ned just forgot.

"That ol' fart probably went to gape at Maggie and forgot all about me sittin' up here in the mountains," he confided to Sweet Pea. The indifferent horse didn't dignify the statement with a response. As the afternoon wore on, Jordan finally decided that Ned wasn't coming, and now he was worried that something might have happened to his friend. "Come on, Sweet Pea, we'd better go back to camp and see why Ned didn't show up."

Something wasn't right. Sweet Pea sensed it. The homely mare cocked her ears forward and broke into the peculiar stutter step that Jordan had come to recognize whenever she approached strange horses. "What is it, girl?" he whispered, his own senses sharpened now.

Approaching his camp from the slope above, he took advantage of the thick stand of pines that shielded their claim on that side. Ned's horses and his own packhorse should ordinarily be nickering a greeting to Sweet Pea, but there was no sound coming from his camp. Then Sweet Pea snorted, as she commonly did when challenging a stranger. Jordan heard an answering snort from the trees on the far side of the camp, and he knew he had a welcoming committee.

He pulled his horse to a stop and slid down from the saddle. Leaving Sweet Pea in the pines, he started working his way around the camp on foot, his rifle cocked and ready. His immediate concern was for Ned. If there was an ambush awaiting his return to camp, something must have happened to his partner. Stopping when approximately halfway around the clearing where he and Ned had set up their camp, he paused to take a look. Moving down to the edge of the trees, he studied the camp. Ned's horse was gone, as well as both packhorses. Scanning the clearing slowly, his eyes settled on Ned's pan. It was still perched on the split table rock where Ned had left it the day before. *Ned never came back from town.* No wonder he had failed to show up at the waterfall. Jordan at once felt a cold sensation of dread clutching his throat. If Ned were in trouble, Jordan felt it was mainly his fault. He shouldn't have let Ned talk him into taking to the hills while the old man went into Deadwood. More anxious than ever now, he moved back into the trees and continued the circle around his camp.

Johnny Cabel left the cover of the rock he had been lying behind and crawled over closer to Web Dupree. "Did you hear that? Somebody's comin'."

"Yeah, I heard it," Web replied. "Most likely, he heard that damn horse of your'n, too." Never taking his eyes off the clearing, he lamented, "He might decide not to come on in now. Get on back behind that rock and keep your eyes peeled."

Web Dupree had enjoyed very limited success as a prospector. He had found some traces of the precious dust in the three different claims he had mined, most of which was lost right away in the saloons and gambling houses that sprang up in Deadwood almost as soon as the first nugget was discovered. His lack of success had served to turn him bitter and envious of those who seemed to have better luck. He and Johnny Cabel decided to go in partners on the last site, a venture that seemed hopeless from the start. Johnny, like Web, was becoming more and more morose as each week passed without sign of color. It was getting to the point where they seldom had a civil word between themselves. Hope was rekindled, however, in Sweeney's saloon when they, along with Sam Morris and Barney Lipscomb, were among the first to grab Ned Booth.

When that leather pouch fell out of Ned's coat and plopped on the floor, Web's eyes grew as large as saucers. He glanced at Johnny, who was looking right back at him, both of their minds locked on the same thought: *Jordan Gray is carrying another one just like it!* As might have been expected, Ben Thompson took charge of Ned's pouch, promising to weigh it and divide it among those riding in the posse. Certain that others would be having the same thought, Web and Johnny hung back from the mob, watching from the fringe of the crowd as Ned was strung up. And while the others stayed to enjoy the final gyrations of the dying man, the two of them slipped away to get a head start.

It was early evening when they had found the camp near the head of the stream. Johnny had been in favor of immediately claiming the two packhorses hobbled near the water, but Web felt like it might spook Jordan Gray if he noticed the horses gone. They talked about it. Johnny argued that it would be difficult to claim the horses for themselves if a posse showed up before they could hide them. When he convinced Web that Jordan would hardly have time to notice since they planned to shoot him down as soon as he entered the clearing, Web changed his mind. "I expect you're right," Web had conceded, so they cut the hobbles and took the horses across the slope and left them to graze.

Now it seemed that their waiting had paid off. Somebody was approaching the camp from the other side of the clearing. There were mighty slim odds that it could be anyone other than Jordan Gray. The question was whether or not he had been spooked when the horses snorted. If their luck was holding, he would merely think it was the packhorses.

"I hope he ain't been anywhere to spend

any of that dust," Web whispered.

"What?" Johnny whispered back.

"Nothin'," Web replied, still in a hoarse whisper. "Be quiet now, and let him come on in." He was already thinking of the possibility of dissolving the partnership. Who could say Johnny wasn't shot by Jordan before Web got him? The thought brought a thin smile of anticipated satisfaction to Web's face. He shifted his body around to the other side of the pine he was using for cover, hoping to get a wider view of the camp. It had been at least fifteen minutes since he had heard the horses snorting. Jordan was being mighty cautious. *Come on in and get your medicine,* Web thought, his eyes straining for the first glimpse of his intended victim. Behind him, he heard his horse whinny. It was answered by another suspicious snort from Jordan's horse on the far side of the clearing. *What the hell's he doing? He ain't moved from that spot.*

"Lay those rifles down and get your hands up where I can see 'em."

Web froze. The voice came from right behind him. "Now hold on, mister," he pleaded. "Me and Johnny was just guardin' the camp." He laid down his rifle gently.

"Where's Ned?" Jordan demanded.

Web hesitated before answering. He

glanced at Johnny and tried to signal him with a furrowing of his eyebrows. Like Web, Johnny had laid down his rifle as directed. His hands up, he rolled over to a sitting position. Jordan's attention seemed to be mainly focused upon Web, so Johnny let his right hand drop slowly until it hovered over the Colt .45 he wore on his hip. Jordan didn't seem to notice.

"Ned's in town," Web replied to Jordan's question.

His answer wasn't enough to suit Jordan. "Whaddaya mean, he's in town? What's he doin' in town?"

"Swingin' from a cottonwood," Johnny blurted and made his move. He was fast. His hand dropped to the handle of his Colt, and the weapon had almost cleared the holster when Jordan turned and fired, sending a bullet ripping through Johnny's chest. Web snatched his rifle from the ground and managed to get off a shot while Jordan cocked his Winchester and spun back to face him. With no time to aim, Web's shot was wide, merely grazing Jordan's shoulder. Ignoring the wound, Jordan put a bullet in the center of Web's forehead.

It had all happened in the time it takes to blink an eye. Jordan stood somewhat dazed over the two dead men, hardly believing what had just taken place. When he had circled around behind the two men, he had no intention of killing anyone. He merely wanted to keep from getting shot himself. He even had slim hopes of convincing the two that there had been a mistake in thinking that he had murdered Bull Brady. Now the man's blurted remark came back to mind. *Swinging from a cottonwood.* Surely that had not been what he meant. But what if he did? Jordan could not control a sudden feeling of panic. What if those crazy sons of bitches had seized upon poor Ned, a total innocent, just as Jordan was innocent? He could feel the muscles in his arms tightening as a wave of anger swept over him, and he knew he had to find out if something had happened to Ned.

He stood where he was for a long moment, still staring at the two bodies, stunned by the thought that they had lain in ambush set to kill him. He realized that he could trust no one in the settlement of Deadwood Gulch, never sure if the next stranger he met might suddenly pull a gun. He might have been inclined to simply climb on Sweet Pea and head for the Powder River country, or the Wind River range, and say to Hell with Deadwood. He might have been, that is, had it not been for his concern for his friend. "If they've touched one hair on that old man's head . . ." he muttered to himself. Knowing there was only one place to find out, he determined to ride into Deadwood.

With no interest in anything that belonged to the two would-be assassins, he nevertheless paused to untie their horses. The only things he took, after second thoughts, were a couple of .45 caliber ammunition belts. He figured he was going to need them. He left the bodies where they lay and walked across the clearing to retrieve his horse. There wasn't much time spent in taking care of his wound. It didn't appear to be serious, so he knelt by the stream and cleaned the blood away, then wrapped it with a clean cloth from his saddlebag. Passing the tent, he paused to take a quick look inside to see if there was anything else he needed. He didn't take much time since he had no way of knowing when someone else might show up looking for him.

Guiding Sweet Pea away from the camp, he deemed it prudent to take a wide swing around the mountain in case there was a posse of vigilantes on their way. Halfway around the eastern slope, he came upon his and Ned's packhorses, peacefully grazing on a patch of bear grass. By this time, it was almost totally dark, but he managed to find a grassy ravine in which to hobble them until he could return for them.

CHAPTER 8

Jordan walked his horse slowly through the darkened alley behind the saloon, Sweet Pea stepping as light as a cat over the muddy wagon ruts. The noisy chatter from inside the building drifted heavily on the cold evening air as the most dedicated drinkers remained. The more conservative drunks had departed long before and were no doubt in their beds. Jordan had given his mission much thought on the ride down the mountain, and had decided that the only people he could trust were Hattie Moon and Maggie Hogg. With that in mind, he had guided Sweet Pea along behind the tents and shacks that made up Deadwood's main street until he pulled the mare up behind the Trough and dismounted. He remembered Ned telling him once that the two women shared a bedroom behind the kitchen, so he led Sweet Pea to the rear of the building.

At this hour, the tent and the kitchen were dark. Since the room that served as the two women's living quarters had no windows, he couldn't be sure if the ladies were still awake or not. He tapped softly on the heavy pine door. There was no sound from inside. Tapping a bit harder, he whispered, "Maggie, Hattie, are you in there?" After a moment, the door slowly opened a few inches, and he found himself staring into the twin barrels of a shotgun.

"Who wants to know?" a gruff voice came from the darkened room.

"Damn!" Jordan recoiled and stepped to one side. "Don't shoot that damn thing."

"Jordan? Is that you?" He recognized the voice now as Maggie's. The door opened wide to reveal Maggie wearing nothing more than long johns. "Get in here, boy, before somebody sees you." She grabbed him by the arm and pulled him inside. After taking a quick look outside, she quickly closed the door. "Light that lamp, Hattie." In a few moments, the modest room was ablaze with light until Hattie, similarly attired, turned the wick down to a comfortable level.

"What are you doin' here?" Hattie asked anxiously. "Don't you know it ain't safe in Deadwood for you?"

"I had to find out what happened to Ned. Two fellows were waitin' to bushwhack me back at our camp, and Ned never came back from town."

"Ned's done for," Maggie informed him. "The sons of bitches hung him."

"Strung him up right in the middle of town," Hattie added.

The sobering news struck Jordan with the weight of a hammer. In his heart, he had known that Ned had met with tragedy. But still he had hoped that there would be a possibility that Ned was merely wounded or was awaiting a trial. To hear that his friend was dead brought a frantic sense of grief to the broad-shouldered young man. It didn't make sense that Ned should die. He wasn't even involved. When Maggie told of how the mob had hauled him out and left him hanging with a sign on him, the anger was too great for Jordan to control.

"Who?" Jordan suddenly demanded, his face twisted with the anger inside him. "Who are the ones who killed him?"

"I know how you feel," Maggie said, "but this ain't no time to go off half-cocked."

"Half the men in town was in that drunken mob," Hattie added.

"I want to know the names of the men responsible," Jordan insisted.

"You can't kill the whole damn town," Maggie replied. "Some of 'em didn't have nothin' to do with the hangin' besides watchin'."

"Maggie's right," Hattie said. "By the time they was all drunk, the whole town was singing the hangman's song. Besides, you've got your own neck to worry about. They're goin' after you next. You ought not even be here. Ben Thompson's called for a posse to ride out at first light, headin' up to your claim. You'd better be long gone from here before then." She could see that he wasn't really listening, his mind still obviously racing with thoughts of revenge. "Jordan, there's nothin' you can do for poor Ned now. It's time to look out for yourself. Get on that ugly horse of yours and leave this place."

"Ben Thompson, huh?" Jordan repeated the name his mind had seized upon, the balance of her statements left unheeded.

Quick to try to shift his thinking, Hattie said, "Ben's just the head of the committee. He ain't the one who pushed for Ned's hangin'. In fact, he tried to keep 'em as calm about it as he could."

"That damn preacher was the one that done most of the damage," Maggie said, causing Jordan to jerk his head up at the

174

sound of the word *preacher.* "He said he saw Ned with you at Bull's claim."

"Preacher?" Jordan questioned. "What preacher?"

"Never saw him before last evening. He just showed up at Sweeney's while they was havin' the meetin' — said he saw Ned hidin' in the bushes while you shot Bull."

"Big man?" Jordan pressed. "Did he have two sons with him?"

"I don't know," Maggie replied. "I believe there was someone with him, but I ain't sure."

So I've crossed trails with Preacher again. Jordan was sure it was the man who called himself Preacher Rix — the devil's own disciple. Who could say how he figured to benefit by lying about Ned? "Listen," Jordan cautioned. "You both better watch your backs around that man, if it's the preacher I think it is. He seems to show up damn near every time somebody gets killed."

The women assured him that they would be cautious, but immediately resumed their efforts to persuade him to flee. He knew it was the smart thing to do, but he was still smoldering inside. Immediate retaliation against the town was what he most craved. "You can't kill the whole town," Maggie repeated. "You've got no way of knowin' who had a hand in it and who didn't." He thought about that for a moment. Maggie was right. While at the moment, his anger was directed at the entire town — it was really only a few who actually caused Ned to be hanged. "And don't go anywhere near your camp this mornin'," Hattie warned, " 'cause that's where the posse will be headin' first thing." Her warning made his decision for him.

Every man riding with that posse will damn sure have a hand in it. There would be no later qualms of conscience over the possibility that innocent lives had been taken. Every man riding with the posse would be coming to take his life. "All right," he abruptly stated, his mind made up. "I'm leaving."

"Six men," Jordan whispered softly to himself, as he watched his camp from the cover of a waist-high boulder high up the slope. Content to merely observe the actions of the vigilante posse for the moment, he was interested to see how they planned to approach. Earlier, before daylight, he had built up a good fire and rolled a sizable tree limb in Ned's old blanket before taking the horses across to the other side of the ridge. Selecting a boulder halfway down the slope, he then settled himself in to await the posse.

Just as the first rays of the sun found their way over the east ridge, he saw the men approach. On foot, they led their horses quietly up from below, following the stream until just below the camp. Then one man — Jordan assumed he was Ben Thompson — directed them to fan out in a half circle. On his signal, they vanished from sight as they disappeared in the pines below his camp. Jordan waited. In no more than a few minutes' time, he caught sight of two of the six at the edge of the clearing, crawling up into a thicket of small pines. Jordan brought his Winchester up to rest on the boulder. He scanned the lower edge of the clearing, but could not sight any of the other men.

Silence lay like a foreboding shroud upon the tiny valley as daylight began to creep up the streambed; even the water's constant grumble was stilled in the cold mountain air. Suddenly Jordan flinched, startled by the eruption of gunfire below him. Without shout or warning, the posse had opened fire on the camp, and the silent valley was now in the throes of a hailstorm of rifle and shotgun blasts ripping countless holes through the tent and peppering the blanket-covered limb with lead. Angered by the blatant attack with no option of surrender, Jordan sighted his rifle toward the pine thicket, but he held his fire, not yet satisfied that he had a clear target. *Come out where I can see you,* he pleaded silently. He wanted to see the faces, memorize them, so as to leave no one to go free. *Come on, you heroes.*

The barrage went on for several long minutes before tapering off to one or two random shots. Emboldened by the total lack of return fire, the vigilantes left the cover of their hiding places, and one by one ventured cautiously into the clearing — all except one. Barney Lipscomb, eager to be the first to find the body, charged straight into the camp, blazing away with his rifle, sending bullet after bullet into the blanket by the fire. "You'll be the first," Jordan muttered softly, but still held his fire. He wanted to know the other faces.

Barney was soon joined by the other five, who now hurried to get in on the kill. Racing up to the camp, rifles ready, they descended upon the tent, a couple of them firing again into the shredded canvas. Above them on the mountainside, Jordan stared at each man's face, intent upon making sure he would never forget even one.

"Bamboozled us," Barney complained loudly as he kicked at the bullet-riddled limb. "He lit out." Thoroughly frustrated at having been deprived of being the one to claim the kill, he pulled up a corner of the tent and dragged it over to the fire.

Sam Morris couldn't resist the temptation to jape him. "You sure kilt that there pine log." A couple of the others laughed.

Barney didn't appreciate the humor. He scowled as he promised, "Well, he might think he's outsmarted us this time, but he ain't gonna —" Stopped in midsentence, he dropped the tent corner. Those standing next to him heard only a dull thump when the rifle ball smacked into his chest, followed almost immediately by the crack of Jordan's Winchester. Killed instantly, he stood there a moment before falling backward to land in the middle of the fire.

The next seconds were filled with chaos as everybody scrambled for cover. Two more shots rang out, one catching Bob Wooten in the back as he ran for the trees, the other ripping into Harvey Perkins' shoulder. Running for their lives, Ben Thompson and Sam Morris both veered around Harvey Perkins as he was spun around by the rifle shot and dropped to his knees, neither man opting to help the wounded man. "I'm shot!" Harvey cried out in desperation, but his companions ignored his plea for help.

Once the safety of the trees was reached,

the survivors stopped to try to decide what action to take. Harvey, the last to stagger in, complained bitterly, "Thanks a lot. It's damn lucky I didn't git hit in the leg. I'd still be out there waitin' for you bastards to help me. That Booth feller put a curse on all of us."

"Quit your bellyaching," his partner, Sam Morris, snapped. "Be glad you ain't layin' on that fire with Barney. You better stuff a rag or somethin' on that shoulder. You're bleedin' like a stuck hog."

"Anybody see where those shots came from?" Ben Thompson asked.

Answering for everybody, Tom Bowers said, "I was too damn busy gettin' my ass outta there to be lookin' around."

"Had to be from up on that slope to the east," Ben said. "Barney was facin' that way, and he got it square in the chest." He scanned the slope for a few moments before turning his gaze back to the clearing and the body lying just inside it. "I can't tell if Bob's movin' or not. He might still be alive."

"Yeah, well, I ain't gonna go out there to find out," Sam was quick to inform him.

"We ought not just leave him," Bowers said.

"Tom's right," Ben said, feeling the responsibility as head of the committee.

"Hell, he's dead," Sam protested. "If he wasn't, he'd've done crawled outta there."

They huddled there for a few minutes more, the valley ghostlike in silence, knowing that death's messenger waited somewhere up on the side of the mountain. Finally, Ben Thompson's conscience got the best of him. "I'm goin' to see if Bob's alive," he announced and hesitated a moment for volunteers to go with him. There were none. He snorted his disdain for their lack of courage and scurried out to the body. The others watched, anticipating the shots that would come. "He's alive!" Ben shouted and started dragging him toward the trees. When there were no shots fired, Tom Bowers darted out to help drag the mortally wounded man. Their reward was a slight grateful flickering of Bob's eyelids moments before he died.

"Dammit, I told you he was a dead man," Sam Morris commented, attempting to justify his lack of courage.

"It needed to be done," Ben replied, his temper flaring.

"It was a foolish thing to do," Sam shot back, "just like this whole fouled-up posse."

During the argument that ensued, the rifleman up on the slope moved across the ridge to take up a new position, having seen where the posse had left their horses. Moving swiftly through the trees, he made his way down the mountain almost to the bottom before taking cover in a thicket of young pines. From there, he had a clear view of the horses tied in the trees just below him. He had just settled himself in position to shoot when the four remaining members of the posse appeared, cautiously moving through the trees. The thickness of the forest prevented him from getting an unimpeded view of all the men, and with the speed in which they hurried to mount and ride, he had to take the first target that presented itself.

Once again, the cold morning quiet was split by the crack of Jordan's rifle, and Tom Bowers staggered against his horse's belly before slumping to the ground. Pandemonium took over again, as the other three men scrambled frantically into their saddles and fled, their horses weaving left and right through the trees. Jordan quickly fired three more shots after them, hoping for a lucky hit, but the forest offered too much protection.

Getting to his feet, he stood staring in the direction taken by the frightened posse. Remaining there until the sounds of their horses lashing through the brush could no longer be heard, he then turned and began making his way back up the slope to his horse. As he climbed up through outcroppings of rock and dark green ponderosas, he thought about what had just taken place and wondered if his actions were morally right. It was the first time he had allowed such questions to arise in his mind since he had learned of Ned's murder. The three men he had killed on this morning were not shot during the heat of his anger. They were calmly executed with a steady hand. Now he wondered if he had just killed three innocent men. *No!* His inner voice insisted. *They killed Ned, and they were coming to kill me.* Then he thought about the way they had fired upon his camp without warning, shredding the blanket and tent. They had no intention of taking him alive. His resolve strengthened, he determined that the other three should not avoid paying the same price as their three dead partners.

It was a sorry-looking posse that limped back into Deadwood. As soon as Hattie heard someone call out that the vigilance committee was back, she placed the stack of plates she held on the table and called Maggie. The two women hurried out to join the small crowd already gathering in the street.

Seeing only three survivors, and one of them wounded, those gathered began to exchange comments among themselves. Finally, when the three rode up to where the crowd awaited, someone asked, "Did you git him?"

"No," Ben Thompson answered calmly.

"Where's the rest of 'em?" someone else asked.

"Barney, Tom, and Bob Wooten are dead," Ben answered without emotion, feeling the burden of his responsibility as he gazed back at the stunned expressions facing him.

Sam Morris, always eager to excuse his failures, insisted, "It'd've been a helluva lot different if he hadn't been hiding up in the rocks. Them poor fellers never had a chance."

"Where are the bodies?" This came from Maggie Hogg. "Didn't you bring 'em back with you?"

Ben shook his head sadly. "We couldn't, Maggie. That feller had us in his sights. We had no choice but to get the hell outta there, or none of us woulda come back."

"Don't seem right to come back without 'em," Maggie spoke softly aside to Hattie. Then loud enough for Ben to hear, she added, "Reckon somebody ought to go back up there and bury 'em." She looked around at the men gathered there. "They were supposed to be your friends." In truth, she would not mourn the passing of any of the three. As far as she was concerned, they were just three drifters who had lit for a spell in Deadwood. Even so, it seemed inappropriate for the posse to leave their dead behind. On the other hand, she was relieved to learn they had been unsuccessful in killing Jordan Gray, even though she was somewhat surprised to see how costly their mission had been.

"We'll be goin' back to take care of 'em," Ben Thompson offered weakly.

Maggie had her doubts. Finished with the matter for the moment, she turned her attention to Harvey Perkins. Some of the men had helped him down from his horse while Hattie stood by to take a look at the wound. "How bad is it?" Maggie asked.

"Clean through the shoulder," Hattie replied. "Hole in the front, hole in the back." Harvey grunted in pain when she pulled the coat sleeve away. "Oh, quit your cryin'," she scolded. "You ain't hurt bad at all."

"It hurts like hell, Hattie," the wounded man complained.

"It's gonna hurt for a spell, but you bled out pretty good. It'll heal up all right. Come on in the Trough, and I'll find somethin' to bandage it with." She led him away while Maggie remained to talk to Ben. "You oughta known better than to go after Jordan Gray with that sorry bunch," Hattie scolded. "They ain't got sense enough to know what they're up against." Once inside the tent, she sat him down on the end of one of the benches and went to fetch a clean cloth and a pan of water. When she returned, she sat down, facing him, and began cleaning the wound. "Now," she said softly, "suppose you tell me just what happened up that mountain."

Back in the street, Ben and Sam were answering the many questions from those who had gathered around them. The one common question that continued to arise was "What are you gonna do about Jordan Gray?" Ben was undecided at this point whether he wanted to do anything beyond hoping Jordan was already on his way out of the territory. One spectator who was more than a little interested was a large shaggy-bearded man wearing a bearskin coat and a black flat-crowned hat. Preacher Rix listened to the discussion, the twinkle in his eyes the only hint of the broad smile behind his heavy beard. He waited patiently until most of the men decided to adjourn to the saloon to hear more embellishment of the story from Sam Morris.

"A word with you, brother," Preacher said, stepping in front of Ben. Ben stopped short and looked up at the bear of a man. "I reckon I can help you in this hour of need," Preacher confided.

Ben, feeling in no need of spiritual guidance at this particular point, took a backward step from the huge man's overbearing presence. "I don't mean to be disrespectful, Reverend, but I guess I already did a gracious plenty praying back there on that mountain."

"There are two kinds of preachers," Preacher persisted, stepping in front of Ben again when he tried to go around him. "There are them that sing the praises of the Lord, and there's them that swing the mighty sword of the Lord. That last kind is my callin'. I have smote many heathens that didn't see the straight of things. Me and my boys will go get this Jordan Gray for you before he kills more innocent folks. Whaddaya say to that?"

Thompson was surprised. He hardly expected a man of the cloth to offer anything more than prayers. Peering into the fearsome countenance of the brute blocking his way, he suddenly had little doubt that

Preacher could back up his boast. And after that morning's encounter with Jordan Gray, he was open to most any alternative plan that would preclude his involvement.

Seeing Ben's hesitancy, Preacher pressed further. "The sooner we get this Philistine, the more innocent lives we save." His voice rumbling down like thunder, he went on. "I've seed it happen before. This boy's got the bloodlust now. The devil's got in his gizzard. There ain't no claims safe around here till he feels the terrible vengeance of the Lord."

Ben was compelled to give it some thought. Maybe it would be easier to mount another posse with Preacher's formidable presence at the head. After his posse's experience that morning, he was expecting a great deal more hesitancy on the part of the men of Deadwood. "Maybe some spiritual guidance might make some of the men more willin' to ride with another posse," Ben conceded.

"No, friend," Preacher patiently replied. "That ain't what I mean. Just me and my boys, that's the way I work best."

Meeting the sinister gaze emanating from under the heavy dark brows, Ben suddenly felt sympathy for any man with Preacher Rix on his trail. Feeling he had nothing to lose, he said, "All right, Reverend, if you're sure you wanna risk your neck, it ain't for me to tell you no."

Preacher smiled. " 'Course, me and my boys is gonna have some expenses. If this sinner is on the run, it might take a few days to track him down, and we're kinda hard up for supplies right now."

Ben realized then what Preacher was actually proposing. This shed a different light on the situation, and he was quick to make it clear. "The men just elected me to head up the vigilance committee. I ain't the mayor or nothin'. We ain't got no budget or nothin' like that to pay a tracker."

Preacher's face relaxed into a broad smile. "No, no, brother. I don't look for pay to do the Lord's business. Cuttin' down the enemies of the Lord is all the pay I need. But a man's gotta eat. All I was sayin' is that we could use a little help with supplies, whatever the town could contribute. That's all I was askin', just a little Christian help. And for that, you get your Mr. Jordan Gray, and no risk to you and your townsfolk."

It was a tempting proposition — too tempting at that particular moment to pass up. Ben glanced at the remnants of the crowd as the last stragglers followed Sam Morris into Sweeney's. The odds of mounting another posse from that bunch before morning were pretty slim. They'd have to get liquored up enough to volunteer, and by that time, they'd be too drunk to ride. He shifted his gaze toward the edge of the muddy street to Maggie Hogg, standing, hands on hips, an interested spectator. She would be waiting to question him again about going to bury the dead. He wished they had never elected him head of the committee.

"All right," he abruptly conceded. "I'll go in and talk to the boys and pass the hat, but we'll want to see Jordan Gray's body."

Preacher grinned. "Shore," he replied. "I'll bring him all wrapped up like a Christmas turkey." *And just as dead,* he thought to himself. "Just tell 'em inside to stay outta my way while this killer's on the loose. There's no tellin' where he's liable to strike next. It's best if they all stay away from their claims."

Ben nodded and turned to follow the crowd into the saloon. He avoided eye contact with Maggie when he passed her. His gaze aimed at his feet, he tossed her a platitude to placate her. "We'll see about takin' care of the dead." He hurried past her before she had time to comment.

Preacher looked at Maggie and grinned

190

before turning on his heel and striding off to round up his sons. She stood, transfixed, staring at his broad back as he walked away from her. A sudden shiver ran down her back, and she felt like she had just looked into the eyes of evil. Why, she wondered, had no one questioned the sincerity of the man's claims to be a man of God? She was suddenly swept with a wave of compassion for Jordan Gray, and she knew that she had to warn him.

Inside Sweeney's, the crowd of miners was already heating up with most of the spark provided by Sam Morris. "Ain't no one of us safe with that mad dog roamin' around these mountains," Sam exclaimed to a chorus of agreeing grunts. "We're gonna have to go up there and root him out. By God, he can't stand up to the whole damn town."

"Sam's right," someone at the bar chimed in. "We need every man with a gun to go up there and get that bastard." His comment was met with several hoots of approval. "Just like we've always done," someone else shouted. "Ain't but one way to handle a backshootin' claim robber, and that's with a rope."

"Hold on a minute!" Ben Thompson raised his voice above the din. "What you're sayin' is true, but let's hold off for a day or two."

"What for?" Sam blurted.

Ben then related the proposition just offered him from Preacher Rix. The men were as surprised as he had been, and several of them immediately questioned his reasoning.

"You have a mad dog walkin' down the middle of the street, you shoot him. You don't send no preacher out to talk to him," Sam stated.

Ben waited a moment for the crowd to quiet down again after Sam's remarks. Then he explained that Rix didn't have prayer in mind. He had assured Ben that he and his sons stood a better chance of tracking Jordan Gray without a noisy posse to get in their way. "And he guarantees he'll bring Gray in, dead or alive, and after talkin' to the man, I don't believe he cares which way it is." He paused while the miners thought it over, then said, "Let's give him a chance. Then if he don't bring him in, we'll get up another posse."

They might have run over the first body, that of Tom Bowers, if Maggie's mule had not sidestepped to avoid it. It lay where it had fallen, among the dark pines where the posse had left their horses. "Let's git him on a mule," she said to Manuel and slid off to help him lift the body. They picked up the cold, stiff corpse that had once been Tom Bowers, Maggie at the head, Manuel at the foot, and hoisted it up on one of the extra mules they had brought. Once it was balanced, Maggie stepped back and scratched her head. "I reckon we're gonna have to tie his hands and feet together to keep him from tipping one way or the other." Manuel did as she instructed, using as much force as he could muster in an effort to bend the body to fit the mule's rump.

With one of the dead secured on a mule, Maggie led them toward the clearing. "Jordan," she called out, lest he mistake her for more of the posse, "it's Maggie Hogg. I got Manuel with me." There was no answer, no sound at all except the solitary hoot of an owl, watching from a tall pine. In spite of her confidence that she had nothing to fear from Jordan Gray, Maggie felt a cold shiver run the length of her spine.

Bob Wooten's body was several short yards from that of Tom's. They hefted it up beside the first corpse. Once it was secured, they proceeded cautiously into the clearing, Maggie calling out Jordan's name every few minutes. She had come with a feeling that Jordan would stay close by his camp to see if the posse was going to try it again. It was beginning to look like she was wrong, for her husky voice echoed through the narrow gulch, coming back to mock her.

"Miss Maggie," Manuel softly uttered and pointed toward the tent. At almost the same instant, a strange odor reached her nostrils, and her eyes followed Manuel's outstretched hand to the charred corpse of Barney Lipscomb.

"Damn," Maggie swore softly. She walked up to the remains of the fire and stood staring at the body that had extinguished it. Reluctant to touch it, she nevertheless forced herself to grab Barney's boots. Manuel took hold of the wrists, and they threw the body on a mule as quickly as they could manage. That done, she walked from one side of the clearing to the other, calling out for Jordan again and again.

"I'm here, Maggie."

"Jesus Christ!" Maggie blurted. She and Manuel both jumped at the sound of his voice right behind them.

"I didn't mean to spook you," Jordan apologized.

"You gave me a fright. I can tell you that," she confessed. "Are you sure you ain't part Injun? Damn!" She took a moment to compose herself, then told him why she had come. "I kinda figured you'd stay close around this camp, figured you didn't have sense enough to run. But you'd best light out now, boy. The whole damn town is talkin' about stringin' you up. Ben Thompson's sending that scary-lookin' preacher after you, and I wouldn't trust that man to guard a rattlesnake."

This captured Jordan's attention in a fraction of a second. "So the preacher's coming after me?" Why, he wondered, did that not surprise him? He remembered his meeting with Preacher Rix and his two sons, and the gut feeling he had had at the time. They were standing over a grave like wolves over a carcass, and his natural instincts had told him not to turn his back on them.

"I was standin' there listenin'," Maggie said. "He talked Ben into lettin' him and them two half-wits of his'n come after you alone. Now I ask you, what kinda preacher is that?" Jordan didn't answer, but he had a fair idea what kind of preacher Rix was. He was thinking about the couple near Fort Laramie, the two miners south of Deadwood, and Bull Brady. He wondered if he would have found a hoofprint with a spur at Bull's camp if he had been given time to search for it. He'd be willing to bet on it.

Maggie spoke again. "If that man's a

preacher, then I'm a Sioux Indian."

"He's a murderin' son of a bitch," Jordan said, "the worst kind."

Maggie looked hard into Jordan's eyes. There was no fear there, only impatience. "You'd best run, Jordan. You've already settled Ned's account." He didn't answer right away, and she figured what was in his mind. "You're gonna wait for him, ain'tcha?"

He again ignored the question as he thought about Preacher Rix. "So those other three who came up here to kill me have decided to hire that butcher to do the work they set out to do," Jordan said. "I'm sorry I let 'em get away this mornin'." He owed Ned, and he had every intention of balancing the account. "I don't aim to spend my time lookin' back over my shoulder for that grizzly bear," he replied softly.

"Well, I knew it was a waste of my time, ridin' up here to warn you, but you've been warned. Good luck to you, Jordan Gray. Now I've got to get back and help Hattie in the kitchen."

"Much obliged, Maggie," he said and stood back to watch her grab the lead rope on one of the mules. He remained there until she and Manuel disappeared into the trees below the camp.

CHAPTER 9

"Why are we goin' after that feller, Pa?" Zeb questioned. It didn't make a lot of sense to him to go after someone who had demonstrated the ability to fight back. Six men had already gone after him, and not but three of them came back — and one of them wounded. Even Zeb's simple mind could see the folly in chasing such a man.

Preacher snorted in disgust for his elder son's lack of cunning, but he answered patiently, "Them fellers in town is so scared of Jordan Gray that they're all huggin' each other in the saloon, a-feared to go back to their claims. Hellfire, Zeb, we ain't goin' after Jordan Gray. I expect he's halfway to Montana territory by now. And while them yeller-tailed miners is huddled up together in town, why, we'll just help ourselves to whatever we find, with nobody to bother us."

"Ain't everybody in town," Quincy

pointed out. "What about all them people still settin' on their claims?"

"Why, that'll be the Lord's business as usual, like we've always done," Preacher explained. "The beauty of it is anybody gets killed, they'll blame it on Jordan Gray." He paused while his two offspring beamed their admiration for their father's guile. "And it was mighty nice of 'em to take up a collection to take care of our supplies, warn't it?" He chuckled at the thought.

Preacher took a long look at his two sons as they climbed up in their saddles. They weren't the brightest pennies in the purse, but they were good boys. They feared the Lord and their daddy. Preacher felt a great deal of pride in the job he had done, rearing two rambunctious sons without benefit of a mother's guidance. Cora very seldom crossed his mind anymore. The boys' mother was not worthy of his thoughts, although he should probably give her some credit for the line of work he undertook. Thinking about her now caused Preacher to grin to himself.

As a young man, Preacher had never been predisposed to honest labor. For that reason, he had been drawn to Cora's father's calling as pastor of a little church near Omaha. He had never heard a calling himself and admitted as much to Cora's father, and the old man advised him to find other work. After Quincy was born, Preacher bounced from one job to another, usually leaving or being fired, most often for breaking some fellow worker's skull in a trivial disagreement. It was after one such altercation at a sawmill that Preacher came home early one afternoon to find Cora lying on their bed with her ankles locked behind her cousin's bare backside. It was like the touch of a match to an open keg of dynamite. He was still smoldering from the rage that had just sent a fellow worker to the doctor with a broken jaw, and the sight of his wife in the embrace of another was enough to cause the explosion that took two lives.

Cora had sent Zeb and Quincy up to the woods to cut firewood when her cousin Wilbur stopped in to visit. It had never occurred to Preacher until that day that the boys had been sent to cut wood so often that there was enough firewood stacked back of the house to last for three or four winters. On that day, when the boys came back with another wagonload of wood, it was to find their father standing over a freshly dug grave. "Just throw that load off right on top of the grave," Preacher had ordered.

When Zeb asked what was buried in the grave, Preacher had explained to his two sons that he had been called upon to dispatch two sinners to Hell. "Ma and Uncle Wilbur?" Zeb had asked at once. When Preacher answered that it was, Zeb looked at Quincy and grinned. "We knowed they was sparkin', didn't we, Quincy?"

Quincy reflected his brother's grin. "Yeah, we sneaked back to the house one time and peeked at 'em through the window." He chuckled. "They was goin' at it like a couple of hounddogs." Then he furrowed his brow when a deeper thought struck him. "Sinners is the Lord's enemies. Ain't they, Pa? So you're doin' the Lord's work when you kill a sinner."

His son's simple statement had profound impact upon Preacher. *Out of the mouth of babes,* he had thought, and he knew at that moment that he had received a sort of calling. It might not have been from above, but it would serve his needs and satisfy the simple minds of his sons. "We've got to leave here now," Preacher had then told them. "The Lord's called upon me to seek out other sinners and let them know the mighty sword of the Lord."

Before leaving, he stood before the monument of firewood and said a few words of prayer for the benefit of his sons. The fact that neither son seemed to feel any sorrow over the passing of their mother did not strike Preacher as being that unusual. Cora had never showed much in the way of affection for either boy, and her cooking left a great deal to be desired as well. So, he reasoned, there was very little about her to be missed. It was strange, indeed, that his calling in life had been showed to him through his younger son, the one who seemed less likely to have intelligent thought. Quincy was always kind of special to him after that, even taking into consideration that the boy held a striking resemblance to Cora's cousin Wilbur.

Now, as Preacher thought back over the years since he had left his wife, he felt satisfied with his chosen path. He had never felt remorse for any of the many *sinners* he had sent to their glory. At times, he even believed he really was doing the Lord's work. He turned in the saddle to take a look at Zeb and Quincy, following blissfully along behind him. As full-grown men, the boys were strong and enthusiastic disciples of their father's work, young men a father could be proud of.

Preacher Rix was not the only man contemplating his path in life at that moment. High up in the pines, near the summit of a rocky-faced mountain, Jordan Gray sat quietly waiting for the unholy preacher. The smoldering rage that had driven him to seek total vengeance upon every man who had a hand in Ned Booth's lynching had left him now. Maggie was right. The vigilante posse was just a confused mob of drunken fools. The one who had instigated Ned's murder was Preacher Rix, and Jordan was resigned to wait for him to settle up for Ned.

It was time to think with a calm mind. Maybe Maggie Hogg was right about another thing, too. Maybe he should ride out of these mountains after he settled with Preacher, and leave all that had happened here behind. He had taken three lives. Was this not compensation enough for the loss of his partner? But three of the six men who had come to kill him had managed to escape, and he was pretty sure that he had recognized two of them as the very two who had attempted to hang him at Bull Brady's camp. The leader of the posse, Ben Thompson, was a fair man according to Maggie, but Jordan could not forget that he had allowed the mob to hang Ned. It was a great deal to consider for a man who held no fondness for taking a life. As for Preacher

Rix and his sons, Jordan felt no compassion for the blatant murderer, and no fear with the knowledge that Preacher was now searching for him. If he got the opportunity, he could rid the world of Preacher Rix with no qualms.

Finish what he had started here or leave before more lives were taken? It was time to make the decision. A squeal from one of the packhorses caused him to snatch up his rifle, ready to fire, but it was only the result of Ned's packhorse standing too close to Sweet Pea. The ornery mare was not yet comfortable with Ned's horse and wouldn't hesitate to take a nip out of its flank if it crowded her. Jordan could not help but smile.

Kathleen Beard — the name suddenly jumped to the forefront of his conscience mind, an occurrence that often happened when he did not discipline his thoughts. This time, he permitted the name to linger. He wondered if she was now Mrs. Thomas Jefferson Wallace. The thought of it still caused pain. When he left Fort Laramie, she had not formally accepted the lieutenant's proposal, but she made it plain that she intended to. He could not deny a strong desire to find out for certain. *Maybe I'll ride back to Laramie and find out,* he thought.

Without really realizing it, he had just made up his mind to leave the Black Hills and the trail of vengeance. If he could have known of the hornet's nest being stirred up in Deadwood, he might have decided it best to strike out immediately instead of waiting to let his horses graze on the new grass.

The sun was not quite directly overhead when Grady Bostick drove his lathered horse recklessly down into the gulch and pulled up in front of the saloon. Without taking time to loop the reins over the rail, he charged into Sweeney's, shouting the news. "Fraiser's dead! Dry gulched!" he exclaimed breathlessly. "I just come from his claim!"

His frantic announcement brought a momentary silence to the noisy saloon, and then the joint erupted into a chorus of angry cries. Although early in the day, there was a sizable crowd in Sweeney's due to the supposed threat of a killer stalking the mountains. Many cried out for action. The loudest voice belonged to Sam Morris. "By God, he's gonna kill us all one by one. We've got to go up in them hills and run him to ground."

"What about the preacher?" someone asked. "Ben said he didn't want nobody in his way."

"I don't know about you fellers," Sam retorted, pushing his way to the center of the crowd, "but I ain't got much faith in no Bible-thumpin' preacher." He looked around him to see how many agreed with him. "We got us a mad dog here. I say we go up and git him."

The room filled with the din of excited voices, as everyone tried to speak at once. "Somebody better go get Ben," a man standing next to Sam said.

"To hell with Ben!" Sam immediately exclaimed. "It was Ben's idea to set here while that jackleg preacher went after that killer. If we hadn't listened to him, we mighta already had Jordan Gray strung up to a tree."

"Sam's right," someone said. "Let's get mounted and go after that bastard while there's still plenty of daylight left." There were only a few dissenting voices while the majority in the gathering expressed excited support for immediate action.

"All right then," Sam said, his face flush with bloodlust and whiskey. "Grab your guns. We're gonna go get us a badger." In a matter of minutes, the saloon was emptied as the crowd of miners, drunks, and hangers-on spilled into the muddy street, yelling and hooting with drunken courage. Sweeney, left standing alone behind his bar, walked to the door to watch the disorganized posse assemble. He shook his head slowly. *If Jordan Gray is anywhere within five miles of that mob, he'll damn sure hear them coming.* As he turned to go back to the bar, his eye caught a glimmer of metal under one of the tables. Bending over to take a closer look, he discovered a silver dollar protruding from a crack in the plank floor. He picked it up and brushed it off. *A sign of good luck,* he thought. Then another thought occurred. He had been trying to decide on a formal name for his saloon. *The Silver Dollar — that's what I'll call it.* "Now I reckon I'll sweep up a little while I've got the chance. I expect they'll all be back in here before dark."

Making his way carefully down through a narrow passage chiseled out of the rocky face of a cliff, Jordan leaned back in the saddle, one hand resting on Sweet Pea's rump. *She might be ugly as a goat for a reason,* he couldn't help thinking, smiling to himself. The steepness of the path had caused him to consider finding another way down to the spring where he had temporarily left the packhorses while he had waited in vain for Preacher, but Sweet Pea had shown no hesitation. So Jordan let the cantankerous mare make the decision. Halfway down, when her front hooves slid a few feet in the loose gravel, he had to wonder if maybe he was giving the horse credit for more sense than she actually had. It wouldn't have taken much before man and horse went head over heels in a rock slide. Undeterred, the mare found her footing again and proceeded down to the bottom of the passage without mishap. "You had me worried there for a minute, girl." He gave her a pat on the neck and guided her toward a ring of trees that circled the mountain's base.

Striking an old game trail, he rode down through the pines until he came to a clearing, where he paused to get his bearings. The clearing, a mountain meadow, extended toward the eastern side of the slope. The spring where the horses waited would be to his right, toward the western slope. He had climbed up to the top of the mountain to take a look around and determine the best way to circle back south, avoiding his camp. He had spent enough time hunting in these mountains to know them as well as Ned Booth had. Confident that he was swinging wide enough, he turned Sweet Pea toward the west and the waiting horses.

He had no sooner entered the dark pines again when he heard the shots. A barrage of gunfire, the shooting went on for several minutes, the sound reverberating through the trees below him as if a major skirmish was in progress. Finally, the shooting tapered off with a few random shots and then silence again. Whatever it had been was apparently over. With real cause for alarm, Jordan urged Sweet Pea forward. His packhorses were in that direction.

Closer to the spring now, he picked up the sound of voices. White men, he determined immediately, yelling to one another. He continued on toward the sound, his senses alert, his eyes taking in everything before him, lest he stumble into an ambush. Close enough now to make out the words being flung back and forth among the members of the posse, Jordan dismounted. Pulling his rifle from the saddle sling, he made his way on foot to a spot some one hundred yards above the spring. Below him, he could see the source of the noise. It looked like half the town of Deadwood had stormed up the slope. There was little need for speculation upon their intent. Next to the little trickle of a stream, he saw his two packhorses, their bodies riddled with bullet holes while riders crashed around wildly in the brush, looking for any target to shoot at. Jordan felt his face flush hot as the anger filled his veins. The useless slaughter had been meant for him.

A voice rang out loud and clear above the others, and Jordan shifted his gaze to spot Sam Morris emerging from the trees, his rifle raised above his head. Jordan didn't know the man's name, but he recognized him from earlier encounters. While he watched, Sam yelled to the others, "He can't be far away! He wouldn't run off and leave his horses." He then lowered his rifle and fired several times into the carcasses.

Jordan's temper snapped. Without thinking about it, he pulled his rifle up and aimed. A single shot from the Winchester and Sam Morris suddenly jerked upright in the saddle, his rifle falling from his hand. Then he leaned to the side and slid out of the saddle, landing in a heap on the ground. Instantly chambering another cartridge, Jordan sighted down on a rider next to Sam as chaos took command of the posse. With his sights set on the rider's back, he followed the man's frantic dash for cover, but he hesitated to pull the trigger. It was an easy shot, one he couldn't miss, and yet he decided not to take it. He pulled his rifle down and knelt, watching the pandemonium taking place below him. The posse had scattered in all directions, seeking the nearest cover they could find. Shots were being fired blindly from both sides of the little stream because no one in the posse could see where the shot that killed Sam Morris had come from. In a few moments, someone cried out in pain as a wild shot claimed a victim. The madness of it all was not lost on Jordan Gray, and he was inexplicably calm as he grasped the folly of the situation. He was suddenly sick of the senseless killing. These were not bad men who had come to kill him, but merely a confused mob incited to take up an unjust cause. It was time to leave *Paha Sapa.* White men had no right to be here in the first place. Turning his back on the chaos below him, he started back to his horse.

Making his way up through the trees, he paused when within about thirty yards of the gully where he had left Sweet Pea. He could see the horse from where he stood, and something about her triggered his sense of caution. Usually content when left to graze, the mare was shifting about nervously, her ears twitching in the wind. Something was bothering her. Jordan dropped immediately to one knee. As he did, a pine branch snapped in two directly over his head, and he saw the muzzle flash of a rifle from a thicket no more than fifteen yards from him. There was no time for thought as he pumped two rounds into the thicket and chambered another. The cry of agony he heard told him that he had hit his target. A moment later, a man staggered from the thicket and collapsed.

Jordan waited, scanning the trees around him until sure his assailant had been alone. Then he advanced toward the body slowly, still holding his rifle ready. The man was dead, two slugs no more than a hand span apart in his chest. Jordan knew he had seen the man before, but he couldn't place him at once. Then he recalled. The last time he had seen him, the dead man was wearing a heavy bearskin coat. He was one of Preacher's sons, Zeb or Quincy, he wasn't sure which. Jordan cocked his head to the wind, listening. Preacher Rix could not be far away.

Having already decided to put Deadwood far behind him, he had to reconsider his decision. He was convinced that it would be all right with God and everybody else if Preacher Rix was stopped. On the other hand, he no longer felt that it was up to him personally to correct God's mistakes. He had done enough killing. Maggie Hogg's words came back to him: *You can't kill the whole town.* After a few more moments' thought, he decided to leave Preacher Rix and the confused posse of miners to take care of themselves. "Come on, Sweet Pea," he said to the waiting mare. "Let's get the hell outta here."

"Where's your brother?" Preacher asked when Zeb pulled his horse to a stop before the fire and dismounted.

"Said he was gonna take a look at what all that shootin' was about on the other side of the ridge," Zeb replied.

Slightly irritated, Preacher said, "I thought I told you to stay on this side of the ridge until that crazy bunch of miners was gone." Zeb merely shrugged indifferently. Preacher and his sons had spotted the posse when they were first starting up the western slope of the mountain. Annoyed that Ben Thompson had not kept the mob away from the claims as he had agreed, Preacher had decided to cross over to the far side of a high ridge to avoid contact with the posse. So far, the pickings had not been as good as he had hoped, with little to show for the few claims he and the boys had raided. The only gold he had found was on the one man they had killed.

"Might as well rest the horses," he had told his sons and selected a spot down the slope to wait out the posse. The spot he picked was a long, narrow gully, where he felt a small fire would go unnoticed from the opposite side of the ridge. "Cup of coffee wouldn't be bad either, would it?" By the time the coffee water was brought to a boil, they heard the eruption of gunfire reverberating across the ridge tops. Alert to possible trouble coming his way, Preacher had stood up, his ear to the wind. After a while the shooting had stopped. "Zeb, you and Quincy go back up to the top of the ridge and keep your eyes open," Preacher had instructed. "But don't go off down the other side. I don't want none of that crazy bunch to spot you."

Now Zeb was back without his brother, and it riled Preacher when he was disobeyed. He decided to let it go. *Boys will be boys, I reckon.* To Zeb he said, "Set yourself down and have some coffee. Quincy'll just be too late to get some." Zeb was still blowing his coffee to cool it enough to drink when they heard three more shots. These last shots sounded closer than the original volley. Preacher was immediately concerned. "We'd better go find Quincy," he said and dumped the remains of his cup on the fire.

CHAPTER 10

"Yonder's his horse," Zeb called out and wheeled his mount to intercept Quincy's.

Preacher turned his head and followed Zeb with his eyes for only a moment before turning his gaze back to a thicket of heavy brush below him. His brows knotted in a dark frown, he peered intensely into the tangled branches of young pines and laurel bushes whence Quincy's horse had bolted. There was no sign of his youngest son. It didn't look good. It wouldn't be the first time Quincy had simply fallen off his horse, if that was the case. Were it not for the gunshots he had heard, he might have suspected as much.

With the possibility of ambush in his mind, Preacher dismounted before the thicket and took a good look around before entering. There was plenty of sign to paint a fairly accurate picture of what had taken place. Aside from the obvious path Quincy's horse had created when it bolted, the underbrush was still bent and broken where a body had lain in wait. Preacher looked beyond the impression to see a small clearing a few yards ahead. He pushed on through the tangle and almost stepped on the body lying at the edge.

"Quincy!" Preacher howled upon finding his youngest a lifeless corpse. "Quincy!" he cried out again, this time wailing like a mother wolf over her fallen pup.

When Zeb rode up, leading Quincy's horse, it was to find his father on his knees beside his brother's body, tears streaming down the ominous face. He had never seen his father stricken this way before. "Is he dead?" Zeb asked in his simple way.

Without turning away from his son's body, Preacher replied angrily, "They got my boy, my favorite, shot him in the chest. I always liked him the best, too."

Oblivious to the slight, Zeb edged over to get a closer look at his late brother. "Dang!" he exclaimed. "Got him dead center."

"I'll kill every last one of 'em," Preacher vowed.

"I don't think it was any of them in that posse," Zeb said. "They scattered and run off down the other side of the ridge. I could still hear 'em ridin' like hell."

His son's comment stopped Preacher cold. Zeb was right. It was unlikely that Quincy had been shot by a member of the posse. "Jordan Gray!" he exclaimed softly. It had to be. There was no doubt in his mind, and he knew he would track Gray down if it took the rest of his life. Getting to his feet, he snapped, "Look around this clearing. Find the bastard's trail!"

They scoured the perimeter of the small clearing until Zeb called out that he had found what they were looking for. Pointing at two faint hoofprints at the south edge of the clearing, he said, "He lit out yonder way, most likely headin' for that canyon."

Preacher studied the tracks for a few moments. Then, agreeing with his son, he said, "Let's ride."

"What about Quincy?" Zeb asked. "Ain't we gonna bury him?"

Preacher hesitated, one foot already in the stirrup. "Of course we're gonna bury him," he said reluctantly and withdrew his foot from the stirrup.

"What are we gonna use for a shovel?"

This stopped Preacher for a moment longer, his mind already working on the thought of Jordan Gray getting farther and farther away. "Our knives," he finally answered, drawing his skinning knife from its sheaf.

The rocky soil, laced with pine roots, proved to be a formidable task for gravediggers armed with nothing more than skinning knives. After laboring for almost half an hour with no more to show for their efforts than a shallow seam scratched into the hard ground, Preacher gave it up. "We'll just lay him down here and cover him up good with rocks," he said. So they spent another half hour collecting enough rocks to form a mound. When he was satisfied with the grave, Preacher prayed to the Lord above to receive his younger son in Heaven and promised that he would seek out and slaughter Quincy's killer. Finished with the prayer, he said, "Let's ride. The trail's already gittin' cold."

Unaware that he was now the object of an intense manhunt far more perilous than the haphazard effort by the miners' posse, Jordan was on his way out of the Black Hills. It would have been better if he could have somehow cleared his name before leaving Deadwood. But with the mind-set of the men there, he knew there was very little chance. Still grappling with the decision to return to Fort Laramie, he decided to make his way back to the Cheyenne River. Once he reached the river, and was out of the mountains, he would decide whether to continue on to Laramie or turn west to the Big Horns or maybe the Wind River Mountains.

The call of the mountains was a powerful force upon Jordan. He thrived upon the solitude they offered, but there was still a nagging thought that continued to return to plague him. *Kathleen Beard is at Fort Laramie.* And he had given up trying to deceive himself about his indifference to her engagement to Lieutenant Wallace. Kathleen was the only person who could lure him away from his mountains, and he admitted to himself that he would work as a scout, farmhand, or most any other job to be near her. More and more, he wondered if it would have made a difference had he expressed his feelings for her instead of simply slinking off to the Black Hills like a whipped dog. "God," he confessed to Sweet Pea, "what a damn fool I was. She may have changed her mind about marrying Wallace." Deep down, he doubted it, but he felt he needed to know for sure. Otherwise, he could never be free of the nagging thought of what might have been.

■ ■ ■ ■

After a half day's travel, making his way through the many narrow canyons that wound through the mountains, Jordan came upon a strong spring that formed a small pool at the base of a sheer rock cliff. With darkness rapidly closing in, he decided he'd better camp there for the night. For the previous hour and a half, he had been following a game trail that led in a generally southern direction. He hoped that it would lead him around the mountain that had seemed intent upon blocking his way.

He was probably a day's ride east of the trail Ned and he had followed into the Black Hills, so this area of the mountains was new to him. Without Jordan giving it conscious thought, his mind was already beginning to settle into the peaceful state that almost always descended upon him when he roamed alone and free in the high mountains. Away from the greed and destruction that mining towns like Deadwood cast upon the land, he could appreciate the art of the Creator in the steep, dark mountain slopes and the green valleys. There was a spiritual feeling about these mountains that he could not recall experiencing in the Big Horns or the Wind River range. He allowed that it could simply be his imagination, but he fully understood the Lakota's reverence for the Black Hills, for he felt it too.

Several miles behind him, Preacher Rix stood up in his stirrups, glaring angrily at the steep wall of a box canyon. His son pulled his horse up beside him. Gazing at the pine-covered slope, now rapidly releasing the last rays of the sun, Zeb stated the obvious. "I don't think he come this way. He musta took the other fork back yonder."

Preacher glowered at his surviving son, his patience already threadbare. It had never been an obvious trail that Jordan Gray had left for them to follow, and now they were even farther behind after making the wrong guess at the confluence of two streams some two miles back. They had not found a track along the entire two miles, but Preacher had been almost certain it was the fork Jordan would have taken. It just looked to be the easier route. Preacher stared at the ground around him, still looking for sign and unwilling to believe he had lost the trail. "Dammit!" he bellowed. "Don't that horse ever shit?" *Damn him. He must know we're trailing him.*

But Jordan was not concerned with being followed. At the fork where Preacher had made the wrong choice, Jordan might have taken the same trail had it not been for the simple decision to try to work his way back toward the west in hopes of crossing the original trail Ned and he had taken into the hills.

The cold night air that settled onto the canyon floor as soon as the sun had disappeared brought a chill that made him long for the warm buffalo robe he had left behind when his packhorses were slaughtered. He wrapped his blanket around him and lay close to the fire, thinking about the coffee that had also been left behind. Luckily, the pouch of gold dust was safe in his saddlebags. It would be needed to buy new supplies when he got to Fort Laramie.

The thought of Fort Laramie caused him to create a picture of Kathleen in his mind. Choosing not to dispel it this time, as he usually tried to do, he turned over to put his back to the fire and drifted off to sleep, taking her image with him into his dreams. Sweet Pea ambled over and stood next to the sleeping man. Jordan had long since dispensed with hobbling the homely beast, knowing the horse would not wander. She had become firmly attached to her master, almost like a pet dog, and she stood over him now for a few moments, sniffing his blanket, before settling in for the night herself.

Stiff and cold, Jordan awoke when he heard Sweet Pea blow and snort a couple of times. He instinctively grabbed his rifle and sat up, pushing his blanket aside. The first rays of morning light were filtering through the trees on the mountainside above him, yielding enough light for him to look around his campsite. Nothing seemed to be amiss. Sweet Pea would normally blow through her nostrils when she heard or saw something that concerned her, followed by a snort if she felt there might be danger. Sometimes it was a real danger; sometimes it might simply be a fox or a coyote investigating his camp. As there was almost always something slinking around out there, Jordan decided it most likely some small animal. He put his rifle down and turned his attention toward reviving his fire.

A strip of pronghorn jerky would have to suffice for breakfast, for he had not taken time to hunt. Carrying the cold hard meat in his saddlebags was a habit he had acquired during the long, cruel months of winter in the mountains when game was sometimes scarce. The jerky was enough to quiet the arguing in an empty belly when there was no fresh meat to cook. His brief breakfast finished, he warmed his hands over the fire for a few more moments before saddling his horse.

Sweet Pea held still while she was being saddled, but Jordan noticed that the horse was still uneasy about something. Her ears, which were constantly in motion, were now standing rigid, instead of loosely erect as when nothing troubled her. Jordan had learned that it was best to pay attention to Sweet Pea's sounds and signs, so he paused to take another look around him. As he carefully scanned the trees at the base of the canyon, the sun peeked over the ridge behind him, casting slender beams to light the tips of the pines.

It was no more than a fraction of a second, but his eye caught the flash of sun reflecting from a metallic surface, and then it was gone. Immediately alert, he nonetheless took care not to show signs of alarm. The flash of metal had come from a point where the pines were thickest. He could see nothing out of the ordinary in the trees, but he knew for sure that God had made no part of a pine tree out of metal, and he was certain of what he had seen. Moving without apparent haste, he slipped around to the other side of his horse. With Sweet Pea between himself and the pines, he pretended to adjust the saddle while he peered over the horse's back, trying to spot any sign of movement. *Indians?* he wondered. There was no thought of the posse from Deadwood. There was no possibility that they could have caught up to him, even if they had ridden through the night while he slept. There was no way they could see to follow him through those narrow canyons and over the ridges in the dark. Preacher? He doubted it. If it was Preacher, he would already be shooting, instead of simply watching. Yet Jordan was certain there was something or someone out there watching him. Sweet Pea was certain of it as well. She tossed her head around and snorted defiantly. Considering his options, he decided there were only two. He could take cover behind a low rock ledge beside the stream, or he could make a run for it down the length of the canyon. Although he was not certain where the canyon might lead him, he favored that option over digging in to stand off a possible attack when he wasn't sure of the odds.

"Well, girl," he whispered low, "let's get the hell outta here." With one foot in the stirrup, he gave her a slap on the rump, and she immediately responded. Before he swung his leg over and settled in the saddle, she was in full gallop. In the next instant, he heard the distinct snap of a bullet passing over his head, followed by the crack of a rifle. Behind him, he heard war cries, and glancing back over his shoulder, he saw several warriors running from the trees to take a shot at him. Lying low on Sweet Pea's neck, he urged the mare for more speed, and she held nothing back as several more bullets zipped around them. Then the shooting stopped while the warriors ran back into the trees to get their ponies. Jordan and Sweet Pea raced toward the end of the canyon and the mountain that appeared to close off the passage.

The homely mare soon exposed her inner beauty, gliding over the grassy valley floor with long, steady strides that increased the gap between them and the war party. Behind him, Jordan could hear the war cries of his pursuers echoing against the rocky walls of the canyon. Still lying low against Sweet Pea's neck, he could feel the power of her strides surging up through her shoulders and withers as her hooves pounded a steady rhythm over the ground, rapidly consuming the length of the valley. In no time at all, they reached the southern end of the canyon and, much to Jordan's relief, a narrow passage that led to another canyon.

Due to the confined space and the winding curves of the passage, Jordan had to hold Sweet Pea to a slow walk for a distance of close to seventy-five yards. He sat patiently, glancing up at the sheer rock walls on either side as Sweet Pea followed the narrow trail. Angry cries of Lakota warriors came closer and closer as they approached the mouth of the passage. Finally, the narrow pass opened to a canyon much the same as the one he had just fled. Sweet Pea immediately jumped to a gallop without waiting for Jordan's urging.

Recognizing his advantage at this point, he quickly made a decision. He was confident in Sweet Pea's ability to outrun the war party. On the other hand, the warriors were sitting ducks when they reached the end of the passage. Being only wide enough to permit riders to go single file, the passage presented the opportunity to stop the war party in its tracks. Some fifty yards into the valley, Jordan brought Sweet Pea to a stop and wheeled her around. Without dismounting, he drew his Winchester, cocked it, and waited for the first warrior to reach the end of the passage. Even though he was being chased, he had no real desire to kill his pursuers, only to stop them. He was a trespasser in their sacred land. He couldn't really blame them for coming after him.

He didn't have to wait long. In what seemed to be only seconds, the first warrior appeared near the opening of the pass. Pulling the trigger and cranking each round in the chamber almost in one action, Jordan sent three shots ricocheting off the rocks on both sides of the warrior's head, driving the startled Lakota back into his friends. Jordan cocked another cartridge into the chamber and waited. Before long, he spotted the head of a warrior cautiously peeking around the base of a boulder guarding the mouth of the passage. Jordan held his fire, letting the man inch forward on his belly until he could get a good look into the canyon. Clear of the boulder, what the warrior saw was a rifle leveled at him. Jordan's shot chipped off a shard of rock inches from the warrior's cheek, and the Indian immediately scrambled back to safety.

In the confines of the narrow passage, the Lakota war party was in a state of confusion as those in the rear tried to push forward, not sure what was confronting those in the lead. After several chaotic seconds with Indian ponies pushing and shoving against one another, the word was relayed back to wait.

Painted Wolf, after narrowly avoiding being shot, crawled back to define the situation. "We are trapped here," he said. "The white man sits and waits to shoot us one by one if we try to get out of here."

Frustrated, yet reluctant to see any of his war party killed, Red Feather recognized the futility of trying to press the attack. It was difficult to acknowledge defeat of a war party eighteen strong by a lone white man with a repeating rifle, but it would be suicide to continue. "We must go back," he finally stated. "It is foolish to push on."

Painted Wolf, always reluctant to admit defeat, complained, "Maybe we should ride out as fast as our horses will run. I think he is not such a good shot. He missed with every shot."

"I think he is a very good shot," Red Feather replied. "I don't think he meant to kill. He does not look like he seeks the yellow dirt like the others. He has no packhorse, none of the tools the miners use. I think he merely wants to pass through our lands. I think he is saying let me go in peace. I say we should back out of this trap and go back to our village. Maybe we will catch him on the other side of this mountain. If not, I'll go alone to look for him to make sure he is leaving *Paha Sapa,* but the rest of you should return to our camp. If he is on his way out of these hills, I say we should let him go. But I only speak for myself."

Those close enough to hear decided Red Feather spoke with wisdom. They had been on their way back to their camp on the Cheyenne River when they had discovered this white man. They had been away for many days, and all felt the need to return since there was word that the army had sent out patrols looking for Lakota who had left the reservation. "It is best that we hurry back to our camp," Two Kills said. "We must see that our women and children are safe. I agree with Red Feather."

Even Painted Wolf was persuaded. "I'll go with Red Feather," he said. "The rest of you hurry back to the camp, and we'll catch up as soon as we see that this white intruder is on his way." The word was passed back, and the war party started backing out of the passage until reaching a curve where there was enough room to turn their ponies around and proceed.

Out in the open valley, Jordan watched and waited. After a few minutes, when there was no sign of further attempts by the warriors to gain a position to shoot from, he wheeled his horse, and Sweet Pea once again sprang into full gallop. Racing down the length of the valley, he fully expected to hear gunshots behind him, but to his surprise, the Indians did not come after him. Ned Booth had often said you could never figure out what a Sioux Indian would do. *I guess he was right,* Jordan thought.

"Pa, look!" Zeb Rix pulled hard on the reins, causing his horse to stop and back up a few paces.

"Stay back," Preacher warned. He had already spotted the Lakota war party entering the lower end of the valley. "Just hold still right there till we know for sure they ain't seen us."

Edging the horses back into the trees, they watched, ready to run for it if necessary. After a few minutes, it was obvious that the Indians had not seen them, for they headed off over a ridge to the west. "They come from the way Jordan Gray had to have rode," Preacher said. "Maybe that was what the shootin' was about." Maybe Jordan Gray had run right into the Sioux war party, and the Indians had settled the score for Preacher. He hoped Jordan had escaped because he wanted the satisfaction of dealing with his son's killer personally.

As the Rixes watched the war party climb the ridge, two members of the party broke off from the others and headed back across the lower end of the ridge and the other side of the mountain. "Now where are them two goin'?" Preacher wondered aloud. Quincy's death had sparked an unrelenting lust to spill someone's blood. If there was a chance the war party had killed Jordan Gray, then Preacher would at least demand satisfaction from those who had killed him. Besides that, he never passed up an opportunity to kill an Indian, and he liked the odds when there were only two. "Let's follow them two," he said to Zeb.

"What about Jordan Gray?"

"We'll git back on his trail, but first, we'll see what these two heathens is up to." He waited a couple of minutes longer until the last of the war party disappeared over the ridge; then he left the cover of the trees and made straight for the point where the two warriors had crossed.

Topping the ridge, the father and son paused long enough to make sure they hadn't been seen by the two warriors they were stalking. The two Indians were not in sight, so the Rixes descended to the base of the ridge to find a game trail that circled the mountain before them. From the hoofprints they found, Preacher determined that the Indians had followed the trail. Riding as fast as they could while still maintaining a cautious eye, Preacher and his son followed the narrow, winding trail, skirting the mountain, which was on their left now, then down through a rocky gulch that separated it from another mountain on their right. There was no sign of the Lakota warriors. Up through the pines, then down again to weave its way around huge boulders, the trail led them almost completely around to the valley beyond the mountain. Unknown to Preacher, it was the valley where Jordan had turned back the war party in the narrow passage. He was about to leave the game trail and ride down into the open meadow when he spotted the two warriors some fifty yards below him.

He quickly held up his hand to halt Zeb behind him. "Hold the horses," he whispered as he dismounted and handed the reins to his son. Drawing his rifle from the saddle sling, he made his way a little farther down the slope to a point where he could get a better look at the Indians. They were completely unaware of the two white men following them. Sitting on their ponies, they appeared to be discussing something, as one of them pointed toward the south end of the valley. A slow grin crept across Preacher's dark face as he raised his rifle and sighted down on the shoulder blades of the warrior closest to him.

Below Preacher, Painted Wolf jerked upright when the bullet slammed into his back. He appeared to brace himself for a moment before sliding sideways from his pony. At the sound of the shot, Red Feather rolled off his pony, narrowly avoiding the second slug that ripped the air over his horse's back. With his rifle in hand, the Lakota warrior crawled over to Painted Wolf. Keeping low to the ground, he managed to drag Painted Wolf to cover behind an outcropping of rocks. Searching desperately, he tried to spot the source of the attack on the hill above him while glancing back frequently to determine the severity of Painted Wolf's wound. His friend made no sound, lying as still as the rock he was behind, and Red Feather soon realized Painted Wolf was dead, the bullet having severed his spine. Red Feather turned his full attention back to the slope. A movement in the trees below the game trail caught his attention, and he turned in time to see the muzzle flash of a rifle. The bullet ricocheted off the rocks behind him. He quickly raised his rifle and returned fire, his shot answered almost immediately by three shots in quick succession. Hunkering down behind the rocks,

Red Feather loaded another cartridge into the chamber and crawled over to the opposite side of the largest of the rocks. With only three more cartridges in his belt, he wished he had been able to grab Painted Wolf's bullet pouch before the shots caused both ponies to bolt. Glancing back over his shoulder, he could see the ponies standing some one hundred yards away in the grassy meadow.

Not far away, Zeb was unable to contain his excitement any longer. He tied the horses to a tree limb and scrambled down to join his father.

"I thought I told you to mind the horses," Preacher scolded.

"They're all right," Zeb replied, all the while searching for a target. "I tied 'em to a tree."

"I got one of 'em," Preacher said. "The other one's behind them rocks down yonder." He pointed out the mound of rocks just as Red Feather fired another shot. Anxious to get in on the fun, Zeb squeezed off three rapid bursts, sending shards of rock flying. "Dammit, boy," Preacher rebuked sharply. "Wait till you can see somethin' to shoot at." Zeb responded with a nervous giggle. Understanding his son's passion for killing, Preacher said, "Don't fret yourself. You'll git your turn."

Content for the moment to sit and wait for the Indian to make a run for the ponies standing in the open meadow, Preacher rested his rifle barrel in the fork of a small limb. "Come on outta there, you heathen," he muttered patiently. Zeb, on the other hand, was possessed of very little patience for anything. He stood up and cranked out three more shots, chipping away at the rocks. His barrage was immediately answered by a single shot that barely missed his head, sending him scrambling behind a tree trunk. "Dang blast it, boy," Preacher snarled. "You done pinpointed our position for him. We'd better move."

With Zeb following, Preacher quickly made his way farther down through the trees to a new position behind a sizable rock. There was a short pause before the Indian fired another shot at the trees Preacher and Zeb had just fled. The pause was enough to make Preacher think, *He ain't got nothing but a single-shot rifle.* He looked around him then, deciding the best place to move to next. "Zeb, throw a couple more shots at him, then hustle your ass after me." Zeb did as he was told, and ricocheted two more slugs off the rocks. As soon as he fired, Preacher reached up and pulled him roughly to the ground. The return fire he expected was short in coming. As soon as Red Feather fired, Preacher ordered, "Come on," and made a dash for a pine thicket a few yards farther down the slope. Once within the cover of the thicket, Preacher paused to study the bastion of rocks. "He sure is stingy with his bullets," he mused aloud. "He must not have many." The thought brought a grin to his face. He turned to Zeb. "Let's just see how many he's got." Raising his rifle again, he aimed at the edge of the rocky fortress and blasted away. Zeb followed suit. After a volley of more than a dozen shots, they hugged the ground and waited. As Preacher expected, a single shot answered the barrage and then nothing.

Enjoying the game now, Preacher moved again, this time down to a gully roughly on the same level as the outcropping of rocks. He could not be sure, but he was willing to gamble that the heathen had very little ammunition left, for the warrior failed to fire at them when they scrambled for the gully. Had he known that his enemy had already fired his last cartridge, he would have strolled boldly across the short expanse of grass that separated them.

Red Feather's situation was desperate. It would only be a matter of time before his assailants realized that he was out of bullets. Death was certain. His only chance was to make a run for the horses, but to do so meant sprinting across approximately one hundred yards of open meadow. He knew there was very little chance he could make it, but it was his only option. Laying his rifle aside, he crawled to the edge of the rocks and prepared to run. After taking a deep breath to make sure he had plenty of wind, he braced himself to spring forward. After a short prayer to Man Above, he launched his body into the open, sprinting as hard as he could.

Preacher, watching the rocks intensely, immediately jumped to his feet and fired. His bullet caught Red Feather in the thigh, causing the sprinting warrior to crash heavily in the grass. With his evil grin in place, Preacher reached up and grabbed Zeb's rifle barrel before his son could squeeze the trigger. "Hold your water," he said. "He ain't goin' nowhere."

In no particular hurry now, Preacher stepped out into the open, paused a moment to look around, then leisurely walked toward the wounded man, reloading his rifle as he walked. Zeb, anxious to get to the helpless Indian, ran ahead of his father, giggling gleefully, like a schoolboy one third his age. By the time Preacher reached Red Feather, Zeb was standing over the fallen warrior, his rifle pointed at Red Feather's head. "Let's turn him over so he can see it comin'," Preacher said as he walked up. Red Feather tried to resist, but Preacher was too powerful. He grabbed Red Feather's ankles and flipped him over on his back. Red Feather grunted in pain. Zeb, the muzzle of his rifle only inches from the warrior's face, cocked his weapon and prepared to fire.

"What's your hurry?" Preacher asked. "I ain't never skinned no Injun before. Whaddaya say we skin this one?" He glanced up at his son. Noting the look of disappointment in Zeb's face, he added, "You can try your hand at it." Zeb's face immediately lit up again. Red Feather, understanding English very well, tensed perceptively and struggled to free himself from Preacher's powerful grip. The huge man merely laughed at the Indian's efforts. "Go fetch some rope off my saddle," he said. "I'll hold this buck here. And bring the horses up with you," he called after Zeb, who was already running toward the slope. He knew his son wouldn't think to do it on his own.

"Well, Mr. Redskin," Preacher gloated, "I reckon you ain't as lucky as your friend back there. You ever seed a man skinned before?

I ain't myself, but I bet it's a pretty sight. I'm gonna let my boy do the work. Zeb loves to work with a knife." He studied the dark eyes gazing unblinking up at him. "You understand what I'm sayin', don't you?" Red Feather didn't answer. "Shore you do," Preacher went on. "I can see it in your heathen eyes." Preacher chuckled. "Does that leg pain you some? I'll have Zeb dig for the bullet when he skins your legs." Red Feather suddenly lunged backward in an attempt to break his captor's hold on his ankles. His unexpected surge caught Preacher by surprise and resulted in his freeing one ankle, but the big man reacted quickly enough to hold him fast with the other hand. Red Feather kicked violently with his free leg until Preacher grabbed his rifle and knocked him senseless.

"Let's do this right," Preacher said and dragged Red Feather back to meet Zeb at the trees on the edge of the meadow. With Zeb's enthusiastic help, he tied ropes from the Indian's ankles and wrists to four young saplings, spreading the barely conscious warrior's limbs wide apart. When he was satisfied that Red Feather was stretched as far as his limbs would permit, he told Zeb to fetch a hatful of water from the stream that divided the valley. When Zeb returned with the water, Preacher instructed him to throw it in Red Feather's face. "We wanna make sure he don't miss any of the fun."

Content now that all was ready, Preacher sat down on a rock. "All right, son, go to it. Let's see if it's the same as skinnin' a deer."

"He ain't got much fur, has he, Pa?" Zeb chortled. "I reckon it's best to split the hide down his belly first." He held the long skinning knife up before Red Feather's face so his victim could see it. Red Feather's eyes were wide with terror. But in one last show of defiance, he spit in Zeb's face. Startled by the spittle dripping from the end of his nose, Zeb looked at his father.

Preacher threw back his head and laughed. "By damn, he's got sand, ain't he?" Then, just as suddenly, his face turned dead serious. "Cut him," he ordered. "Let him know the wrath of the Lord."

Zeb thrust the knife downward into the warrior's chest, just deep enough to pierce the skin. Red Feather stiffened with the pain, but made no sound. Zeb grinned and held the blade there for a moment. Watching the fun, Preacher was about to tell his son to go on and rip his belly apart when he heard what sounded like a solid thump and saw the ragged hole that suddenly appeared in Zeb's throat. Less than an instant later, he heard the crack of the rifle. Too stunned to move at first, he watched in horror as his only remaining son stood for a long moment, his eyes bulging, staring into eternity before crumpling to the ground. Then Preacher's natural instinct for self-preservation took command and he rolled away from the bound Indian, seeking cover in the trees. His first thought was that the rest of the war party had heard the shooting and returned to investigate. He searched the ridge above him frantically, but could see no one. Not ready to take on an entire war party, he jumped on his horse and sped away across the open meadow toward the ridge on the far side.

From his vantage point; Jordan sighed in relief. He had not been sure he could hit his target two hundred yards away. He wasn't sure where he had hit his target. He had aimed at Zeb's back. But at least he had hit him somewhere that had dropped him.

Even at that distance, he had recognized the pair — Preacher Rix and one of his half-wit sons — up to their evil tricks. Jordan had heard the gunfire and, after some deliberation, decided to go take a look. At present, he didn't know if he had been in time to save the Indian's life. The way the

242

man was strung up by his limbs, it was hard to tell if he was living or dead.

Jordan watched until Preacher reached the far side of the valley and disappeared into the trees that covered the ridge beyond. He could have thrown another shot in Preacher's direction, but the huge brute was already out of range, so Jordan decided not to waste the ammunition. He stepped up into the saddle and guided Sweet Pea down the steep slope toward the captive Lakota warrior.

Suspended between four saplings, the muscles in his arms and legs screaming in pain, Red Feather could scarcely believe the sudden reprieve from torture and slow death. He could now hear the horse approaching from behind him, but if he had been saved by his friends as he assumed, he was puzzled that he heard no cries from familiar voices. A few moments later, he was again cast into a state of uncertainty, for it was another white man who approached. Again, he waited helplessly to know his fate.

Jordan rode slowly around the captured warrior before dismounting and drawing his knife from its sheath. Not a word was spoken by either man. Red Feather watched the broad-shouldered white man dressed in animal skins. He could not tell from the quiet, steady gaze if he were to be spared or if his execution had merely been delayed. He involuntarily tensed when Jordan knelt before him to cut the ropes binding his ankles. He released his breath in a long sigh, not realizing until then that he had been holding it.

When the last rope was severed, Jordan just managed to catch Red Feather by the arm to prevent the weakened Indian from collapsing. Red Feather could not suppress a groan of pain when his tortured joints were suddenly released. Jordan lowered him gently to the ground. Assuming the Indian spoke no English, Jordan pointed to the bullet wound in Red Feather's thigh and tried to motion that he intended to examine it. He was surprised when Red Feather spoke.

"Why have you saved my life? You are my enemy."

Jordan looked up into the dark eyes that stared unblinking at him. "I'm not your enemy," he stated simply.

"All white men are enemies of the Lakota people."

"I reckon I can understand why you think that way, but it ain't necessarily so. That man that just rode off from here — he's my enemy. You ain't my enemy unless you raise your hand against me." His gaze locked on the warrior's for a moment. "Right now, I'd best take a look at that wound while you've still got some blood left in you."

Red Feather considered Jordan's words. Then he thought about the incident back in the narrow pass when Jordan could have very easily killed Painted Wolf, but chose to spare him, taking only warning shots to hold the war party at bay. The white man was right. These were not the acts of an enemy. "How are you called?" he asked.

"Jordan Gray."

"Jordan Gray," Red Feather pronounced slowly, memorizing the name. "I am called Red Feather. Thank you, Jordan Gray, for saving my life."

"You're welcome," Jordan replied. "I'm glad I came to take a look-see." He paused to glance at Zeb Rix's body. "It was a pleasure."

With Jordan supporting him, Red Feather hobbled over to the stream to clean his wound. Afterward, Jordan searched through his saddlebags until he found an old cotton shirt he used for rags. Tearing off a strip, he used it to bind Red Feather's wound. "I ain't very good at this," he apologized, "but I reckon it'll stop the bleedin'." A picture flashed though his mind of the gentle touch of Kathleen Beard's hands when she had once bandaged his wounds. Just as quickly, he banished the image from his thoughts. "I best get those horses in," he said, looking at the Indian ponies grazing in the meadow.

From the top of the ridge on the other side of the valley, Preacher Rix stood watching the man round up the two ponies. He could feel the angry blood pulsing through the veins in his neck, filling him with a hot hatred that cried out for vengeance. *Jordan Gray.* The name was a curse on his family. Now Jordan Gray had taken another son from him. Calling for God to witness his oath, he vowed to cut Jordan's heart out and eat it. If he had known it was Jordan alone when Zeb fell dead, he would not have fled. Checking his rifle now, he prepared to return to the meadow to extract his vengeance when something at the head of the valley caught his eye, causing him to hesitate. Sixteen Sioux warriors suddenly appeared, their ponies prancing smartly as the warriors guided them out on the valley floor.

Circling around behind the two grazing ponies, Jordan let Sweet Pea herd them back toward the stream, where Red Feather waited. His mind on the horses, he was not aware of the war party until the shots rang out, and the slugs ripped into the grass before him. His first reaction was to reach for his rifle.

"No!" Red Feather immediately cried out and struggled to his feet. Waving wildly, he called out to his brothers to hold their fire. "Come!" he yelled to Jordan. "Come stand by me."

Jordan did as Red Feather directed, but he kept his rifle ready. Although they had stopped shooting, the war party was now charging toward them at full gallop. Jordan could not be sure if they understood Red Feather's signals or not. He wheeled Sweet Pea around behind Red Feather and dismounted. It was too late to run. He hoped Red Feather hadn't changed his mind about being friends.

In a matter of seconds, Jordan and Red Feather were surrounded by Indian ponies, their hooves stomping and sliding as their riders pulled them to a sudden stop. The warriors slid off their ponies and crowded around Jordan and Red Feather, their voices loud and excited. Jordan knew very few words of the Lakota tongue, and the voices sounded angry to him. He was not certain that he had chosen wisely. It might have been better to give Sweet Pea his heels when he first caught sight of the war party. Then, as one, the warriors turned to look toward the edge of the meadow where Painted Wolf's body lay, and Jordan figured Red Feather had just given them the news of the warrior's death. While several members of the party went to take care of Painted Wolf's body, the rest turned their attention to Jordan, as Red Feather told them that the white man had saved his life. The angry glances disappeared, and the warriors nodded to Jordan, smiling their approval. One of the Indians, who appeared to be older than the others, spoke directly to Jordan, causing those around him to laugh and nod their heads in agreement. Puzzled, Jordan turned to Red Feather for explanation.

"Many Horses says he knew you were a brave man. It would take a brave man to ride a horse that looks like a coyote."

Jordan grinned and once again received nods of approval from the Lakota warriors. Several of them repeated the words *sung ma he tu* while glancing from Jordan to Sweet Pea. Jordan nodded in return, then looked again to Red Feather for explanation.

"Coyote," he translated.

Suddenly, a high-pitched war cry rang out, and Jordan turned to see a warrior standing over Zeb's body by the pine saplings. He was holding a bloody scalp over his head.

The other warriors joined in the triumphant cry. After some discussion, with most of the warriors looking to Many Horses for his opinion, the warrior with the scalp came up to Jordan and presented the grisly trophy to him. Jordan had no desire to have the bloody piece of hair and scalp, but he was not sure if it would be an insult to refuse it. Glancing at Red Feather, who nodded approval, he mumbled, "Much obliged," and accepted it.

Up on the ridge top on the far side of the valley, Preacher Rix observed the scalping of his son, and he could barely control his agony. Moaning helplessly, he watched as the warrior handed Zeb's scalp to Jordan, and the sight almost blinded him with rage. Desperately needing some way to vent his fury, he grabbed a limb of the pine he had taken cover behind and snapped it in two. He cursed Jordan Gray, the Lakota warriors, even God Himself. That done, he vowed to follow Jordan Gray, no matter where, until he had an opportunity to kill him. "If it takes the rest of my life," he stated, "I'll track him down until I catch him alone, and then I'll feed his guts to the wolves." He would have to be patient, for across the meadow the war party mounted up and started toward the southern end of the valley, Jordan Gray with them.

There had been some discussion among the warriors about whether or not they should go in search of the man who had killed Painted Wolf. Most had been reluctant to return to camp without avenging Painted Wolf, but Many Horses had reminded them of their obligation to protect their women and children. "The soldiers have already sent patrols out to other camps to punish the people for ignoring the white father's orders to return to the reservation. We have been away for a long time. We must see that our people are safe, and move our camp to the Powder River valley to join Sitting Bull and the others." He had turned to look at Jordan. "This man is our friend. He has killed one of the white men and avenged Painted Wolf. I think it best to return to our people now."

Jordan rode beside Red Feather as the Lakota war party filed out of the valley. It was not his preference to accompany the Sioux back to their camp. He had other issues on his mind that could only be resolved back in Fort Laramie. But his new friend, Red Feather, was intent upon showing his gratitude, so Jordan agreed to ride with them, thinking it might be impolite to refuse the invitation. It would be a two-day ride to the

Sioux camp, but it was in the general direction of Fort Laramie, so it would not be that much out of his way. Also, he had never been to an Indian village before, so he had to admit to a mild curiosity to visit one. Sweet Pea was still a little leery of the Indian ponies, so Jordan was careful to keep a safe interval between the mare and Red Feather's pony lest she take a notion to take a bite out of the unsuspecting animal.

As Jordan rode along in the midst of a Lakota war party, his mind was busy sorting through a mental stew of random thoughts. His decision to accompany Ned Booth to Deadwood had resulted in a series of unfortunate turns of fate. There was a definite feeling of guilt on his part, for Ned would in all likelihood still be alive if he had not been Jordan's partner. As for Deadwood, the town regarded him as a wanton murderer who stalked isolated mining claims, and he saw no way to disprove it. Now he questioned the reasoning behind his decision to return to Fort Laramie. Kathleen had given him no reason for hope — or had she? He found it difficult to remember now why he had thought so. Maybe he was a fool to think she had feelings for him. She was going to marry her handsome lieutenant. He shook his head to clear his mind. He glanced up to see Red Feather watching him, a questioning look in his eye. Jordan smiled at the Lakota warrior, and Red Feather returned the smile. *Maybe,* Jordan thought, *I belong here with the Sioux.*

From his position, when the last warrior rode out of the little valley, Preacher Rix guided his horse down to the grassy floor. His mind gripped in a partial daze, he rode to the edge of the meadow and dismounted by Zeb's body. Long minutes passed while he stood transfixed, staring down at his elder son's lifeless eyes. The expression on Zeb's face, now eternal, told of the sudden shock when his life ended. A flash of anger flooded over Preacher when he looked at the ragged wound where once Zeb's hair had been. In Preacher's life now, there remained but one certainty, and that was the fact that Jordan Gray was a dead man. No matter where he had to go, or how long it took, he would follow Jordan Gray. He would not rest until Jordan Gray's body was rotting in the sun. With the patience of a man who knew the inevitable truth, Preacher took his time burying his son before following the party of Lakota. They would not be hard to track, especially with the trail left behind by the travois carrying Painted Wolf's body.

CHAPTER 11

The Lakota war party arrived at their campsite to find the village gone. Much to Many Horses and his followers' alarm, there were signs of a fight there on the banks of the river. Tipis were left standing, although some of them were half burned and most were riddled with bullet holes. Articles of clothing and utensils were scattered about, evidence of a hasty flight. The bodies of several ponies lay dead where the herd had grazed. Near one of the tipis, the body of a cavalry mount gave testimony as to who had raided the village.

"Soldiers," Many Horses uttered in anger. All about him, his warriors moaned in despair as they searched for any sign that might give them news of their families' fate. After a careful, though hasty, scout, it was determined that most of the village must have escaped. There were no bodies found, other than those of the horses, although there were some patches of blood on the grass, telling of wounds or possible deaths. The route of escape by the village was easy to determine. The people had fled along the riverbank, the men taking cover in the gullies to hold the soldiers at bay while the women and children crossed over to the other side. All signs indicated that the village had escaped with minimal casualties. The soldiers had evidently stopped short of following the fleeing Lakota across the river. After an attempt to burn the tipis down, they had retreated to the southeast, apparently headed toward Fort Laramie.

Jordan found himself in an uncomfortable position as the lone white man in the midst of an apprehensive war party. He felt compassion for the warriors who had returned to find their families and friends gone. It was difficult for him to decide how he felt about the raid on the Lakota village. Was it in retaliation for a raid on a white farm or settlement? He did not forget that Many Horses and his warriors were just returning from a war party to chase miners from their sacred land in the Black Hills. He had to admit that he could sympathize with the Indians' attitude on that particular problem. The white man had no business in *Paha Sapa*. Now he wondered if the friendly attitude exhibited by Many Horses' warriors might suddenly turn on the lone white man. *A man might make friends with a pack of wolves as long as they're well fed. It might be a different matter if they're hungry.* With that thought in mind, he nudged his rifle slightly to make sure it was riding free and easy in the saddle sling. Then he gave Sweet Pea a gentle kick and guided her toward the riverbank. He had it in his mind to be ready to take a quick swim if the Sioux decided to turn on him.

"This is the second time the soldiers have attacked our village." Jordan turned to see Red Feather riding toward him. "They want us to live on the reservation and give up our way of life. So they come into our villages to kill our women and children. A Lakota warrior cannot live on the white man's reservation. My people have hunted this land for many years before the first white man ever set foot on it. How can the white man claim that all the land belongs to him?"

Jordan had no answer for that. He knew in his heart that he could not dispute Red Feather's words, realizing also that he would feel the same way if he were in his Indian friend's place. He felt as if he should apologize for the greed of his race, but he was smart enough to know that it was inevitable that civilization, as the white man knew it, would push the red man onto reservations — or wipe him out completely. Like most white men, Jordan had never given the right or wrong of the conflict with the Indians a great deal of thought. This was the first time he was forced to view it from the Indians' point of view.

Red Feather did not expect an answer to his question. He could see the empathy in Jordan's eyes and knew that his friend could not answer for the government's policies. "We must go now to find our people," he said abruptly. "You, my friend, must go your own way. There may be some in my village who would want to avenge their loss by killing you. They may be in too much grief to understand that you are not our enemy."

Jordan nodded solemnly. He could not deny a great feeling of relief, now that it appeared he was not going to have to fight his way out. "Much obliged," he said and turned his horse toward the open prairie.

Red Feather reached over to place a hand on Jordan's forearm. "I will never forget that you saved my life."

Jordan nodded and nudged Sweet Pea with his heels. As he started along the river-bank, Many Horses pulled his pony to a halt to watch the white man leave. When Jordan looked his way, the war chief called out something in the Lakota tongue and, knowing Jordan could not understand, made the sign of peace. Jordan again nodded and returned the gesture.

Once he was free of the village, Jordan let Sweet Pea lope along for a distance until he was sure some of the younger hot bloods in the war party didn't have it in their minds to come after him. If he had been fluent in the Lakota tongue, he would have known that Many Horses had reminded his warriors that Jordan was a friend to the Lakota.

The lone dark figure that lay flat on the top of a hill, his massive body hidden by the sage and the new spring grass, watched the warriors as they searched through the ruins of their village. For two days, he had followed the war party, sleeping very little each night as he slinked around the perimeter of their camps, searching for the opportunity he prayed for. But there had been no occasion when Jordan Gray was apart from his Indian friends. The blood that pumped through his veins was filled with his bitter hatred for the white man who had slain his sons. His frustration grew daily while he had followed the party's trail. The few hours at night when he closed his eyes were filled with visions of his sons and, most often, Zeb's ragged scalp. Out of the mountains and over the hills, he had trailed them, lagging far enough behind to escape their detection. Each mile intensified his anger to the point he had now reached. He demanded vengeance. His tormented mind insisted that God deliver his enemy unto him. And just as he was set to admonish God Himself for protecting the Philistine, the Lord yielded to his demands. Jordan Gray parted from his heathen friends and rode off alone.

Knowing that vengeance was his at last, Preacher backed away from the brow of the hill and hurried down into the ravine where he had left his horse. Once mounted, he rode along the ravine to its lower end, paralleling the route Jordan had taken. By the time he emerged from the mouth of the ravine, his quarry had turned toward the south. *Heading straight for Fort Laramie,* Preacher thought, a satisfied smile spreading across his face. *I'll have him long before he gets there.* Taking a cautious glance over his shoulder to make sure the Lakota war party was riding west, he set out after his prey.

Preacher, sure of himself now, was content to trail Jordan at a distance. The open prairie made it difficult to catch up without being discovered, so he took care not to get too close. He would claim his vengeance in the black of night, striking out of the darkness with the swiftness of the Lord's mighty sword. His tortured mind told him that the Lord was pleased that he was going to slay this Philistine. *I will cut off his head and mount it on a stake in the ground as a monument to the wrath of the Lord.*

Jordan let Sweet Pea set the pace as he set out across the rolling hills of grass. The Niobrara River was perhaps a day's ride, maybe more. He was in no particular hurry. The more he delayed in reaching Fort Laramie, the longer he could entertain the possibility that Kathleen might have changed her mind about marrying Lieutenant Wallace. As the afternoon wore on, and the sun settled lower and lower, he turned his attention toward finding a place to camp. There was going to be a full moon that night. He could already see it hanging large and ghostly silver in the afternoon sky.

Just at dusk, he came upon a deep ravine and a small stream that ran down the center. *Probably runs down to the Niobrara,* he thought, figuring that he could not be that far from the river. *Right here is about as good as I'll find.* Sweet Pea, making a decision on her own, walked down to the water and stopped. She tossed her head back to give Jordan a look that told him this was as far as she intended to go.

With flint and steel, he started a fire in the crook of a gully, where he was protected from the cool breeze. Feeding the flames with dead grass and pine twigs, he soon kindled a healthy blaze. It was going to soon be a cold camp, he figured, because the branches were not plentiful. Since there had been no opportunity to kill any game, he was also going to have another supper of hard jerky. Even that was going to be lacking, for upon rummaging through his saddlebags, he found he was down to his last two strips of the tough meat. *Tomorrow, I hunt,* he promised himself.

Like the unblinking eye of God, a full moon rode low over the lonely prairie. Bathed in its light, the rocks and ridges stood out in stark relief, casting deep shadows that filled the draws and gullies with deep pools of darkness. Aided by the moon, and knowing in his mind that it was sent to light his way, Preacher guided his horse down into a shallow ravine and dismounted. With the unhurried calm of an executioner, he checked his rifle to make sure it was fully loaded, then cranked a cartridge into the chamber. Satisfied that all was ready, he climbed the side of the ravine and stood at the top, staring out across the moonlit prairie. His intense gaze sweeping slowly across the rolling hills, he searched for the clue that would pinpoint his prey. Patiently, he scanned the prairie before him, firm in the knowledge that Jordan Gray was close, too close to proceed on horseback, so he started walking, leaving his horse to graze in the ravine.

All afternoon, the trail had not wavered in its direction. It had been easy for Preacher to determine that Jordan was following a line of distant hills. That much was obvious. Once, he had topped a ridge and caught sight of Jordan, causing him to quickly back down the slope lest his prey happened to turn to look behind him. Now, as he stepped cautiously forward, avoiding the patches of sage scattered carelessly along the rim, he constantly searched back and forth, stopping every few seconds to listen. After listening for a moment, he started to step again when he was stopped cold by a sound off to his right. He waited, straining to hear. There it was again, and he was sure now. It was a horse whinnying. He stared in the direction whence it had come, seeing nothing for a few seconds. Then he caught sight of what he was searching for: a thin, dark wisp of smoke barely discernable in the bright moonlight. A smug sinister smile spread slowly across his dark face. *Vengeance is mine,* he thought and started toward the ravine, each foot carefully placed so as not to make a sound that might announce his presence.

As he approached the rim of the ravine from which the smoke was rising, he dropped to one knee when he heard the horse snort and blow. *Damn you,* he thought, picturing the homely mount that Jordan Gray rode and fearing that she would alert her master. Rising once more, he hurried over the side of the ravine, and dropped to one knee again. Beyond the dying campfire, he could see the dark outline of the horse standing in the shadows of the ravine, but nothing else. *Damn you,* he again silently cursed Sweet Pea and raised his rifle to settle with her, but he stopped before pulling the trigger when common sense told him that shooting would give his position away. *When I'm done with him,* he silently promised her, lowering his rifle. Knowing that Jordan had to be in the gully somewhere, he moved to a better position to cover the narrow opening. Shadows in the gully made it too dark for him to see his target, but he was content to wait for daybreak when the sun would light the ravine for him. He was ideally positioned to trap his quarry when Jordan tried to come out of the gully.

While Preacher knelt, waiting and watching, Jordan crawled up the far side of the ravine, working his way around the dark assassin. He had been sleeping fitfully, trying his best to keep warm by the puny sagebrush fire, when he was awakened by Sweet Pea's whinny. Accustomed to paying attention to warning noises from the cantankerous horse, he was instantly alert and listening. When the horse snorted, Jordan didn't hesitate. He grabbed his rifle and rolled over the edge of the gully into the shadows. Something, or someone, was approaching his camp, and whatever it was, it was approaching without announcing its presence. It could be a wolf, he considered, but it was more likely an Indian. Red Feather had told him that there had been other war parties sent out from his village. He hoped this was not the case, having just made friends with Many Horses and the rest of the Lakota war party he had recently left. He didn't care for the prospect of killing one of Red Feather's brethren.

Out of the shadow of the ravine now, he kept as low as he could manage. The moon had drifted almost to the opposite horizon since he had fallen asleep, but it still bathed the prairie in its light. Consequently, Jordan judged it safest to make a wide circle around his camp in hopes of getting behind his visitor, still not certain there was anything out there. *What if the damn fool horse was just blowing at the wind?* He would feel pretty damn silly if that were the case. But Sweet Pea generally did not snort at the wind. Seconds later, Jordan's doubts were dissolved when he crawled up to the rim of the ravine to discover a dark figure kneeling in a patch of brush some fifty yards down the ravine. He knew at once who his visitor was. *Preacher Rix!* There could be no mistaking the massive bulk of the self-proclaimed preacher. There was no hesitating on Jordan's part. He raised his rifle and aimed at the center of the dark mass. In his resolve to rid the world of this evil that preyed upon honest men, Jordan forgot that his rifle was not cocked. He had not wished to alert anyone to his location by throwing the lever of the Winchester while he had crawled out of the ravine, so he had waited until he was ready to fire. Now, having forgotten the chamber was empty, he squeezed the trigger slowly, only to realize his oversight. As quickly as he could, he reached up and cocked the rifle.

Below him on the slope of the steep ravine, Preacher reacted to the metallic sound immediately. His nerves already taunt and anxious, he flung his body to the ground, rolling over and over down the slope amid a hailstorm of forty-five slugs ripping the ground around him. Frustrated after having missed his chance, Jordan cocked and fired as fast as he could, hoping for a lucky shot as Preacher disappeared in the deep shadows of the ravine.

Realizing the dangerous position he was now in, Jordan scrambled to his feet and ran down to the bottom of the dark draw, anxious to escape from the moonlight. As he expected, his flight was spurred on by a barrage of return fire from Preacher. Both men were at the ravine bottom now. Jordan splashed across the tiny stream and knelt to reload his rifle. He guessed Preacher was doing the same thing.

At the far end of the ravine, Preacher snarled in anger as he sought to catch his breath. He had lost his black hat in his desperate roll down the slope, and he could feel the chill of the night wind on his bald dome. The sensation served to make him even more angry. His rifle reloaded, he fired several shots toward the opposite end of the ravine. Jordan watched carefully, noting the muzzle flash in the darkness; then he returned fire. Preacher grunted in pain as one of Jordan's shots caught him in the shoulder and spun him around. Hearing Preacher grunt, Jordan knew he was hit. He started to advance along the stream toward his adversary, moving carefully, his eyes straining to peer through the darkness. Preacher was wounded, but how seriously? Jordan was not willing to rush headlong into an ambush. *A wounded bear was a dangerous bear.*

Cursing the lucky shot that now burned in his shoulder, numbing his right arm, Preacher crossed the stream to seek better cover. Grunting with pain, he tried to hold his rifle up to take aim, but his arm seemed to have lost all feeling, and try as he might, he could not raise it to even grasp the trigger. His brain almost choked with rage, he cursed God for forsaking him, knowing he was doomed if he stood his ground. There was no choice but to run. With his rifle in his left hand and his right arm hanging uselessly, he lumbered toward the gully and the horse standing there. Sweet Pea, having bolted when the shots were fired, had stopped several yards from the dying camp-fire and now stood there watching the strange man stumble toward her. She remained motionless until it became apparent what Preacher had in mind. Certain in her independent way that she had no desire to be ridden by the desperate man, she promptly turned tail and galloped up the side of the ravine, leaving Preacher to hurl curses after her. With no other option before him, he ran along the stream until he felt it safe to climb up from the ravine and scramble down the other side.

Back in the shadows, Jordan could not see what was happening on the other side of the gully where he had built his fire, but he heard Preacher cursing his horse. Moving carefully along the stream, he was startled by the sudden charge of Sweet Pea out into the moonlight. He would have called out to her, but he was still not certain what he was facing. When he finally spotted Preacher, it was too late to get a clean shot because the huge man was disappearing over the edge of the ravine. Without hesitating, Jordan took off after him, running without regard to safety now. Preacher was wounded, but it was hard to say if the wound was mortal. He was moving pretty fast for a dying man. Jordan could only guess why Preacher chose to run instead of fighting back. It was unlikely the relentless stalker would give up this easily unless he was hurt too badly to fight.

Sprinting up the slope of the ravine, Jordan flung himself on the ground at the top. Panting from the exertion, he lay flat on his belly while he peered over the rim of the ravine, searching for Preacher. There was no sign of the huge man. Jordan scanned the moonlit prairie from horizon to horizon. It lay before his gaze, an endless sea of rolling hills and shadowed gullies and cutbacks. Preacher could be in any of a number of dark channels that ran between the hills. Jordan hesitated before exposing himself in the moonlight. He would be an easy target silhouetted against the rim of the ravine. Gradually his breathing settled down, and he listened for any sound that might lead him to Preacher. There was nothing until a distant pounding of hooves toward the east suddenly caused him to jerk his head in that direction. Preacher was getting away! Still Jordan could not catch sight of him. He sprang to his feet, and ran toward the sound, just in time to catch one final glimpse of the fleeing man as his horse came up from a dark draw and crossed over a ridge several hundred yards away. In that brief second, Jordan couldn't tell how badly the man was hurt. Preacher was lying low across his horse's neck. Whether it was because of his wound, or just to present as small a target as possible, Jordan couldn't say. One thing was certain — he had too great a lead for Jordan to go after him.

"He made his move and got himself shot for his efforts," Jordan observed aloud. "Maybe that'll be the end of it." He stood there, staring at the last place he had glimpsed the murderer. "Maybe he's draggin' his ass off somewhere to bleed to death." He turned around and gazed back toward the narrow gully where he had made his camp. *If it wasn't for that ugly coyote of a horse of mine, I'd probably be lying dead in that gully.*

He suddenly felt weary of the killing and fighting that had become his life over the past year. It was not a lifestyle for a man who craved peace as much as he. Yet it seemed that trouble had a way of finding him. "I need to change my life," he announced to the pale moon now hanging low on the horizon and already fading in submission to the coming sun. Having automatically started thinking about tracking Preacher when daylight allowed, he abruptly made a new decision. "To hell with him!"

he blurted. "I'm goin' to Fort Laramie." Suddenly he felt an urgency to return to the army post as quickly as possible. There might still be a chance he could persuade Kathleen that he could settle down and raise a family. It might give her pause to consider him. He couldn't stand the thought of her with that arrogant lieutenant. The decision made, he hurried back down to the gully to round up his horse. It would still be an hour or so before the sun cleared the hills to the east, but he was intent on starting out at once. He was convinced that he had seen the last of Preacher Rix, but it didn't make sense to remain in a spot where Preacher could find him. He was soon in the saddle and heading south, although his stomach reminded him that there was still the problem of food.

CHAPTER 12

Lying flat in the knee-high grass, Jordan took careful aim at the rearmost of the three pronghorns that made their way down to the river's edge to drink. On second thought, he waited. *Might as well let them get a drink of water before I scare them to hell and back,* he thought. He gave the antelope a few minutes to slake their thirst; then he sighted down on his target again. He slowly squeezed the trigger, and the pronghorn dropped to its knees before falling over dead on its side. Startled, the other two bolted in opposite directions before racing toward the hills.

Jordan didn't move at once, waiting to see if the sharp crack of his rifle had summoned any wandering war parties. When there was nothing to disturb the quiet of the river after several long minutes, he got to his feet and went to retrieve his horse. Since the antelope's carcass was lying handy to the water's edge, he decided to butcher it right where it was. He was no longer concerned about Preacher Rix. There had been no sign of anyone following him since leaving camp that morning. So he went to work with his skinning knife, slitting the animal's hide along the belly.

He was well into his work, quartering the animal when two Indians suddenly appeared on the low bluff about a hundred yards down river. They held their ponies in check while they looked the white man over. Jordan paused and stared back at them, wondering what the next move was going to be. He glanced over his shoulder, upriver, to see if there were any more in that direction. Then he glanced across the river to make sure that way was clear in case he was forced to make a quick retreat. There wasn't much else he could do at this point. It would depend on what the two Indians had in mind, so he continued to watch them, waiting for them to call the play.

After some discussion between the two warriors, they turned their ponies toward him and walked slowly along the bluff. Jordan casually wiped his skinning knife on the pronghorn's hide and returned it to its sheaf. Without a pause, he reached over and picked up his rifle. Within fifty yards now, one of the Indians held up his arm and made a sign of peace. Jordan returned it, but kept his rifle ready to fire at the first hint of deception. As the warriors approached, Jordan recognized Iron Pony, one of the Crow scouts who rode with the patrol he had accompanied. The Crow scout recognized Jordan at almost the same time. A smile appeared on his face then, and he urged his pony forward to greet Jordan.

"If I was a Sioux, I could have shot you back there," Iron Pony said, grinning widely.

"That's a fact," Jordan admitted. "At least you coulda shot *at* me." He pulled out his knife again and resumed his butchering. "What are you two doin' out here? You're kinda close to Sioux country, ain'tcha?"

Iron Pony dismounted and helped Jordan wrap the meat in the pronghorn's hide. "We're scoutin' for your friend Lieutenant Wallace," he said, grinning as he watched Jordan's face for his reaction. "The patrol's about a mile behind us."

Jordan merely grunted in response as he loaded the meat up behind his saddle. When it was secure, he asked, "What brings the army out this way?"

Iron Pony went on to explain that there had been several raids on some of the ranches in the outlying areas, some within a half day's ride of the fort. "Lieutenant Masters led a patrol that raided a Sioux camp upriver from here, but most of the Sioux got away. Wallace is set on findin' them and wipin' them out." The grin returned to his face. "He said if he had been leadin' the patrol instead of Masters, none of the Sioux would have got away."

"I just came from that camp," Jordan said. "There are about fifteen or twenty more Lakota warriors with that bunch than there were when Masters hit 'em. You're pushin' mighty deep into their territory. They may even have joined up with some of the other bands that jumped the reservation. I'd be mighty careful if I was you. How many men on this patrol?" When Iron Pony replied that there were twenty, not counting the lieutenant, Jordan shook his head solemnly. "That ain't enough. I rode a-ways with this war party, and they're all armed with rifles."

Iron Pony shrugged. "Wallace says he ain't scared of the Sioux — says they can't stand up to a real cavalry attack."

"Is that a fact?" Jordan shook his head, a picture in his mind of the arrogant young officer. "Just the same, you'd better watch yourself if you're goin' after this bunch." He stepped up in the saddle, and the other Crow scout called out from the bluff above them that the patrol was in sight. Jordan and Iron Pony rode up to meet them.

Riding a few paces out in front, Lieutenant Wallace led the patrol, looking very much like he was passing in review on a parade ground. Jordan and the two Crow scouts pulled up and waited for the soldiers to reach them. Curious upon seeing someone with his scouts, Wallace scowled when he recognized the insolent scout who had invited him to kiss his behind. Corporal Macy sprouted a wide grin when he saw Jordan sitting beside the two Crows.

"There ain't no tellin' what you'll run into out here," Macy joked after Wallace halted the patrol. "What are you doin' in these parts, Jordan?"

"Just tryin' to get by," Jordan replied, smiling.

Lieutenant Wallace chose to ignore Jordan's presence, speaking directly to Iron Pony. "Any sign of the hostiles?" he asked.

Iron Pony told him that there had been no sign of Sioux war parties on the move, then relayed the information given him by Jordan. He concluded by advising, "Jordan says the camp has more warriors now, maybe fifteen or more."

Skeptical, Wallace asked, "How does Mr. Gray know this?" When Iron Pony told him that Jordan had ridden with them to the Sioux camp, Wallace turned to acknowledge Jordan's presence. "He rode with them?" Staring accusingly at Jordan, he sneered. "That would make him a renegade, wouldn't it?"

Jordan was tempted to inform the egotistical officer that the invitation to kiss his ass was still open, but he felt an obligation toward the men under Wallace's command. Directing his comments to Macy, he warned, "I wouldn't go after this bunch with less than a full troop of cavalry. That camp Masters hit a few days ago has been reinforced, and they're madder'n hell about the raid on their village."

"Thank you for your expert opinion, Mr. Gray," Wallace said, his tone heavy with sarcasm. "But I think I'll rely on my scouts for information about the enemy." Turning to Iron Pony, he ordered the scouts out again. Returning his gaze to Jordan, he said, "If you're thinking about joining this patrol, you can tag along behind. Just be sure you don't get in the way."

Jordan couldn't help but laugh. "Join your patrol?" he replied. "Hell, I've got better sense than to join any patrol you're leadin'. If you find that Lakota village, you're gonna have more than this patrol can handle, and that's the fact of the matter." Feeling the anger rising in his blood, he abruptly turned Sweet Pea's head and took his leave. Passing Macy, he said, "Watch yourself. If you find that camp, it ain't gonna be no picnic."

He turned once to watch the patrol start out along the bluffs, following the river. Then he urged Sweet Pea forward, looking for a good spot to build a fire and cook some meat. He felt that if he didn't have something to eat pretty soon, his stomach would be growling loud enough to summon a Sioux war party down upon him.

Selecting a wide gully that ran from the bluff to the water's edge, he soon had a fire going. Cutting some of the raw meat into strips, he fashioned a spit out of a willow branch and squatted on his heels watching it cook. While he waited, his mind formed a picture of Lieutenant Thomas Jefferson Wallace sitting rigidly erect in the saddle as if on parade. Jordan had an overwhelming dislike for the man. He would have disliked Wallace even if he wasn't betrothed to Kathleen. And he sincerely believed that if Kathleen could see her fiancé in the field, she would see him for the arrogant son of a bitch that he was.

His empty stomach churning with the sizzle of roasting antelope, he pulled the first strip off before it was thoroughly done and devoured it. Satisfied for the moment, he was content to wait for the rest of his dinner to cook. While it roasted over the flames, he climbed up on the bluff to have a look around. The patrol was long out of sight to the northwest, and there was no sign of any movement on the prairie. He turned slowly around in a complete circle, searching every direction. Satisfied that the patrol had not attracted any curious Lakota scouts to his fire, he descended the bluff to enjoy his meal.

After being empty for so long, his stomach, when finally filled to capacity, began to exert weight upon his eyelids. Like a mountain lion after a kill, he felt a strong temptation to take a short nap while his meal digested. Giving in to the urge, he climbed the bluff again to make sure he was alone, then settled himself by the fire, content that Sweet Pea would warn him of any danger.

Jordan awoke with a start. Immediately alert, he sat up and reached for his rifle. There was no sound but the gentle sigh of the river as it slid by the sandbar behind him, creating tiny eddies near the bank. He looked at Sweet Pea, only to receive a questioning gaze from the horse. Puzzled by the feeling of urgency, he scrambled up to the top of the bluff and searched the prairie around him once more. There was nothing. It then registered that it was late in the day. He had slept the afternoon away. It would soon be dusk. Maybe that explained his feeling of urgency when he awoke. He was wasting daylight when he could have been on his way to Fort Laramie and Kathleen. *Maybe I should just go ahead and make camp right where I am — start out for Laramie in the morning.* It suddenly dawned upon him that he was looking for excuses to stay, and he realized that it was the fate of the cavalry patrol that caused his concern. They were riding into certain trouble.

"Hell," he blurted. "I warned 'em. If that pigheaded lieutenant has to see for himself, it's not my problem." Still, his conscience was not placated. There were the lives of the scouts and the enlisted men to be concerned for. Maybe he should have been more persuasive in his warning, instead of bristling before his rival. *Well,* he conceded, *it's too damn late to do anything about it now.* Returning to the gully where he had built his fire, he unsaddled Sweet Pea and prepared to make camp. After collecting enough wood to feed his fire all night, he cut some more of the antelope meat for supper.

It was close to dark when the first of the column appeared along the far bluffs. Jordan, already alerted by Sweet Pea's nicker, stayed low behind the lip of the riverbank until he identified the riders. Still, he didn't expose himself for a few minutes. Something didn't look right about the formation, and he soon realized what it was. Lieutenant Wallace was not out in front in his usual position, and the column was strung out with long intervals between some of the troopers. He counted only fourteen men. Where were the others? This didn't look good. Climbing up from the bank, he hailed the column.

The call from the riverbank startled the limping column of soldiers, and there was an immediate rustle of weapons bristling. "Hold your fire!" Macy yelled. "It's Jordan Gray." He turned his horse and loped over to meet Jordan.

"What the hell happened?" Jordan asked when Macy stepped down.

"It was a damn massacre," Macy replied, his face streaked with gunpowder and grime. "They musta seen us comin'. They led us right into it. We were lucky the rest of us got out alive." He shook his head slowly, recalling the battle scene. "They got the lieutenant. I don't know if he's dead or alive. They killed six for sure. The rest of us fought our way back. There wasn't nothin' we could do for the dead. There was just too many Injuns."

"Are they followin' you?" Jordan wanted to know first.

"Not no more. They chased us for a couple of miles, but me and a couple of the men dropped back and picked off three or four of 'em. They turned back then."

Jordan looked over the weary troopers as they gathered around him and Macy. Some wore makeshift bloody bandages. All were spent. "Where are your Crow scouts?"

"Don't know," Macy replied. "Lieutenant Wallace sent 'em out on the flanks, and we ain't seen 'em since. The Sioux mighta got 'em. They mighta seen what happened and decided to save their own scalps. I couldn't say."

"You might as well make camp here," Jordan said to Macy. "These men look too worn-out to go any farther tonight. You can set up some sentries on the bluffs to make sure the Sioux didn't decide to come after you. And you can cook the rest of that antelope carcass if you want to."

After Macy organized the guard detail and

the horses were taken care of, he filled Jordan in on the details of the ill-fated raid. "We were comin' up on a line of hills when we saw the first of 'em: half a dozen of 'em on top of a hill. We took off after 'em. They fired a couple of shots at us, then disappeared down the other side of the hill. We tried to cut 'em off. There was a long draw running between the ridges, and it looked like the shortest way to head 'em off. But when we got to the end of it, there weren't no Injuns in sight. Then about two hundred yards off to the right, a party of maybe a dozen or more popped up out of a ravine and started shootin' at us. Lieutenant Wallace ordered us to charge 'em."

Here he paused to look Jordan directly in the eye. "I told him maybe we ought to hold back till we found out where the other six Injuns had got to. But he was rarin' to go after that bunch in the ravine — said they'd scatter soon enough when they saw a genuine cavalry charge. For a minute, it looked like he was right, 'cause they took off down the ravine. The farther we rode, the tighter that ravine got, till it couldn'ta been no more'n forty yards wide near the end. I tried to call the lieutenant back, but he was out in front, chargin' like hell. I didn't like the look of it, but I didn't have much choice but to follow him.

"When we got to the end of the ravine, it took a sharp turn, and we found ourselves out in the open with hills all around us — and there was them Injuns settin' there lookin' at us. Any fool could see right then what was gonna happen. I halted the men, but Lieutenant Wallace just kept on, chargin' at 'em in full gallop. He hadn't gone ten yards before the hills on both sides of us came alive with Injuns. I swear, there musta been a hundred or more. The lieutenant's horse went out from under him. Bullets were flyin' everywhere. We lost three men before we could retreat back to the ravine, but by the time we pulled back, they had closed that door behind us. There wasn't nothin' to do but climb up over the side and ride like hell. They picked off three more of us before we made it to the clear." He shook his head, obviously feeling some guilt. "The last I saw of the lieutenant, he was fightin' with four or five Injuns. We couldn't do nothin' to help him. There was too many of 'em, and I had to save as many of the men as I could."

"No," Jordan said, "it wouldn't have done any good to sacrifice the rest of your men. You didn't have much choice." In all honesty, Jordan could not say he felt a great deal of sympathy for Wallace. He was more inclined to feel that the brash young officer got what he deserved. It was the men he had caused to sacrifice their lives who bothered him. He was stunned by Macy's next comment, however.

"I never cared much for Wallace," Macy began, "but it's a shame to have to tell a woman she's a widow after she ain't been married but a week."

"Kathleen? Married?" Jordan blurted, barely able to believe his ears.

Macy, puzzled by Jordan's reaction, replied, "Yes, sir, Kathleen Beard, the surgeon's daughter. They got married about a week ago. You know her?"

Jordan didn't answer at once, couldn't in fact. His brain was flooded in a confusion of thoughts. He had no notion that they would marry so soon. Somehow, he had harbored the impression that Kathleen would plan a big wedding, and it would take time to have a wedding dress made and lots of other things that a girl found necessary to prepare. He had been counting on that time to give her opportunity for second thoughts. *Kathleen married!* How could he have been so wrong about her? Evidently he had been the only one who felt an attraction. The blunt impact of Macy's words left him speechless for a long minute. Then he realized that the corporal was staring at him, openly curious about his sudden paralysis.

"I know her," he replied softly. "I reckon I didn't figure they'd get married that quick."

"Well, her husband is most likely dead by now," Macy said. "And it's a damn shame. She's a right nice little lady."

"You said you saw him fightin' with some Indians. Did you see him actually killed?"

"Well, no," Macy said. "I didn't have time to do much lookin'. He was so far out ahead of the rest of us that they cut him off, and I had the men to worry about, too."

Jordan could picture Wallace in his mind, riding ramrod straight in the saddle, charging ahead, expecting the Sioux to scatter and run before him. He couldn't help but wonder if the corporal might have made more of an effort to rescue the lieutenant if Wallace had been more popular with his troops. He couldn't deny the thought that flashed through his mind that it meant that Kathleen was no longer married. He wasn't proud of it, but the thought was there.

"What are you plannin' to do now?" Jordan asked.

Macy shrugged. "Nothin' much I can do," he said. "I ain't got the men to go against that many hostiles. I reckon it's up to the brass to decide if they're gonna mount a regiment or somethin' to clean that village out."

And in the meantime nobody's really sure if Wallace is dead or a captive, Jordan thought. The picture of a grieving Kathleen entered his mind, a new bride, now a widow, and he knew what he had to do. "Damn," he uttered softly. Noting the quizzical expression on Macy's face, he answered the corporal's unspoken question. "Nothin' — there's just somethin' I've gotta do." He rose to his feet and picked up his saddle. Macy didn't say anything until Jordan started for his horse.

"What are you fixin' to do?"

"I'm gonna go see if the lieutenant's body is out there in that ravine. If I can't find it, I'm gonna find that Sioux camp. He might still be alive, and it's somethin' I need to know for sure." He somehow felt that he owed Kathleen that much.

"It'll be dark soon," Macy said. "You might better wait till mornin'."

"Mornin' might be too late if he *is* a captive. There's gonna be another full moon tonight. There'll be plenty of light to find that ravine."

Macy found it hard to understand Jordan's concern. He knew the contempt the broad-shouldered young man held for the lieutenant. What he was planning to do might very well place him in danger of being killed or captured as well. Macy was about to say as much when one of the sentries called out a warning.

"Riders comin'!"

The alert was sufficient to cause every man to seek some form of cover and prepare to repel a possible attack until the sentry called out again. "It's Iron Pony and Otter."

In a few moments, the two Crow scouts rode in, their horses showing signs of hard riding. Macy strode forward to meet them, curious to know where they had been all this time. Iron Pony recounted the series of circumstances that separated them from the column. They had ranged out about a mile or so from the patrol. When the shooting started, they tried to reach the column, but were intercepted by the Sioux — the same party of six who had originally baited the soldiers. The Crows had to make a run for it, eventually losing their pursuers in the hills. During the chase, they had almost blundered into the Sioux village. By the time they were able to make their way back to the ravine where the ambush took place, the soldiers had retreated. Iron Pony and Otter watched from the western ridge while the Sioux warriors scalped the fallen troopers. When asked about Lieutenant Wallace, Iron Pony told them that Wallace was taken captive and was still alive when they last saw him.

Jordan's task was clear to him now. He had to make an attempt to rescue Wallace — not for the lieutenant's sake, but for Kathleen's. Upon hearing that Wallace was alive, Macy volunteered to take a few of the men and go back with Jordan. Jordan rejected the offer, figuring the chances were better for one man to sneak close enough to the Sioux village to see what was going on. "I'll take Iron Pony," he finally decided, "to show me where the Sioux camp is — if he's willin' to go." The Crow scout readily agreed to guide him to the camp. "I can wait till you get somethin' to eat," Jordan told him. Turning to Macy, he said, "He's gonna need a fresh horse."

Iron Pony tore off a portion of the antelope meat and ate it while one of the soldiers put his saddle on an army mount. In a matter of minutes, he was ready to follow Jordan. Macy and the rest of the patrol watched as the two filed out of the camp and disappeared into the bluffs, just as the full moon made its first appearance over the distant hills.

CHAPTER 13

The time it took to reach the Sioux village was considerably shortened with the help of a guide. Still it was a two-hour ride through the moonlit hills and draws before they sighted the rosy shroud over the camp created by the many campfires.

"Big camp," Jordan commented.

"Big camp," Iron Pony agreed.

They proceeded with caution from that point forward until reaching a low ridge that guarded the western flank of the camp. Jordan dismounted to look the situation over. There was a broad expanse of level grassland between the ridge where he now stood and the outer ring of tipis. The other side of the camp was protected by the river, with the pony herd in between it and the lodges on the east. Jordan and Iron Pony remained there on the ridge for a considerable period, searching for sentries, but finally decided that none had been posted.

The Sioux, they concluded, had little reason to concern themselves with an attack by the badly outnumbered army patrol. There was a great deal of activity in the camp, with many people walking back and forth between the tipis. Their voices, light and cheerful, carried on the evening breeze.

"I reckon they're feelin' pretty good about whippin' that patrol this afternoon," Jordan commented quietly. "We need to get closer." He climbed back in the saddle and guided his horse along the ridge paralleling the center of the camp.

When they had reached a point opposite the camp's center, they left the horses below the ridge and moved in closer on foot, using the tall grass as cover. Before leaving the protection provided by the ridge, Jordan turned to look Iron Pony in the eye. The Crow scout understood the intense question behind the gaze and nodded his head solemnly. Firmly assured that Iron Pony was willing to risk his neck, Jordan moved into the waist-high grass.

If there had been dancing to celebrate the war party's victory, it was evidently over at this point. Close enough now to hear voices in casual conversation, Jordan scanned the open area at the center of the tipis until he saw what he was looking for. A crowd of men, women, and children had gathered near one of the tipis, forming a circle. As the crowd shifted, moving back and forth, he was able to catch glimpses of the object of their interest. Lieutenant Thomas Jefferson Wallace was tethered to a stake in the ground, his hands bound behind his back and tied to his ankles. Trussed up like a hog for slaughter, he was helpless before his tormentors. Some of them, mostly the women, were amusing themselves by throwing sticks and small stones at his bloodied body. His bare chest and back bore evidence of the beatings he had suffered at the hands of his captors. If he had shown defiance, it had long since been beaten out of him, for he lay unmoving, dead for all Jordan could tell.

"Maybe too late," Iron Pony whispered.

"You might be right," Jordan replied, "but we might as well make sure." He studied the situation carefully, knowing that whatever he decided to do, he'd better not waste much time in doing it. One thing was certain, there was no hope of getting anywhere close to Wallace with so many Sioux around him. There might be a chance if a sizable diversion was created, but it would have to be big enough to distract the entire village. His mind went immediately to the large pony herd peacefully grazing between the village and the river. Whispering to Iron Pony to follow, he withdrew from the edge of the village far enough to talk without fear of being overheard by any of the Indians milling about the clearing.

Iron Pony listened to Jordan's plan, nodding his understanding when Jordan emphasized the danger and assured him that he would understand if the scout was unwilling to take such a chance. Unfortunately for the lieutenant, it would take some time to implement the plan. Iron Pony would have to skirt around the lower end of the camp, cross the river, and come up on the other side. He would then have to cross the river once more to get to the Sioux horses.

"Once you get 'em moving," Jordan warned, "you're gonna have to ride like hell. Make plenty of noise, because I ain't likely to get but one chance to get to Wallace. I'm hopin' you attract everybody's attention long enough for me to get to him. As soon as you clear the upper end of the camp, just cut out for the hills and worry about savin' your own neck. Don't wait around for me. If we're lucky, I'll see you somewhere along the way back."

"If they catch you, it will be very bad for you," Iron Pony said.

"It'll cost 'em. I guarantee you that," Jordan replied, already having second thoughts about risking his life to save a man he had no liking for. "I just hope I ain't stickin' my neck out for a man that's already dead."

Iron Pony placed his hand on Jordan's arm and nodded his head solemnly. Then he was off, making his way through the tall grass, and soon gone from sight. Jordan returned his attention to the Sioux camp, moving back to the place where he had caught sight of Wallace. It would take a while for Iron Pony to circle the camp, and while Jordan waited, his mind was busy with worrisome thoughts. *I'm a damn fool for trying to save the arrogant bastard,* he thought, knowing he was betting on extremely long odds. Iron Pony might not be able to get to the Sioux horses. If he was successful in driving off some of the horses, there might still be a lot of people who just didn't run to save them. And of course, Wallace might be dead. *Damn fool,* he condemned himself, but thoughts of a grieving Kathleen could not be repressed. *What's the use of fretting about it? You're going to do it, damn fool or not.* He determined to put any wavering thoughts out of his mind and concentrate on the job he was about to do.

It was probably no more than half an hour, but it seemed much longer to the lone white man crouching in the high grass so close to the hostile camp. Twice during that time, he feared that he was going to be forced to retreat from his spot when a couple of the Sioux walked in his direction. Once he lay flat, watching a small boy relieve himself no more than ten yards from him in the thick grass. *Come on, Iron Pony,* he pleaded impatiently.

As the night progressed, and the moon rode closer to the dark hills in the distance, the gathering started to thin out. The people began to lose interest in the captive soldier and sought the comfort of their beds. Jordan shifted his position, advancing even closer to the outer ring of tipis. There were now no more than a dozen people in the clearing near the fire and the tormented white soldier. Jordan estimated the distance between him and the lieutenant to be right at fifty yards. Turning to look back over his shoulder, he figured it to be another fifty yards to the spot below the ridge where he had left his horse. Suddenly the still night air was split with the sound of gunfire and a high piercing Crow war cry.

Jordan, after waiting anxiously for so long, was as startled as the people in the Sioux camp. Warriors poured from the lodges, and the people still milling around the fire joined them as they ran toward the river. "The horses!" someone shouted, and the call was taken up by several as the camp was caught in the panic of a possible Crow raid.

Iron Pony did his job well. Cutting into the pony herd, he drove a bunch of horses, numbering fifteen or twenty, toward the upper end of the camp. Shooting and yelling, he ran them along the western riverbank before veering into a gully that led down to the water. Behind him, the village was alive with excitement: warriors running after the stampeding ponies, others riding on the backs of favored war ponies that had been tethered by their lodges. Leaving the frightened horses to gallop toward the hills, Iron Pony plunged into the dark water, unnoticed by the angry Sioux, and crossed to the opposite bank. Once he was sure he was in the clear, he headed downriver, using his quirt to demand all the speed his horse could provide, effectively disappearing into the shadows. His part of the plan completed, he concentrated upon saving his scalp. There was no way he could know for sure if he had been able to give Jordan the time he needed.

Back at the edge of the camp, Jordan

hesitated for a moment until everyone around the captive had run toward the stampeding ponies. *Now or never!* he thought and sprang to his feet. With his rifle in one hand, and his knife in the other, he sprinted by the first two lodges, straight for the man tethered to the stake.

Wallace, bloodied, confused, and convinced that the charging man was death's messenger, pulled frantically at the rawhide rope binding him. Jordan quickly knelt beside the wounded officer and hacked away at his bonds. "Gray!" Wallace blurted, realizing that he was not about to be executed.

"Can you walk?" Jordan demanded, working away at the cords as quickly as he could manage, while anxiously watching the Indians running toward the river.

"Damn right," Wallace gasped, his voice raspy from thirst. "I'll damn sure walk out of here."

"Well, let's go then," Jordan said as the last cord fell away. He reached down and grabbed Wallace's arm to help him to his feet.

His limbs stiff and sore from lack of circulation, the lieutenant sagged and almost went down before he regained his balance.

"Can you make it?" Jordan demanded

impatiently, still with his eye on the mob.

"I'll make it," Wallace insisted, though he was staggering on unsteady legs.

"You'd better, 'cause I can't run that far carryin' you." Jordan took one last look behind him, then turned to follow Wallace, only to find the lieutenant had stopped. Jordan almost bumped into him. When he looked up to see what had caused Wallace to stop dead, it was to find a solitary Lakota warrior standing in their path. Jordan reacted quickly, bringing his rifle to bear, but the warrior already had his rifle aimed and ready to fire. Both men hesitated, recognizing each other at the same time.

"Jordan Gray," the Lakota pronounced, still with the rifle aimed at Jordan's chest.

"Red Feather," Jordan acknowledged.

Both men stood facing each other for what seemed an eternity, Lakota and white man, neither wanting to make the first move. Frantic to save his neck, Wallace blurted, "Shoot him!"

"Shut up, Wallace," Jordan spat, never taking his eyes from Red Feather's. He knew the warrior hesitated because he felt he owed his life to Jordan. "I don't want to kill you, Red Feather. You are my friend. But I have to take this man with me."

"He is an enemy of my people. He led the

soldiers against us. He is not worth your life, my friend."

"I have to take him back," Jordan stated calmly. Red Feather raised his rifle to point it directly at Jordan's head. "You and I have no reason to fight," Jordan said. He reached over and gave Wallace a shove. "Get going," he said and lowered his rifle.

Red Feather started to step forward to block Wallace's path, but paused, clearly battling with his feelings. "He will be my prisoner now," Jordan said in an effort to appease Red Feather's conscience. "He has committed a greater crime against me." He then walked past the warrior, moving un-hurriedly toward the tall grass at the edge of the camp. Striding tall and deliberate, he resisted the urge to run. It was a gamble, but he was counting on the Lakota warrior's sense of honor toward a man who had saved his life. Almost out of the light of the dying fire now, he could feel the nerves tingling between his shoulder blades, but the shot did not come. The only sound he was aware of was the steady pounding of his own heartbeat drumming in his ears.

They reached the place in the grass where Jordan and Iron Pony had knelt to scout the village when the first cry of alarm rang out behind them. "Run!" Jordan ordered and lunged forward in the waist-high grass. Wallace tried to follow, but stumbled and fell, his legs still unsteady. Jordan stopped and came back to help the weakened soldier to his feet, realizing as he did that Wallace was in no shape to outrun a party of angry warriors. At best, they had only seconds before being overtaken. "Go!" Jordan commanded, pointing toward the ridge. "My horse is below the ridge. I'll try to buy us some time." Wallace did as he was told, staggering as best he could on unsteady legs. Jordan watched for a few seconds to make sure the lieutenant was heading in the right direction; then he turned back to face the pursuit.

Looking back at the clearing, he could see a number of warriors gathering near the fire, shouting excitedly, arms waving in frantic gesturing, and he braced for the coming assault. His only hope was to stop enough of them to discourage reckless pursuit, thereby gaining enough time to get back to his horse. But the pursuit did not come. Instead, the warriors charged out of the camp in a direction clearly ninety degrees from where he knelt, waiting. Puzzled at first, he suddenly realized that Red Feather must have sent them in the wrong direction, knowing that Jordan would not have time to escape otherwise. *Now I'm in your debt,* Jordan thought and, wasting no more time, followed after Wallace.

Sprinting over the backside of the low ridge, he arrived to find Wallace struggling to mount Sweet Pea. With one arm hanging useless, he was trying to pull himself up by one hand on the saddle horn. Sweet Pea, however, was not of a disposition to allow it. As a result, the two, man and horse, were engaged in a frantic ballet, as they went round and round in a circle, Sweet Pea sidestepping each time Wallace tried to put his foot in the stirrup. "Damn you!" Wallace spat at the belligerent horse in frustration as Jordan arrived to grasp the reins.

"Hold still," Jordan ordered, and Sweet Pea immediately obeyed, standing still while Jordan climbed up in the saddle. "Put your foot in the stirrup and climb up behind me," he said. Sweet Pea stood tranquil, with no protest, as she accepted the double load. "Red Feather's givin' us a fair head start, but we're gonna have to make some time while we've got the chance. That war party will soon find out we didn't head outta there that way. I've got an extra shirt in my saddle bag — maybe keep you from freezin' to death." As the moon set beyond the distant horizon, and the dusky light of predawn settled upon the prairie, Sweet Pea loped along the back side of the ridge, heading toward the rising sun.

The first rays of the sun found the two white men approaching a creek with high banks on either side. Jordan remembered crossing it on his way to the Sioux camp the night before. "We'll stop and rest my horse for a while," he said. "Looks like you could use a little rest yourself." There had been no sign of pursuit as yet, but Jordan was not willing to assume the chase was ended. "We won't be long," he added.

Wallace was more than ready to rest, and as soon as Jordan helped him down, he sank to the ground, exhausted. Jordan led Sweet Pea to the water and dropped the reins, letting the mare take her time drinking. When he turned around, it was to find Wallace staring up at him. Jordan handed him his canteen. Wallace took a long pull from it, then handed it back without a word of thanks. He continued to stare at his rescuer for a long moment before speaking.

"Why did you risk your neck to save me?" Wallace asked bluntly.

Jordan shrugged. "It doesn't matter, does it?" He wasn't about to confess that he did it because of his feelings for Kathleen. When

Wallace continued to probe with his gaze, Jordan said, "I wasn't busy at the time." His curt answer didn't satisfy the lieutenant's curiosity.

"I would have expected Corporal Macy and some of the men to attempt to rescue me, but not you. I thought you would be the last person to want to help me."

Jordan was quick to speak in Macy's defense. "The corporal was plannin' to try to come after you, but there was a better chance that one man alone would be able to get close enough to get in and out again. All your men — the ones that made it back — were too worn-out to go back for you. All I needed was for Iron Pony to attract the Indians' attention for a few minutes."

Wallace took note of Jordan's comment: *the ones that made it back.* But he declined to defend his reckless attack upon the Sioux camp. "Well, I suppose I should thank you for risking your life to save me," he finally said.

"Oh, not if it causes you grief," Jordan replied with a half grin, a note of sarcasm in his tone.

"What were you planning to do if your diversion failed to work?"

The half grin spread into a wide smile as Jordan answered, "Why, I woulda shot you to put you out of your misery."

The two adversaries looked at each other, neither speaking for a long moment. Then Wallace asked, "What did you mean back there when you said I was wanted for a crime against you?"

Jordan shrugged. "It was just somethin' to make Red Feather think you weren't goin' to get away without some kind of punishment." He had no intention of giving the lieutenant the satisfaction of knowing that the crime he committed against him was taking Kathleen. There was an awkward tension between the two men, a definite dislike with no middle ground for a truce between them. Jordan hated the fact that he felt compelled to rescue the arrogant officer. Wallace despised the thought of owing his life to a man he held in such contempt. "I'm gonna walk back up to the top of that rise to take a look around. Then we'd best get goin'."

"We would have a better chance if you had brought an extra horse," Wallace said.

Jordan took a long look at him before answering candidly, "You're right, but to tell you the truth, I didn't expect to find you alive."

Macy was undecided as to what he should

do. It was a little after sunup when Iron Pony showed up, his horse lathered and blowing. The scout related the events of the night just passed, but he could not say what had happened to Jordan and the lieutenant. He had done as Jordan had instructed: stampeded the pony herd, then made sure of his escape. The last he had seen of Jordan, he was kneeling in the grass at the edge of the Sioux camp. Whether to wait any longer or to start out for Fort Laramie right away — that was the decision Macy had to make. According to what Iron Pony had seen, Lieutenant Wallace was badly beaten and most likely needed help. He could even be dead. But Macy could not know for sure if Jordan had been successful in rescuing Wallace, and he felt he could not wait too long to find out. He had wounded of his own to consider. Also, he was in no condition to fight if the Sioux decided to come after them. In the end, he concluded that there was but one course of action, and that was his obligation to the men under his command, especially the wounded.

Jordan walked back down to the creekbank to find that Wallace had passed out from sheer exhaustion. Since he had seen no sign of a war party searching for them, he decided to let Wallace sleep for a while. It wouldn't hurt to rest Sweet Pea a little longer as well. The sun was well up in the sky when he finally shook the lieutenant awake. "We'd best get goin'."

Jordan held Sweet Pea to a slower pace in an effort not to tire the horse too quickly. Consequently, it was close to midday when they reached the bluffs where the cavalry patrol had waited. Surprised that they were allowed to approach without being challenged, Jordan reined his horse to a halt, thinking it wise to take precautions. Macy and the men were either gone or they were mighty careless about posting sentries. As soon as he nudged Sweet Pea forward, following a gully down the bluffs to the water's edge, he discovered it was the former.

"Looks like your boys gave you up for dead," Jordan commented as he pulled the horse up before the remains of his campfire. He dismounted, then helped Wallace down.

"They can't have been gone long," Wallace said, clearly irritated that his command had given up on him.

"Maybe not," Jordan replied dryly. "I can't say as how I blame them. They were in pretty bad shape and in no condition to fight if those Sioux decided to come after them." After he got the lieutenant settled, he knelt to examine the ashes of the fire. "Still warm," he said. "Three or four hours, I'd say." That wasn't much of a lead, but with Sweet Pea hauling double, it might as well be a day and a half. It wasn't likely they would catch up before reaching Fort Laramie. He turned to look at the lieutenant, slumped on the bare ground, looking as if he were too weak to hold his head up. "Are you gonna make it?" Jordan asked.

"I'll make it," Wallace replied with a faint spark of defiance. There was a moment of silence. "I'm hungry."

It occurred to Jordan then that he had been far too busy avoiding a war party to even think about food. Wallace could not have eaten in two days. Jordan had nothing to offer the officer. "I'll see what I can find," he said. "It wouldn't hurt to rest up a little while, anyway." He paused to bend over him. "That arm of yours don't look too good, either. It's swollen pretty bad behind your wrist. I think it's broke. We may have to fix it." Straightening up again, he said, "I'll get this fire goin' again, and then I'll try to find you somethin' to eat."

The prospects for finding game were slim, since any wild beast would have already been frightened away from the vicinity of the camp, so Jordan made his way down along the riverbank, looking for any small varmint that could provide nourishment. There was plenty of sign that muskrats had been pretty busy all along the bank, but Jordan hoped for something better. He had never been partial to muskrat. What he was looking for was a deer or an antelope that might happen down to the water's edge to drink. After a half hour with no luck, however, he was forced to resign himself to eating muskrat. *I'm not going to eat much of it, anyway.*

He had nothing with which to fashion a trap, so he was going to have to shoot one. Walking along the bank, he spotted many muskrat runs, easily distinguished by the lack of silt along their tiny trails, a result of repeated trips made back and forth by the rodent. It didn't take long before he caught sight of one about to slip back into the water.

The force of the forty-five slug caused the animal to turn a complete flip in the air before it landed in the shallow water along the edge. The impact of his rifle slug made a sizable hole in the carcass, and ruined the shiny winter fur — which was of no concern to Jordan at the moment. As soon as he pulled the trigger, he wondered if he might have summoned a Sioux war party. The odds were in his favor that he had not because he was within a day's ride of Fort Laramie. Still, he had to think about it.

He skinned the critter, taking care to avoid puncturing the musk glands near the long flat tail when he cleared the entrails. Wallace was starved to the point where he didn't care a great deal what was roasting over the fire. When it was done, Jordan tore off a quarter of the small rodent, and Wallace accepted it, although he puzzled over it for a few seconds. "What is this?" he asked.

"Chicken," Jordan replied. "It's meat. Eat it."

Wallace ate it without complaint.

When Wallace had finished his feast of roast varmint, Jordan broached the subject of the lieutenant's injured arm. "From the look of it, I'd say that arm's broken. You can't even lift it without pain, can you?"

Wallace stared at his swollen wrist. "I think you're right. It must be broken. It's painful as hell. I think we'd better get back right away so Captain Beard can treat it."

Captain Beard, Jordan thought. *I guess he hasn't been married long enough to call the post surgeon Pa.* The thought served to irritate him, but he immediately discarded it. "We can't go just yet," he said. "My horse is lookin' kinda spent." He returned his attention to the broken arm. "That thing don't look too good. It's still swellin'. We probably oughta try to set it. If we don't, it's liable to be so infected your pappy-in-law might have to saw it off."

They discussed the issue for a few moments more. Wallace was reluctant to attempt setting the bone. He felt his arm was more important than Jordan Gray's homely horse, but he didn't care for the prospect of having to walk the final miles to Fort Laramie if the horse foundered. As far as Jordan was concerned, the decision was not Wallace's to make. Sweet Pea needed to rest, so they were not leaving for the post until his horse was ready to go.

Wallace's concern for saving his arm finally convinced him to agree with Jordan's diagnosis. As for Jordan, it was actually immaterial to him whether Wallace lost the arm or not. He was simply pointing out what seemed to him to be the obvious course of action. "Have you ever done anything like this before?" Wallace wanted to know.

"Oh, yeah, several times," Jordan lied.

"Let's get it over with, then," Wallace said.

The procedure they decided upon was for Wallace to stand firm and pull back on his arm while Jordan took hold of his hand and yanked against him. Wallace flinched with pain, however, when Jordan simply laid a hand on his arm where the fracture had occurred. "I need to be able to feel when the bones are back in place," Jordan explained. He could feel the jagged edge of the bone as it protruded into the flesh of Wallace's arm. "The bones ain't meetin'," he reported. "We're gonna have to pull 'em apart so they'll go back together." He looked into Wallace's eyes. The lieutenant's forehead was beaded with drops of sweat. "You ready?" Jordan asked. Wallace nodded in reply, biting his lower lip firmly.

With his gaze locked on Jordan's eyes, Wallace steadied himself while Jordan took hold of his wrist. With a slight nod, Wallace signaled, and both men pulled. The lieutenant yelped in pain, but he was determined to stand the treatment. The muscles and ligaments of his arm proved to be firm in their resistance to yield, however. With his other hand, Jordan could feel no movement of the broken ends of the bone. The two men continued to pull against each other, Wallace's eyes staring unblinking into Jordan's.

Suddenly, Wallace's eyes rolled upward until Jordan could see nothing but white. In the next instant, Wallace dropped to the ground, fainting dead away. Frustrated by the lack of success at first, Jordan quickly realized that now was the time to proceed. With Wallace flat on his back, Jordan placed his foot on the lieutenant's arm just above the elbow. Then he took hold of the wrist again and pulled hard until he felt the bone move. Gripping the arm with his other hand, he continued to pull until he felt the two ends line up properly, and it was done. With nothing to use for a sling — the only extra shirt he owned was on Wallace's back — Jordan searched for something to substitute. He had to settle for using a length of rope with which to fashion a sling. Cutting three strong willow branches, he formed a splint, wrapping the rope securely around them. Then he slipped a loop of it over Wallace's neck while the stricken officer was still unconscious.

Wallace came to with a start, immediately aware of the throbbing pain in his arm. Confused to find himself on the ground, he tried to sit up, but was suddenly overcome by a wave of nausea. When Jordan asked him how he felt, he couldn't answer, sinking back down to lie flat again. Jordan had no choice but to wait until his patient was recovered enough to ride.

By the time Wallace was stable enough to continue on to the fort, it was already getting dark. "Hell, we might as well wait till mornin' now," Jordan said when Wallace was on his feet again, still reeling while he adjusted his makeshift rope sling. The lieutenant was obviously embarrassed over the fainting incident, but he knew that any attempt to make excuses for it would only make matters worse. Still, he was certain Jordan perceived it as a sign of weakness, and the thought galled him to no end. Jordan, for his part, gave no thought to the matter. "I'm gonna find us somethin' to eat besides muskrat," he announced, for now he was feeling hunger pangs, having eaten very little of the rodent.

Once again, he left the lieutenant and strode off down the river, searching for suitable game. As before, he had no luck in his hunt for a deer or antelope, but he was fortunate to catch a raccoon scurrying back from the water's edge. One shot from his rifle, and the raccoon was supper. The critter was not what he had hoped for, but it was a definite improvement from the previous meal.

Morning found both men anxious to get under way. They weren't fond of each other's company, so awkward silences between them lasted for long periods, broken only by words of necessity. Sweet Pea plodded along without protest, although Jordan figured she was getting damn tired of carrying double. Wallace was forced to revise his evaluation of the homely beast and even admit a begrudging admiration for her, but only to himself. After another night's rest, and the nourishment of raccoon meat, Wallace was a great deal better, although there was still a good bit of discomfort with the injured arm. Some of the swelling was already beginning to show signs of going down, and most of the cuts and lacerations administered by the Sioux were scabbing over. It appeared that Jordan had been right in insisting the arm should be set right away, and this, too, irritated Wallace. So they rode, rocking gently in motion with the mare's steady gait, each man deep in his own thoughts.

It was the middle of the afternoon when Jordan spotted the cavalry column riding in their direction. He estimated the distance to Fort Laramie to be about twenty miles at that point and figured the patrol had most likely started out from the fort that morning. "I expect they're lookin' for you," he commented.

As the column drew closer, Jordan recognized Iron Pony and Otter out front. When they spotted him, they raced forward to meet him. Behind them, the column broke into a canter to catch up. "I wasn't sure you'd make it," Iron Pony called out, grinning broadly as he reined up beside them. "I thought maybe your scalp was tied to a Sioux lance by now."

"Why, hell," Jordan replied, reflecting the grin, "you did such a good job running off those ponies we just strolled out of that camp pretty as you please."

Within minutes, they were joined by the thirty-man detail, led by Lieutenant Martin Scales, a stranger to Jordan. "Thank God you're safe, Thomas," Scales called out. "We had almost written you off as dead." He yelled back over his shoulder, "Bring that extra horse forward." Then he dismounted to help Wallace off Jordan's horse. With Wallace safely on the ground, he glanced briefly at Jordan and said, "Good job, Gray."

Jordan simply nodded in reply. He watched as Scales, with the help of an enlisted man, led Wallace to the waiting cavalry mount. He then turned to find Iron Pony grinning at him. "He didn't waste no time thanking you for risking your life, did he?" Iron Pony said, laughing.

Jordan smiled. "At least he didn't insult my horse," he replied.

Chapter 14

It was well after dark by the time the rescue column filed into Fort Laramie, but a small crowd of soldiers soon gathered to welcome the lieutenant back. News of the return of the rescue column spread rapidly throughout the post, and the crowd swelled in number. Apart from the gathering, at the edge of the parade ground, Jordan sat on his horse, watching the hero's homecoming with the two Crow scouts. He felt apart from the celebration, an outsider, much like the Indians beside him.

After politely refusing an invitation from Iron Pony to camp with the Crow scouts, Jordan turned Sweet Pea toward the stables. He preferred the solitude of the tack room in the rear of the stables if the space was still available. Sergeant Hamilton Grant had arranged for the room when Jordan first signed on as a scout, and Jordan had left a few incidental belongings there. There was also a distinct aversion to a chance meeting with Kathleen, and he suspected it would only be moments before she arrived to welcome her husband home.

Jordan was challenged by the sentry walking the guard post by the stables, and it took a few minutes to convince the young soldier that he had permission to enter. Finally, the skeptical young man accepted Jordan's word that it was all right for him to bed down there. It helped to point out that he was leaving a horse, not taking one.

With the guard back walking his post again, Jordan led Sweet Pea through the stable to the corral. Before turning the mare in with the other horses, he unsaddled her and helped himself to a generous portion of the army's oats. He figured the mangy-looking horse had done a hell of a job in hauling one of their officers safely home and deserved a good supper. When Sweet Pea had finished eating, he turned her loose in the corral and watched for a moment while she walked casually over toward the far fence. A group of army mounts gathered there no doubt remembered the ornery mare, for they immediately dispersed, seeking space elsewhere. Jordan couldn't help but smile.

■ ■ ■ ■

Exhausted, Jordan slept soundly, not even aware of the changing of the guards during the night. He was finally awakened by the sound of the bugler blowing reveille at five thirty. A half hour later, when the bugle sounded stable and watering call, he was standing in front of the stables, ready for breakfast. As he stood watching the men as they arrived to take care of their horses, he saw a familiar figure approaching.

"I thought I'd find you here," Hamilton Grant called out cheerfully. The big first sergeant extended his hand, and Jordan shook it, grinning back at his friend. "Come on, and we'll go get somethin' to eat."

"That's exactly what I wanted to hear," Jordan said, and the two men started toward the enlisted men's mess.

The cooks weren't quite ready, since it was still almost an hour before mess call, so Grant and Jordan sat down and had coffee while they waited. "God, that's good," Jordan proclaimed, upon sipping the hot coffee. "It's been a spell." It *had* been a long time since he had anything but water to drink.

"I heard Lieutenant Wallace's account of

his capture and escape last night. I was wonderin' if you had any details to add."

Jordan shrugged indifferently. "Not much to tell — Wallace was in pretty bad shape. Iron Pony scattered the Sioux pony herd, and when the Indians went after 'em, it gave me a chance to get Wallace out. That's about it."

"The lieutenant said the two of you had to fight your way outta the Sioux camp."

"He did?" Jordan asked, surprised. "We weren't in much of a position to fight." He went on to explain that their escape was only possible because of his friendship with a Lakota warrior. "Naw, we just got on my horse and ran like hell. The Indians didn't even know which way we were runnin' until it was too late to catch us."

Sergeant Grant was about to express an opinion about the brash cavalry officer when they were interrupted by a clerk from the post adjutant's office. "Excuse me, Sergeant," the soldier said, nodding first to Jordan and then to Grant. "Captain McGarity sent me to ask Mr. Gray if he could come by the adjutant's office after morning formation."

Only mildly curious as to why McGarity wanted to see him, Jordan shrugged and said, "All right. Tell the captain I'd be glad to."

When the clerk turned to leave, Grant got up from the table. "Come on," he said to Jordan. "Let's get us a plate. Mess call's in about five minutes, and they'll be runnin' over us." After breakfast, Grant took his leave to report for duty, and Jordan headed for the adjutant's office.

"Come on in, Jordan," Paul McGarity said and got up from his desk to meet him. "That was a fine piece of work you did, going into that camp and bringing Wallace out." He motioned Jordan to a chair. "Colonel Bradley wants me to bring you by to see him." While Jordan was wondering why the post commander wanted to see him, McGarity went on. "Captain Beard told me that Wallace is going to be fine — in good shape, in fact, for what he's gone through. He's keeping him in the hospital for a couple of days if you want to check on him."

Not hardly, Jordan was thinking. He had no desire to ever see the lieutenant again. "I expect you didn't wanna see me just to tell me that," he said.

"No, the main reason was we need men of your caliber to scout for the army. I was hoping you'd reconsider and come back to work for us again. I know you and Wallace had a little falling out when you scouted for him before. But you must have worked it out, considering you risked your neck to rescue him." He paused to gauge the broad-shouldered young man's reaction. "Whaddaya say, Jordan? I might even be able to get you backpay for the time you spent bringing Wallace in."

Jordan had to consider the proposition. He had never really given much thought toward working as a scout again, primarily because he didn't figure the army would consider rehiring him. In fact, he wasn't set on what he would do at this point. He could definitely use a source of income. He still had the pouch of gold dust he had happened upon with Ned, but most of that would be used to replace the outfit he had lost in Deadwood.

McGarity, impatient for an answer, continued. "There's definitely going to be a campaign to strike that Sioux camp that ambushed Lieutenant Wallace's patrol. They could use you, since you know where it is."

Jordan hesitated, thinking of Red Feather and Many Horses before he answered. "I don't reckon I'll take part in a raid on that village. I've got friends there. If it hadn't been for one of 'em, I'd have never gotten

Wallace out." He went on to explain how the rescue had been made possible by the actions of Red Feather.

McGarity registered some mild surprise upon hearing Jordan's version of the escape. It obviously varied to a degree from Wallace's. There was a long pause while he decided what to say to Jordan. "All right," he finally said. "Iron Pony knows where to find them, but I want you to consider working for the army, anyway." He rose to his feet, signaling an end to the interview. "Will you do that?" Jordan nodded. "You know, Jordan, I appreciate the fact that you have friends among the Sioux. But there's going to be war against them and the Cheyenne, and it's going to be soon. A man's going to have to choose which side he's on."

"Yeah, I reckon," Jordan replied. "Doesn't leave a man much choice, does it?"

"No, it doesn't," McGarity agreed.

Jordan turned to take his leave, then paused. "What about Colonel Bradley? What's he wanna see me about?"

"Never mind," McGarity said. "He just wanted to offer you a job. I'll tell him you're considering it."

After leaving McGarity, Jordan returned to the stables to look in on Sweet Pea. Upon spotting her partner at the corner of the corral, the ornery mare immediately walked over to greet him. The other horses parted to give her plenty of room, causing Jordan to smile. "Come here, you mangy-lookin' critter," he said when Sweet Pea nudged her muzzle against his chest. "Let's me and you take a little ride down by the river. We've got a lot to think over." He had decisions to make, and he preferred to be away from the bustle of the army post to do so.

"Why do you ride such a scary-looking horse?"

The sound of the voice caused him to freeze, his muscles tensing in his arms. "Because she's never let me down," he answered, turning to face her. The picture of Kathleen that he had carried in his memory paled in comparison to the smiling vision before him at that moment. He hoped that she could not hear the beating of his heart.

"Sergeant Grant told me I would probably find you here," Kathleen said. "I wanted to thank you for bringing Thomas back to me." He answered with nothing more than a nod of his head, unable to think of an appropriate reply. "Father said that splint you put on Thomas's arm was the crudest he'd ever seen, but it did the job," she added in an attempt to lighten the moment. She searched his face, wanting to say more, but knew she could not. That face, rugged and honest, would always remain in a special place in her heart, tucked safely away to forever remind her of what might have been. Already, in her young marriage, she had to admit to having had second thoughts. When those moments came, she promptly told herself that she had, indeed, made the sensible decision. Thomas presented a predictable future. She recognized the brash, even arrogant, nature of her husband, but she felt he would certainly improve upon those faults in time. And he was always of a gentle nature with her. Yes, she assured herself, she had made the wise choice. Still, whenever in the presence of this quiet mountain man, she felt a certain longing inside to know him like no other man. It was not to be, and such thoughts only made her position worse. "Were you planning to come to see me?" she asked, breaking the awkward silence.

"No . . . I mean, I guess not," he stammered. How could he tell her that he had thought of very little else over the past weeks, until he was told that she had married? It would be wrong to express his true feelings now, so there was nothing left to say. "I guess I should say congratulations and wish you and your husband the best of luck."

"Thank you," she replied politely, a sad smile gracing her lips. Why, she wondered, did she have the feeling that she owed him an explanation, maybe even an apology? There had never been any commitment between them, not even of a casual nature. "Jordan . . ." she started, but could not bring herself to say what was in her heart. Instead, she said, "I wish you the best of luck, too. You'll always be a special friend to me."

There was no reason to linger. Still she was reluctant to walk away, knowing she would be closing a door forever. "Well," she finally sighed, "I must be getting over to the hospital. Thank you again." After a brief glance around to make sure they were alone, she stepped up to Jordan and quickly kissed him on the cheek. Their eyes met as she stepped away. For that one moment, time stood still, and they came together, eagerly following the passion of their hearts. Their lips met in desperate longing, releasing a hunger that was sentenced to die forever after. Locked in his powerful arms, she pressed her body against his, clinging to the moment with complete abandon.

Then she broke away. They spoke not a word. There was no need, for they both knew without speaking that it could not be. She was married. She had exchanged vows with Thomas, and she would be faithful to those vows. He saw the tears in her eyes as she took one last look at him before turning and hurrying away.

It was a long walk back to the hospital, but he stood watching her until she disappeared from his view. He touched his fingers gently to his lips. The fire of her kiss still remained to torment him, and he had a feeling that it would remain in his mind for a long, long time. He turned back to face his horse. "We need to shake the dust of this place off our heels," he declared. As usual, when desperation and consternation set in, he needed the solitude of the prairie or the mountains to free his brain. He could give McGarity his decision regarding a job as a scout again when he got back, but for now he needed to get away from the army and the noise.

"Heard you was back," Alton Broom said cheerfully when he looked up to see Jordan enter the store.

"Alton," Jordan acknowledged, walking directly over to the general merchandise side of the room. "I'll be needin' some supplies."

"Hamilton Grant said he thought you might be getting your job back," Alton remarked as he left the bar and moved to the counter, where Jordan now stood. "You get tired of lookin' for gold with Ned Booth?"

"Ned's gone under," Jordan replied, offering no embellishment. "I ain't made up my mind yet about scoutin' for the army." He reeled off a list of supplies he needed, then stood patiently while Alton picked each item from the shelves.

"Damn," Alton uttered softly. "I'm right sorry to hear about Ned. What happened? Injuns?" He didn't wait for Jordan to answer, but continued. "Rumors I've heard say there's liable to be war with the Injuns. The army will need scouts that know the country around the Powder and the Big Horns." Taking a cue from the list of supplies Jordan was buying, he guessed that his quiet young friend was preparing to leave again. "Look at what happened to Lieutenant Wallace's patrol. It ain't a good time for a white man alone to be traipsing across the prairie." He eyed the small hide pouch that Jordan placed on the counter. "And," he continued, "unless you've got a few more of these, you're gonna need money for cartridges and staples when these give out."

Jordan smiled. "Thanks for the sermon, but I'll be back directly. I ain't made up my mind what I'm gonna do yet." This was true, but what Alton said was also true. It was easy to think about going *wild*, living in the mountains alone, but cartridges for Jordan's Winchester didn't grow on trees. And he had never learned to like the Crow version of coffee, which was made from acorns and whatever. He needed the scouting job. The thing that made him waver was whether he could remain so close to Kathleen. *I should have left the arrogant son of a bitch with the Sioux.* It was a thought he had had many times in the last couple of days, and a picture of Thomas Jefferson Wallace, sitting ramrod stiff in the saddle, came instantly to mind. *She made her choice. Nobody held a gun on her. It's time I let it go.* She had made it pretty plain that a relationship with Jordan was never going to be. His mind back in the present, he said to Alton, "I expect I'll be workin' for the army again."

Alton nodded. "I'll be seein' you around then." Jordan was at the door when he heard Alton say, "Poor ol' Ned, the Injuns got 'em."

Jordan didn't reply. He preferred not to

tell Alton that Ned had been strung up by an out-of-control lynch mob.

CHAPTER 15

With no destination in mind, Jordan followed the river toward the somber heights of the Laramie Mountains, allowing Sweet Pea to set the pace as well as select a path. With no agenda to dictate, Jordan took the time to notice the first signs of a coming spring. It appeared that winter might finally relinquish its grip on the land. Jordan welcomed the change. He was ready for a new beginning. The thought gave him pause. He tried to recall if anyone at the fort had mentioned what month it was. It had to be close to April he decided.

To be alone in the mountains would be his natural salvation. He had come to believe that ever since the death of his wife and son. It seemed like so long ago that raiders had swept down upon his modest cabin, taking away his reason to live and turning him into a wanderer. He had thought then that his life was over when he buried his little family. The mountains had provided the only peace for his tormented mind. He had ridden the vengeance trail, which led to peace for no man. Ned Booth had told him that the mountains knew all the secrets of the earth, because they were closest to the Great Mystery that controls all events. Jordan was not a religious man, but he was becoming more and more convinced that the Indians were more in tune with the spirits than the white man with his starched version of worship. And now he was told there would be war with the Sioux and their allies, the principle reason being that some of them refused to live on reservations and turn their ancestral hunting grounds over to white miners and settlers. Jordan had never spent a great deal of time questioning the morality of it. It just appeared to be the natural way of things. Progress, some called it. Manifest Destiny the politicians back east termed it. Jordan was forced to make a decision as to which side he was on or else withdraw and head for parts unknown. He firmly believed that if he were a Sioux, he would not willingly report to a reservation. Yet he knew, in the end, he would ride scout for the army. As for withdrawing from the conflict, he needed a job. It was as simple as that, and scouting was really all he was qualified to do.

Late afternoon found him at a point where a rocky stream emptied into the Laramie River. It looked to be a good place to camp. Already his mind seemed to be lighter, just from being in the mountains. He dismounted and unsaddled Sweet Pea, then turned the mare loose to graze on the tender shoots along the edge of the stream. In short order, he had a fire going. As he fed the flames with dead branches, he thought again about the Indian's reverence for the land. According to Ned, the Indian thought that all things were alive, and that the spirit that dwelt in these things would speak to you if you were in a mental state to hear them. If an Indian can hear them, why not a white man? In his mind, there were a great many questions that he didn't have answers for. It had never before occurred to him that there was the possibility that a man could commune with the spirits. The thought appealed to him at this point in his life.

The more he thought, the more intrigued he became with the idea. He was about to slice some bacon for his supper when he decided to wait. A Lakota man would fast for several days before going off to seek a vision. Jordan wasn't willing to go to that extent, but he decided to try his hand at speaking to the spirits. Doing so on an empty stomach would be his compromise. He stood up and looked around him. About fifty feet above him, there was a rock ledge that jutted out over the stream. It seemed to him to be the ideal place.

He was about to climb the slope when Sweet Pea snorted nervously. Jordan picked up his rifle. Kneeling on one knee, he carefully scanned the slopes on each side, listening. Something was out there that bothered the mare, maybe a wolf or coyote. He could see nothing at first. Then he spotted the threat: a young mountain lion watching the camp from the trees that covered the lower slope. Jordan rose to his feet and walked toward the tawny cat. The mountain lion abruptly turned and disappeared into the trees. As a precaution, Jordan built the fire up. He waited a few minutes to make sure the cat was not still prowling around his camp. Then he climbed up to the ledge, seeking communion with the spirits of the mountains.

It was restful. He lay there, his eyes closed, trying to clear his mind to receive any message the spirits might have for him. But there was nothing. He found that he could not clear his mind of random thoughts of Kathleen, Ned Booth, Red Feather, and many others. *I guess you have to be an Indian.* He relaxed his concentration. His mind free, he immediately became drowsy. Just before drifting off, he heard the mountain lion making a return visit. Sweet Pea snorted and blew to announce its presence. It didn't concern Jordan. The big cat wouldn't approach the fire. There was nothing else to disturb the silence until —

"Judgment day is here."

Jordan awoke with a start, thinking at first he was dreaming. The voice seemed to have come from directly over him. Deep and ominous, it reverberated with the promise of doom. His eyes blinked open to reveal a dark shadow cast by the menacing bulk that was Preacher Rix. Every muscle in Jordan's body tensed.

"Well, Mr. Jordan Gray, you've led me on a right merry chase, but now I reckon it's time for you to know the vengeance of the Lord."

Trapped like a damn fool. The angry thought flashed through Jordan's mind as he looked up at Preacher's rifle barrel pointed directly at him. Sweet Pea had tried to warn him, but he had been too damn busy trying to commune with the mountains. There was absolutely no doubt that he was about to solve the great mystery that all men were destined to know. *But I ain't that anxious to find out.* He made a slight motion with his hand toward the Winchester at his side.

"Go ahead and reach for it," Preacher gloated, "if you think you can get it before I put a bullet in you." His lips curled in a sinister smile. "Maybe I'll just put one in your shoulder, like this one you put in me. How'd that be?" His smile froze upon his grizzled features when he remembered the wound that had forced him to retreat before. "I thought you had crippled me for good, but the Lord made me whole again so I could call down His vengeance upon you. You have been a pox on my life. You killed both my two sons, but I knew the Lord would cause you to lie before me to beg for mercy."

Jordan wasn't in a begging mood. He was angry at himself for being so lax as to let the menacing brute slip up on him. If this was to be his final moment on earth, so be it. But he was damned if he was going to grovel before this miserable mistake of God's. "If you're waitin' for me to beg, you might as well pull that trigger, 'cause it ain't gonna happen."

"Ain't you the sassy one?" Preacher chortled. "You ain't gonna get off that easy.

No, you're gonna die slow, a little bit at a time, and I'm gonna watch you suffer." He took a step backward in case Jordan had any ideas about making a desperate lunge at his feet. "Now get up on your feet, real easy-like, and we're gonna climb down off this ledge."

Jordan couldn't see much sense in obeying the man's orders if he was going to get shot anyway, but he liked his odds better if he was on his feet, so he did as he was told.

"Now kick that fancy Winchester over here," Preacher ordered, being careful to stay away from the edge of the ledge himself. "I've been wantin' that rifle."

"Go to hell," Jordan snarled and kicked his rifle off the ledge. It clattered against the rocks as it dropped fifty feet to the base of the slope, almost landing on Sweet Pea. The mare kicked up her hind legs and jumped to avoid the bouncing weapon.

Infuriated, Preacher stepped forward and struck Jordan on the back of the head with his rifle barrel. Jordan staggered, his senses reeling, but he didn't go down. With one giant hand, Preacher grabbed the back of Jordan's collar and shoved him toward the path they had climbed up to reach the ledge. Preacher had coveted Jordan's Winchester since the first time the two had met.

"If that there rifle's broke," Preacher promised, "I'm gonna see just how much pain you can stand before you die."

Struggling just to stay on his feet, Jordan grabbed a pine limb as he fought to clear his senses. Staggered again by a blow across his shoulders, he lurched forward, the steepness of the path causing him to stumble and slide on the loose shale. Finally his momentum caused him to tumble, and he went rolling and crashing down to the bottom, almost landing under Sweet Pea's hooves. The mare quickly sidestepped to avoid the tumbling body.

Cautiously watching Jordan's wild descent down the path, Preacher followed, stepping carefully so as not to duplicate it, his rifle trained upon the plummeting man. When Jordan finally came to rest at the foot of the slope, Preacher hurried to gain a position to cover him in case Jordan was game enough to try to make a run for it. A wide grin spread across his face when he saw that Jordan had gained nothing from his fall but an assortment of cuts and bruises. "Now we'll see how tough —"

That was as far as he got before the twilight air was shattered by the angry scream of the mountain lion from the ledge they had just left. Startled, Preacher turned, losing his balance and lurching against Jordan's horse in the process. Sweet Pea had had enough of the sudden surprises. She expressed her dissatisfaction by kicking up her back legs. The well-aimed hooves caught Preacher solidly in the stomach, knocking him to the ground, doubled over in pain.

Jordan was quick to act. Preacher tried to turn the rifle on him, but Jordan was upon him before he could bring the weapon to bear. A desperate struggle to gain control of the rifle ensued between the two powerful men. Jordan strained with all his might to wrest the rifle away from the huge man, but his efforts were useless against Preacher's superior strength. It was all Jordan could do to prevent Preacher from ripping the rifle from his hands. Finally Preacher's strength prevailed, and he snatched the weapon free. Roaring in triumph, his face a mask of fury, he raised the rifle over his head, preparing to use it as a club to strike Jordan down. His hands free, Jordan drew the long skinning knife from his belt and, with one quick step, moved up under Preacher's arms and sank the blade deep into the huge man's gut.

Shocked, Preacher backed away and stared down at the handle of the knife in stunned disbelief. Wasting no time, Jordan dived to the ground, rolling under Sweet Pea's belly, and scrambled for the Winchester lying in the rocks. The one thought racing through his brain was that, if the rifle was busted, he was a dead man.

Dazed by the burning pain in his innards, and fumbling in confusion, Preacher sought to kill his tormentor. But the horse blocked his aim, and to make things even more difficult for him, the mare started bucking when Jordan rolled under her belly. Staggering backward, the desperate man, mindful also of the mountain lion above him on the ledge, lost precious seconds when he looked in that direction before turning back to search for Jordan. When he tried to walk around the frantic horse, the pain in his gut became so intense that it caused him to falter. Oblivious for the moment of the man desperately searching for his rifle among the rocks, Preacher reached down and grabbed the knife to rid his belly of the pain. He bellowed like a wounded grizzly when the blade withdrew and a flood of blood soaked his shirt. The sight of his lifeblood flowing out of his body prompted him to roar out in righteous anger. With one blow on Sweet Pea's rump with his rifle barrel, he chased the excited mare out of his way, only to find himself looking down the barrel of Jordan's

Winchester.

In his agitated state, Preacher's reactions were still quick, but not fast enough to level his rifle before Jordan's bullet smashed into his breastbone. Mortally wounded, the huge man sank to his knees, his rifle slipping from his hands. Through dazed eyes, he saw the blurry image of the man he had hunted, now rising to his feet and cautiously approaching.

"You've kilt me," Preacher mumbled, coughing to keep from choking on the blood now filling his throat.

"I reckon," Jordan replied.

"Damn you!" Preacher spat, a spark of anger flashing in his dull eyes for just a moment. Then his eyes glazed over and seemed to focus on a faraway object. Still on his knees, he gasped, "Zeb! Quincy! I'll be comin' to join you in God's paradise."

"Tell 'em I said hello," Jordan said and pumped another round into Preacher's chest. He felt no sympathy for the man who had preyed upon so many innocent lives. "But I doubt if you'll find 'em in Heaven." He reached down and removed the rifle at Preacher's knees, then turned to look up at the ledge above him. "I guess the shooting scared him away," he said to himself, for there was no sign of the mountain lion. He wondered for a moment if he had just imagined the fearsome beast. If that were true, Preacher had imagined it as well. He turned back then to see Preacher slowly keel over on his side.

The dying man mumbled for several minutes before his final breath escaped him. Jordan stood watching him until there was no longer any doubt that the self-proclaimed messenger of God was dead. Only then did he take inventory of the cuts and bruises he had suffered in his fall down the slope.

He was overcome with a feeling of peace when he realized that there was no longer a threat to his safety. There was the matter of clearing his name in Deadwood, but he knew of no way to prove his innocence. Still, it bothered his mind. *I might have to go back there one day soon.* Looking once more at Preacher's huge body, he thought, *I was damn lucky to come out alive on this one. But I guess I made it with the help of a mountain lion and a coyote-looking horse.* He looked over at Sweet Pea and grinned. "Coyote luck, I reckon."

ABOUT THE AUTHOR

Charles G. West lives in Marietta, Georgia, and was the proprietor of a commercial typesetting and printing business. He now devotes his full time to writing historical novels.